C. Curtis
April, 1978

AFRICAN WRITERS SERIES
Editorial Adviser · Chinua Achebe

20

Child of Two Worlds

AWS

This series makes available a wide range of African writing: both original works and reprints of already well-known books are included. Orange covers denote fiction (F), blue covers non-fiction (NF), and green covers poetry (P) and drama (D).

Peter Abrahams *Mine Boy* F

Chinua Achebe *Things Fall Apart*; *No longer at ease*; *Arrow of God*; *A Man of the People* F

T. M. Aluko *One Man, One Matchet*; *One Man, one Wife*; *Kinsman and Foreman* F

Elechi Amadi *The Concubine* F

Ulli Beier (ed.) *The Origin of Life and Death* F

Mongo Beti *Mission to Kala* F

William Conton *The African* F

David Cook (ed.) *Origin East Africa* F

Paul Edwards (ed.) *Equiano's Travels* NF

Cyprian Ekwensi *Burning Grass*; *People of the City*; *Lokotown and other stories* F

Mugo Gatheru *Child of Two Worlds* NF

Obotunde Ijimere *The Imprisonment of Obatala and other plays* D

Aubrey Kachingwe *No Easy Task* F

Kenneth Kaunda *Zambia shall be free* NF

John Munonye *The Only Son* F

James Ngugi *Weep not, child*; *The River Between* F

Flora Nwapa *Efuru* F

Ferdinand Oyono *Houseboy* F

Lenrie Peters *The Second Round* F; *Satellites* P

Cosmo Pieterse *Ten One-Act Plays* D

John Reed and Clive Wake (ed.) *A Book of African Verse* P

Richard Rive (ed.) *Modern African Prose*; *Quartet* F

Stanlake Samkange *On Trial for My Country* F

Francis Selormey *The Narrow Path* F

Child of
Two Worlds

*

R. MUGO GATHERU

HEINEMANN

LONDON · IBADAN · NAIROBI

Heinemann Educational Books Ltd
48 Charles Street, London W.1
PMB 5205, Ibadan · POB 25080, Nairobi

MELBOURNE TORONTO AUCKLAND
HONG KONG SINGAPORE

First published by
Routledge & Kegan Paul 1964
© R. Mugo Gatheru 1964
First published in *African Writers Series*
1966
Reprinted 1967

Printed and Bound in Great Britain by
Bookprint Limited, London and Crawley

This book is dedicated to
a future Kenya nation in which
tribalism has become only a historic
memory and tribes mere ceremonial units.

Contents

		page ix
	INTRODUCTION	*page* ix
I.	MY PEOPLE, THE KIKUYU	1
II.	SQUATTER CHILDHOOD	9
III.	YOUTH IN THE HIGHLANDS	27
IV.	BECOMING A KIKUYU	45
V.	THE DISCOVERY OF MY PEOPLE	65
VI.	THE MAKING OF A 'SUBVERSIVE'	78
VII.	I AM HIT BY A TRUNCHEON	88
VIII.	JOMO KENYATTA—THE AFRICAN MESSIAH	105
IX.	I DISCOVER 'CANUTISM'	114
X.	BROWN MAN'S WORLD	120
XI.	WHITE MAN'S WORLD	141
XII.	BECOMING AN AMERICAN 'COLLEGIAN'	151
XIII.	BECOMING A 'LINCOLN MAN'	161
XIV.	UNDER THE SHADOW OF MAU MAU	169
XV.	MUGO AS A KIKUYU 'PSYCHOANALYST'	185
XVI.	MY 'STAR' STARTED SHINING	200
XVII.	MY BROTHERS OF THE NEW WORLD	207

Introduction

by

ST CLAIR DRAKE

Professor of Sociology, Roosevelt University, Chicago, U.S.A.
Former Professor of Sociology, University College of Ghana

SOCIAL scientists, as well as journalists, in Britain, Europe, and America, are producing a steady flow of books about the peoples and cultures, the politics and public personalities, of contemporary Africa. But books about Africa and Africans *by* Africans are rare, although an increasing number of scholarly works, novels, and collections of poetry are appearing. Yet, only a few autobiographies by Africans have been published, these mainly by political leaders, and of these, M. Ojike's *I Have Two Countries*, published in the late 'thirties, has been the only account of African student experiences written *before* the author returned home to become a public figure. Mugo Gatheru will undoubtedly become a man of prominence in the new Kenya, but his autobiography has all of the freshness and frankness of one who has not yet taken on those responsibilities of leadership and those attributes of prestige and power which demand that priority be given to developing and sustaining an 'image'.

This is the story of a young African for whom the dream of an education in America became a compelling desire. Baulked in 1948 by Kenya government officials who considered him 'subversive' because he wrote letters to the editor against racial discrimination, and who refused him the 'good conduct certificate' needed in those days to apply for a visa, he went to India, a journey for which no visa was required. Eventually, he found his way to the United States. All of this he tells us in interesting detail. But the book tells us much more than this. This simple, straightforward, and immensely *human* document reveals to us what it has meant to one individual to be a Kikuyu, a Kenyan, and an African amid the complexities of the modern world. It also discusses, with sympathetic insight, ancient tribal customs in which the author participated as a youth, while describing the process by which he gradually adopted new values and new customs. To understand what happened to Mugo Gatheru is to understand the experiences of thousands of other young Africans.

Being a social anthropologist, I, quite naturally, welcome the publication of Mugo's story as an addition to that small but constantly growing group of autobiographies which sensitive and reflective Africans are now producing. All such documents are interesting and significant, but this one has a special significance, for it is a record of the unique experiences of an unusual man. It is hoped that one of its side effects will be to stimulate others of his generation to tell the story of how they, too, became members of that little circle of well-trained men upon whom the responsibilities for building a Kenya nation and a federation of East African states will so much depend. The author of this book is one of that first generation of college-trained Africans which has come into existence in Kenya since the Second World War, for there were less than a dozen graduates among the 5,000,000 Africans of that country when that war began. Now there are hundreds.

Kenya secured its independence in December of 1963 without suffering the kind of crisis which the Congo faced in 1960, lacking, as it did, a corps of highly trained men and women. The story of how an educated *élite* was produced so quickly in Kenya is one that should be told some day, and, when told, it will be a tribute not only to the ingenuity and dedication of Africans, young and old, but also to individuals and educational institutions in England, India, and America, as well as to the staff of Makerere College in Uganda. But this is not that story. This is simply one man's story, one student's story, of how he grew up in Kenya and then secured an education during those stormy days between 1950 and 1960 when the nationalist struggle in his homeland was at its height, of how he was preparing himself to be of service to his country when the time came to consolidate the victory. Since Fate made me a participant in this drama, I have been asked to write this introduction, and I do so not as a social scientist, but as Mugo's friend.

I first met Mugo in 1950—in a railway station in Chicago. From that day to this we have been what the Kikuyu call *muru-wa-maitu* to each other—brothers. We made our own little private blood brotherhood pact during his first year in America, some thirteen years ago. He was a student then, preparing to embark upon the great adventure in America. I was a professor many years older than he. But the experiences of the next five years dissolved any barriers of age or academic degrees that stood between us, for we found ourselves bound together as partners in a number of exciting, frustrating, and sometimes discouraging joint enterprises.

We set ourselves two goals at the beginning—finding a place where he could secure a college education by 'working his way through' and trying to get as many Kenya students over to America for study as we could. Within two years, Mugo was 'settled in' at Lincoln University from which Kwame Nkrumah and Nnamdi Azikiwe had graduated, and he, on his own initiative, had found places there for three other Kenya students. (Only two had come before him, Mbiyu Koinange in 1927 and Julius Kiano in 1948.) Up to this point the only problems we had faced were those of raising money and soliciting scholarships. Then the personal crisis arose in Mugo's life which he has so vividly described in Chapter XIV, 'Under the Shadow of Mau Mau'.

I received a phone call one day in the autumn of 1952 from the American Negro president of Lincoln University, Dr Horace Mann Bond. He was fighting mad. The American immigration authorities had ordered Mugo to leave the country and would give no reason why. To us the reason seemed obvious. Senator McCarthy was leading the lunatic fringe of American politicians in a widely publicized witch-hunt for Communists who were known to foster revolution in colonial countries: Kenya was seething with the Mau Mau disturbance which must therefore have been Communist-inspired; all Africans in Kenya, or so it seemed to the McCarthyites, supported Mau Mau and were therefore all ardent Communists; it was therefore 'logical' that Mugo too was a Communist, a dangerous canker in the wholesome apple of American democracy; Mugo was dangerous and corrupting, Mugo must go. Dr Bond was determined that this would never happen and had already organized a defence committee. Professor Tom Jones of Lincoln's History Department was to head the committee. I was asked to take on some special assignments. For the next year and a half I was knee-deep in what turned out to be a *cause célèbre*—writing letters, making speeches, raising money, helping to plot strategy. I remember that at one point two other friends of Mugo's and I had planned to rush to Lincoln University and to get Mugo and head for Washington, D.C., to chain ourselves to the White House gates if the police ever made a serious move to deport him!

Throughout what must have been a real ordeal for him Mugo not only displayed an amazing degree of calmness, but also such competence in handling his own affairs and planning his own strategies that I nicknamed him 'The Field Marshal'. I remember once when I asked him why he didn't try to get himself shifted out of the U.N. dining-room where he had a part-time job to an office position, he reminded me that he had a chance to meet all the delegates in the dining-room and thus to have a set of allies on hand if a crisis came. This was typical of his own long-range planning. I came out of this experience with profound respect for him added to the affection for him which I had always had.

This experience also revealed to us both the great fund of good will which is latent among liberal Americans whenever injustice is being fought. Mugo managed to stay in America throughout the litigation and won his Master of Arts degree. Then in 1957 he won his battle and was vindicated.

Long before the shadow of Mau Mau fell on Mugo, I had suggested to him that he ought to write the story of his life and he began it in 1951. From time to time he expanded the document, but then he laid it aside due to the pressure of employment, the demands of his court case, and the need to devote all of his time to study. I thought he would never be able to work on it again, especially after he went to England to study for the Bar. And then one day in 1963 I received a package in the mail from London. It was the manuscript! He had stayed by it all those years—and had completed it while studying for his law examinations. I was amazed at his persistence, but I shouldn't have been. This was the same spirit he had shown in battling to remain in America and complete his education.

As I read the autobiography, it evoked memories of some of his manuscripts I had read long before I ever met him—copies he had sent to America of letters he had written to editors and of projected articles with titles such as 'Is Equality a White Man's Burden?' 'Kenya African Women', 'Where is the Freedom of Kenya Africans?' 'Kenya African Economic Chaos'. These were the writings of a passionate, dedicated young man, and I looked forward to meeting him. Then we met. He has retained that passion, now disciplined and seasoned with a sense of humour, and with something of the detachment of the social scientist. Parts of his story displayed the same shrewdness of observation found in A. B. C. Merriam's book written around the turn of the century, *Britons through Negro Spectacles*, a perceptive account of the experiences of a West African traveller. I am proud that Mugo honours me by calling me his friend and am glad I was able to play some small part in helping him to realize the goals he set for himself.

When Mugo came to America the Africans in Kenya were already engaged in a struggle to break the grip of white settler domination in what was then a colony dominated by a European minority which had pre-empted most of the best land. Africans could not vote; very limited educational facilities were provided for them; and they were subjected to segregation and discrimination. When they protested they were labelled 'subversive'. It was to prepare himself for fighting against this system that Mugo dreamed of securing an education in America. But events have moved fast in Africa during the past decade, and Kenya is an independent sovereign state. Mugo will now be able to use his training in the building of a new nation instead of expending it upon protest and revolt. All of the Kenya nation-builders are, like him, 'children of two worlds'. Mugo's autobiography will help us to understand better the struggles and aspirations of the men who will lead the new Kenya.

Mugo is a member of the Kikuyu ethnic group (sometimes called a 'tribe'), but like all of his fellow educated Africans he is committed to the building of a modern non-tribal state in that country. However, in Kenya, as in all African states, a sense of ethnic consciousness, and even of ethnic pride, will remain just as such attitudes have persisted in the United States or in a federation such as Switzerland or in the United Kingdom. But it will be a harmless ethnic pride which stimulates friendly rivalry and not a destructive tribalism.

This is the frank autobiography of an educated Kikuyu who, while devoted to the concept of the new Kenya, is also proud of the role that the Kikuyu have played in making an independent Kenya possible. Such devotion is now a national necessity; such pride, when subordinated to the national interest, demands no apology.

ST CLAIR DRAKE

September, 1963.

I

My People, the Kikuyu

MY name is Mugo, which in the language of my fathers means 'Man of God'. I come from a long line of men who have borne this name, a line stretching far, far back into time. They were highly respected men among their own people, the Kikuyu. My people are Africans, reddish-brown and chocolate-brown men, women and children, living in the highlands of Kenya, East Africa.

The whole world knows something of the Kikuyu, for they are people out of which the Mau Mau sprang. They have had novels written about them and movies made about them, and for several years they were in the headlines of all the world's newspapers. To some people the Kikuyu were 'blood-thirsty savages' ready to kill all white men. To others, the Kikuyu were 'heroes fighting for freedom against oppression'. To me, however, the Kikuyu are simply *my people*. To me, they are neither savages nor heroes. They are my kinsmen and fellow-tribesmen, and I, too, am one of them.

In 1952, when the Mau Mau crisis broke out in my country, I was in school in the United States. I was there throughout a four-year war in my country which cost the British Government some £55,585,424, and during which over 15,000 of my people people died and another 100,000 were placed in concentration camps. During all this time I was studying and reading and thinking and brooding.

When I was born, everyone thought that I would some day be what American Indians call a 'medicine-man' and what we call a 'mundumugo', for I was in the line of those who were believed to have inherited the power, after being properly trained, to control the wind and the unknown forces that make people sicken and die. They had the power, too, to remove the curses known as 'thahu', that wicked people were supposed to to have placed upon others, or that men brought upon themselves. A 'Mugo' knew much, and could do much. He had a great responsibility for helping to keep the tribe peaceful, healthy and unafraid. As the first-born son of one known as Mugo, it was my duty to respect my father and to learn from him, and then, when I was old enough, to take training and to become a 'doctor' myself. This, until I was eleven years old, I fully intended to do, and to see that my son after me did the same, so that the great chain of doctors in which I was but a link would never be broken. But the link with my fathers has now been broken and I, Mugo-son-of-Gatheru, will start a new chain, with new links. My people, the Kikuyu, were great workers in iron, and they discovered many centuries ago how to make the finest of chains. I have long known that the iron must be good if a chain is to be strong. And so I went to America to be smelted and hammered and beaten and drawn, even as our smiths forge useful and ornamental objects from their iron. I have been laid on the anvil!

My people, the Kikuyu, are being smelted, hammered, beaten and drawn, too, by the great forces that I have now learned, after my college education, to call urbanization and industrialization and aculturation. I have learned, too, that I am what the sociologists call a 'marginal man'—a child of two worlds.

Africa is my home. The Kikuyu are my people. To them I shall return. And I will return knowing that the World of Africa and the World of the West and of the East are equally important parts of our One World.

The People in Love with a Mountain

I have seen the beautiful pictures the Japanese paint of a mountain in their homeland called Fujiyama. These Japanese remind me much of the Kikuyu, for they, too, are people in love with a mountain. We live in a very beautiful part of east Africa, some 5000 feet above sea level, among rolling hills, where for many hundreds of years the Kikuyu have planted and reaped and tended their sheep and goats and cattle.

When the first Europeans came to explore these highlands they saw a beautiful snow-capped mountain rising up from the low hills high into the cloud-filled blue skies. They asked my people what it was called in their language, and they were told that it was Kere-Nyaga which meant 'white stripes'. The word was strange to their ears, and as some of our people pronounce it, it sounded to the Europeans like 'Kenya'. So in the geography books it is 'Kenya', but we still call it *Kere-Nyaga*. The early Europeans left, never knowing how important the mountain was to the people, who believed that high up on its snow-capped peak lived Ngai, the great and powerful unseen god who made all things. Then, and even now, when a most solemn prayer is being made for help, the people turn their faces towards the mountain. And it was to Mt Kenya that my father turned when he was healing people. Many are the times I have seen him do it. It was from Mt Kenya, too, that Ngai spoke, in the beginning of time, and called the first man into being.

The Children of Mumbi and Kikuyu

In 1953, during the trial of those who were accused of organizing Mau Mau among my people, frequent references were made to certain alleged secret rituals in which they referred to themselves as the 'Children of Mumbi and Kikuyu'. But I, who was born long before Mau Mau, learned of Mumbi and Kikuyu —the story which was handed down from father to son about the origin of our people. To us it had the same deep and sacred meaning as the story about Adam and Eve in the Bible. There is a Kikuyu 'Garden of Eden', too, and if you were to visit Kenya and catch the train in our modern capital of Nairobi, and were to ride north to the Fort Hall District, any Kikuyu could take you to Mukurwe-wa-Nyagathanga—'The Tree of Nyaga-thanga', a most sacred spot. They would show you the great hole in the ground near the tree, out of which Kikuyu came— the first man of our people—in answer to Ngai's call from the mountain.

According to our legends, Ngai took Kikuyu to the top of Mt Kenya, among the shining snow-covered peaks, where no

3

man's foot had ever left a print, and showed him the beautiful country for miles around. There were great forests of cedars, bamboos and olive trees, and between them were vast open spaces where herds of antelopes and gazelles were peacefully grazing. Many rivers of clear, cool water flowed through the land. Far, far away to the south could be seen the snow-capped peaks of what is now called Mt Kilimanjaro. To the west was the mountain 'Nyandarua' or 'Aberdare' and to the south, the big hill called Kirima-Mbogo—the hill of the buffaloes.

Ngai said to Kikuyu: 'This is yours.'

Kikuyu lifted up his hands and looked Ngai in the face. In a low, singing voice he offered the prayer of thanks which has been recorded by the great African leader and anthropologist, Jomo Kenyatta:

O, my father, Great Elder, I have no words to thank you, but with your deep wisdom I am sure that you can see how much I prize your glorious gifts. O my father, when I look upon your greatness I am confounded with awe. O Great Elder, ruler of all things both on heaven and on earth, I am your warrior, and I am ready to act in accordance with your will.

Ngai turned to Kikuyu and said to him:

My good and brave warrior, your words have touched my heart and I am very pleased. Within the great bowl formed by the mountains your sons and daughters shall roam and multiply. You shall enjoy the beauty of the country and all its fruits. Always remember that it is I who have bestowed this upon you. My blessing shall be with you and your offspring wherever you go.

Ngai commanded Kikuyu to descend from the mountain and to build his homestead in a place surrounded by wild fig trees. Soon afterwards Ngai gave to Kikuyu his wife, Mumbi, and they lived happily together and had nine daughters and no sons.

When the daughters were grown they had no husbands. Ngai told Kikuyu to sacrifice a fat ram near a tree in a sacred grove. This Kikuyu did, and suddenly, standing beside the fire, were nine handsome young men. There was great rejoicing when he brought them home, and the daughters accepted them as husbands, but only on condition that the women should be the

4

heads of the households and that all of the sisters, their husbands, and their children would live together in one village. All of the Kikuyu believe that they are descended from the nine daughters. We are all, today, divided into nine groups—what anthropologists call clans—and each one claims to be descended either from Wacheera, Wanjiko, Wairimo, Wamboi, Wangari, Wanjiro, Wangoi, Waithera, or Warigia (sometimes called Mwithaga or Ethaga).

Each clan has its sacred totem; for instance, the gazelle for Wanjiro, the hippopotamus for Wanjiko, the zebra for Wacheera. We do not worship these animals, but we do not eat them. My own totem, that of Ethaga clan, is 'all wild game'. I was not supposed to eat any wild animal, nor are any who call themselves Ethaga supposed to eat them.

In the old days, before the Europeans came, it is said that a person never married anyone in his clan. Today, however, the rule is just the opposite. One is supposed to marry a girl in one's own clan, but not a close relative. The Kikuyu do not have totem poles in front of their houses as do some of the American Indians, but in the old days we always were taught our totem and we would never forget it. Wherever I meet a Mwithaga, I know he is my relative and we treat each other like sisters and brothers.

According to the legends of the Kikuyu, the men, for many tens of years, kept the agreement to let the women serve as the rulers, but as the men tell the story, the women became heartless and cruel, so the men decided to take their power away from them. Whatever may have happened in the past, the fact remains that the Children of the Nine Daughters have, for many years now, been ruled by men, and although women are respected, we take our names from our fathers rather than our mothers and belong to our father's clan.

Burnt Offerings to Ngai

When the missionaries brought the Bible to the Kikuyu, our people understood the Old Testament right away, for many of the customs of the ancient Jews were very much like ours. Like the Hebrew people of old, the Kikuyu are a God-fearing people, and when they approached Ngai they brought him a sacrifice.

5

The Kikuyu adored Ngai because of the beautiful land which he had handed over to them. They recognized him as the one and only God. They had no idea, of course, about Jesus Christ, the Holy Spirit, or the devil, but they did recognize the existence of ancestor spirits. They had no devil either. There was only Ngai, Creator of Heaven and Earth.

The Kikuyu had no regular worship coming every seven days on a Sabbath or a Sunday. They worshipped God only during times of prosperity—especially during harvests. But they called on Him for blessings in every kind of crisis such as war, epidemic, or disease. And the system was usually the same. A spotless ram would be offered by someone in the village. The elders and *Mugos* or Shamans would then take the ram to a sacred tree where such sacrifices are performed. There were, and still are, very many sacred trees all over the Kikuyu country. The places where these trees grow are equivalent to churches in the Western world or shrines or temples in the Middle East and Asia. They could not be cut down. The ordinary people were not even supposed to go near them or to clear the bushes near by.

When the ram had been got, the wise men, elders, and doctors would take it to the foot of a sacred tree. It was strangled, the skin stripped off, and all parts separated. The meat would then be roasted on the same spot. But 'taatha', or the waste matter in both the large and small intestines, would be saved. After the meat was roasted and ready it was not eaten, except that Shamans or *Ago* were allowed to taste small pieces. The rest of the roasted meat would then be tied with skin and left in the same place in the hope that God would come and 'eat' the roasted meat later on.

The *Mugos* would then take the *taatha* with them and lead a long procession from the sacred tree to the villages throwing *taatha* on the fields, gardens and into bushes, just as the ancient Jewish priest used to sprinkle the blood of the sacrificial lamb on the congregation with a piece of hyssop. While so doing they would be shouting as follows:

LEADER: Ugai thaaai! (Say peace!)
GROUP: Iiihuuuu ithaaai! (O peace!)
LEADER: Ciana thaaai! (Peace to children!)
GROUP: Iiihuuuu ciana thaaai! (O peace to children!)

LEADER: Bururi thaaai! (Peace to the country!)
GROUP: Iiihuuuu bururi thaaai! (O peace to the country!)
LEADER: Migunda thaaai! (Peace to gardens!)
GROUP: Iiihuuuu migunda thaaai! (O peace to the gardens!)

The procession would then disperse slowly and everyone would go to his home.

There was also a holy day, 'muthenya wa mugwanja'. It was regarded with high solemnity. This day is also known as the seventh day in the Western world. No Kikuyu could make a trip or journey on such day for fear that bad luck might fall upon him. Future events, plans, or activities enabled the Kikuyu to determine the seventh day easily. For example, a person would suggest to another: 'We shall do this or that tomorrow, "ruciu", or the day after tomorrow, "oke", or on the fourth, fifth, or sixth day from today, but not on the seventh day.'

Those who planted a Garden

Some learned scholars who have studied the language of my people say that the word 'Kikuyu' or 'Gikuyu' means 'The People of Fig Tree'. It is true that as long as anyone can remember our people have loved trees and our sacred spots are always groves of trees. Yet, the very way that we have settled the land and made our living has caused us to cut down the trees and turn the Kikuyuland into what one traveller referred to many years ago as 'one vast garden'. It is thought that as the Kikuyu multiplied in numbers they gradually spread out from the area near Mt Kenya, clearing the forest, pushing back the animals and planting crops. By 1900 there were about a half million of us, and we were still pushing westward and clearing the forest, even as the Europeans went westward from the Atlantic Ocean to the Mississippi River in America, planting as they went. Today there are over two million of us.

The forests were originally inhabited by two groups of people, those whom we refer to as the Gumba or 'little men'—pygmies—and a taller group of hunters now called the Wanderobo. There were not many of them and the forest was big. We bought the land from them with the crops we grew and the iron we made, using a solemn religious ceremony to bind the deal.

Some of them intermarried with us. Others gradually moved deeper and deeper into the great forest towards the centre of Africa. We were always friends with them and fought no wars against them. Our men cleared the forest and broke the ground with the hoe. Our women planted and tended the crops. The boys cared for the livestock. The men helped with the reaping and did the building and repairing and a little hunting. But the most important job of the men was to stand guard, and sometimes to fight against those who were our enemies.

On the south and the south-west, the brave and fierce warriors called the Masai lived. The Masai have never been a people who planted and reaped. Like the Indians of the American plains they moved about a great deal and valued most highly those who could fight well. They had enormous herds of cattle which they could drive along with them as they went into battle, drinking the blood and milk of their cows. It was, perhaps, from them that some Kikuyu took over the custom of keeping cattle.

To the further west of us was the Rift Valley Province in which the Nandi, Suk, and the Kipsigis—mighty hunters and herdsmen—lived, none of whom took kindly to the large-scale cultivation of the soil—as well as the Luo who did. And so the Kikuyu carved out a garden and in it planted corn and banana groves, beans, millet, squashes, sorghum, and the other good things which man may eat to grow strong and give himself pleasure.

II

Squatter Childhood

In the Rift Valley Province

MY father was born on the Kikuyu Reserve in a section of the country called *Nyeri*, where his fathers had lived for many years before him. Soon after he had gone through the traditional initiation ceremony called *irua* which made him a fully fledged man, he went westward to the 'land of the strangers', seeking his fortune on a European farm. He had visions of prosperity—a little money and many goats. The young men had been coming back to the Reserve telling of how easy it was to become 'rich' in the Great Rift Valley. So my father and other ambitious men bade their kinsmen goodbye and set out to become Squatters.

Squatter system was introduced into Kenya as a result of European settlement in the highlands. It can be defined as a form of modified neo-feudalism whereby a European farmer would permit several Africans to farm on small strips or plots of land, growing only enough food to live on, in return for labour on the European farm. In addition to these small strips of land some European farmers used to pay their Squatters some six to eight shillings a month. Some, too, offered their Squatters large plots or smaller, depending on the discretion of the European farmer concerned. Squatters had to work long hours, from seven in the morning to five in the evening.

A Squatter's life was very frustrating, uncertain, and miserable. For example, there were no medical facilities available for the Squatters, no recreation of any kind, and no schools were encouraged for the children of the Squatters, though certain

9

isolated European farmers did permit some Christian Squatters to build churches near their villages on the farm. There were also a very few individual settlers who had allowed their Squatters to operate small elementary schools at which some Squatter children could learn to read and write in their vernacular languages, and very elementary arithmetic.

The idea was, not to encourage too much education for the Squatter children as they were meant to replace their fathers on the farms when their fathers were too old to work on them. Hence, a Squatter's child could only look forward to becoming a Squatter like his father. Some lucky Squatters could send some of their children to the Kikuyuland to get some education. This process was encouraged after the Second World War, particularly. European settlers were not supposed to know all this. For it was feared that if they did, those who sent their children to get an education away in the Kikuyu Country might be dismissed by their European bosses.

Another peculiar aspect of the Squatter system was that whatever important product was grown by the Squatters on their small plots of land was to be sold to the European farmer who owned the land at a price fixed by him. Other small products were allowed to be sold on the local markets or to the Indian merchants directly. Corn was one of the major products which the Squatters had to sell to their European farmers only.

Squatters who worked for the Forest Department had the advantage of selling whatever they grew to the local Indian merchants or on the markets directly. Prices for these products —for instance, peas, beans, cauliflower, cabbages, carrots, tomatoes, and onions—were fixed very low. But a Squatter had no alternative but to accept them.

Long before my father turned his feet toward the west, other Kikuyu from the Kiambu section of the Reserve had sought their fortunes there. Among those who went to the Land of Promise was a wealthy man, Kuria-son-of-Nguuri. He was a very famous *Mugo*. When he prospered there, he took nine wives. The third was named Wanjiku, and it was her daughter, Wambui-wa-Kuria, who became the wife of my father. I was their first-born son.

When I was born in 1925, three years after the British Government's solemn promise always to defend the rights of the Africans in Kenya, my parents were living as Squatters on a European's farm called *Kwa-bara-bara-miti*—'The Place of the Trees planted in a Line'. As at all Kikuyu births a 'muciari-thania' presided over the event—an old woman trained in such matters, an expert with the 'rwenji', a razor-sharp knife used for shaving, cutting placenta, and female circumcision. She had with her the bell that is rung in the ears of babies who do not cry or make a noise immediately they are born. It was not necessary to ring it in my case, for I have heard that I very promptly squalled. Then the women in the room cried aloud five times the traditional, 'Aaariririri', and shouted out, in fun, 'What are we going to name him, Mugo or Mbugua?' Had I been a girl they would have cried out only four times. Since I was a first-born son they named me Mugo-son-of-Gatheru. My father was Gatheru-son-of-Mugo, and so will my own son be named, for grandfather and grandchild always have the same name. Since I did not talk much as a child, I was nicknamed 'The Silent One' or 'Mukiri'.

Everybody was very happy because a son had been born. Father had selected a very, very fat ram well in advance for the celebration. When it was killed the stomach was eaten by a few of his close friends—men and women—according to custom. The meat was used to make a delicious stew and soup for my mother. The fat was put away in gourds for it was to be used when she weaned me. She would use the fat to soften the potatoes which she would knead in the palm of her hand and force gently into my mouth. (At home on the Reserve she would have bananas and fat, but in the land of the strangers potatoes were used instead.) An old lady came to cook and clean the house for my mother at the appointed time. The house must not be swept for five days, but at the end of that time it was thoroughly cleaned, my mother was bathed and her head was shaved (and mine too) by some young girls. My mother then strapped me to her back in the little sling we call 'ngoi' and went out into the garden for a few hours of work.

The Sun roasted Me

My mother used to work for long hours in the garden while my father was also working for long hours for a European farmer.

II

She didn't have anyone to help her take care of me whilst she was working on the field. She therefore strapped me to her back in the *ngoi* whilst working. This was very tiring as she had to bend down all the time using a long knife for cultivation or a hoe 'jembe'. Sometimes I would be crying on her back or sleeping. But so long as I was fed and dry my mother would continue working.

When I grew a little bigger, my mother couldn't work properly with me on her back and so she used to lay me down at the foot of a banana tree. She would make sure that the sun was not shining directly on me and that the shadow of the banana tree was cast on me so it could protect me from the hot sun.

One day my mother and my aunt, Wangui, were working together, and as usual they laid me under a banana tree. The sun was very hot. They had already fed me and I was nice and dry. They continued cultivating and singing happily. For a while they forgot me and as the time went by the shadow of the banana tree moved away and exposed me to the sun.

The sun started 'roasting' me and though I tossed and cried, both my aunt and mother thought it normal for a baby. Louder I cried and louder, and then my voice grew faint and thin. At this, my mother looked back to my tree and saw me, still, in the full glaring sun—

'Wangui!'

'What's wrong with us?' My aunt had not yet seen me.

'We forgot the baby and he might be dead!'

'Oh, Ngai!' cried my aunt. 'Let's run fast!'

They scrambled up and, dropping their hoes, ran to me. They lifted up the little *nguo* with which they had covered me and to their horror found I was bright red all over, like a pepper! They were very frightened.

'Oh, my dear, lovely son!'

'What shall we tell his father?' asked my aunt.

'He will be extremely angry—we must do something quickly.'

They rushed me to a near-by well and put me in the water. They bathed me all over but I was still as red. Then they covered me with wet mud, but all in vain. At last, back in the garden, they oiled and fed me, and again laid me in the shadow of a banana tree. But this time they watched me all the time. The day passed and they worked on. What could they tell my father?

At last the evening came when they must take me home. Back they went and began preparing dinner for my father who had not yet come. Soon they saw him and quickly looked at me once more. By now, my skin was getting better but there were still red blotches all over me—I certainly looked a very different baby from the one my father used to know. No escape. They must tell the truth.

My father listened intently but, being worried and nervous, interrupted my mother's story—

'Is he all right now?'

'Yes, he is all right,' they replied.

'Then let me see him.'

My mother took me to him. He unwrapped me and examined me carefully all over. At last he gave me back to my mother, saying sternly:

'Please be careful with this boy. Nothing must ever happen to him.'

My father was a good man. Nothing more was ever said about this incident and soon my skin recovered completely.

Although, unlike Europeans, the Africans do not usually suffer from sunburn, the African children do. This can easily be noticed, especially with the very young, who are born with a white or reddish skin which changes only gradually. Sometimes the change takes five months or more.

Several months later, when I was able to sit up unaided as most babies can, and after the sun incident was forgotten, my mother went to work again in the same garden and again she carried me with her. This time I was also able to crawl around.

My mother, like other Kikuyu women, knew how to sit me down on one spot from which I could not crawl easily and so disturb her while working. What she usually did was to dig a little hole in the ground about five to six inches deep. She would then put me in the hole, covering me up to my hips with soft soil as if I were sitting in a deep-seated little chair.

On this particular day, my mother tied a big branch of a tree with a lot of leaves to a banana tree. The branch up in the tree cast a permanent shadow on the ground so Mother didn't have to dig more than one hole because my protecting shadow did not shift.

I was quite happy by myself, playing with potatoes, and Mother went about working and singing. But, because of past experience, she looked over at me from time to time to make sure I was all right. She worked and I played; she sang and I talked away to myself:

'Ma-mu-mum; Ma-mu-mum; eee—eee-e.'

'Daadaa-daadaah; Daa-daah; eee—eee-e.'

Everything was very peaceful until suddenly, while glancing over at me, my mother saw slithering towards me fast a large snake, its head raised and long forked tongue flickering from its open mouth—and only twelve yards away from me!

I was gay and playing and would perhaps even have thought that the snake was another toy to play with if it had reached me! My mother flung herself towards me, throwing her hoe at the snake in a desperate effort to slow its speed. Fortunately, the hoe hit the snake on the head and it twisted with pain, away from me. At that instant my mother reached me and, without stopping, scooped me up in her arms and ran away calling for help.

A couple working near by hurried to my mother's aid but, shocked as she was with the danger and her great effort, she could only gasp:

'Snake, snake, big snake!'

The snake was still sliding towards a bushy side of our garden. A man came with a long stick and hit its head repeatedly until it was dead. He then made a fire and burnt the snake completely.

My mother was very distressed and could work no more that day. Still frightened and worried, she took me home. In the evening my father came from work. Immediately my mother explained to him what had happened.

'Was it very close to him?' Father asked.

'No, I saw it just before it reached him,' she said. 'I rushed and threw my hoe in front of it and hit it on the head. I cried very loudly and a couple working near by came to my aid.'

'Was it killed?'

'Yes, it was killed and burnt,' she added.

'I think I might have seen a snake near the bushy area of the

14

garden, chasing a rat,' my father said. 'But it disappeared before I reached it. Perhaps it was the same snake', my father thought. 'Perhaps we should ask your mother to allow your young sister to stay with us so that she can take care of Mugo when you are working.'

'I think we should,' Mother agreed.

When my grandmother heard the story she too was upset and agreed at once to let her youngest daughter stay with us to be my nurse. And it came to pass that she took very good care of me, though one day she was negligent and burnt my umbilical cord.

When Father and Mother learned about my wound on the stomach they were extremely worried. Both agreed that my young aunt and I should be purified. The reason for this was that, in Kikuyu society, aunts, uncles, and their nephews and nieces are not supposed to hurt each other physically, however slightly. Even if they should shed each other's blood accidentally, a purification involving the strangling of a goat or sheep must take place. Hence *Aihwa matitihanagia*, meaning that uncles and aunts, and their nephews and nieces do not hurt each other. There is no distinction between sisters of the mother and sisters of the father, or again between brothers of the father and brothers of the mother.

A serious purification like this, however simple it may look, had to be performed by a *Mugo*, and Father consulted with a neighbouring *Mugo*, who agreed to help.

A fairly young lamb was strangled by Father, assisted by a few friends who were our neighbours. As usual, a small amount of *taatha*—a collection of the animal's undigested food in the small intestine—was preserved.

After the meat had been roasted in our yard and eaten, my mother was asked by the medicine-man to bring me to the spot where the meat had been roasted. My young aunt, who had burnt my umbilical cord, had also to come.

The medicine-man asked my mother to hold me just near, or by him. He then asked my aunt to come very close and hold a little stick lit with fire. My father and other friends were watching.

'Pretend that you are burning him again,' the medicine-man told my aunt. 'Just pretend, don't actually do it.'

As my aunt was pretending to burn me, the medicine-man put his right hand between us, throwing bits of *taatha* down as if he were trying to intervene between two quarrelling people and saying words like 'Peace be between you'—*Nindamuhorohia*.

My family was now happy with a restored confidence that Mugo and his aunt would henceforth have no more misfortune.

All of this I have been told as the way in which Mugo-son-of-Gatheru came into the world.

My first memories are of a farm called Kwa Maitho or 'The Place of Him Who Wears Glasses'. The European gentleman who owned that farm not only wore glasses, but also created a crisis for his Squatters by committing suicide. He had been a general in the First World War and then retired to Kenya. One day some of the Africans reported that they had heard him say: 'They want to fight again some day against Germany. They want to call me again. I don't go. I will not.' A few days later he killed himself. The Africans talked for days about the strange ways of white men who kill themselves. Most of the Squatters were not sorry to see him die, for he was very rough and free with his curses and kicks. But the farm closed down and the Africans had to find somewhere else to go. Father was very prosperous—he had over 100 sheep and goats, the most valued form of wealth, and even though I was very small then, I can still remember him boasting, when he was warm with beer, about his ten fat and lovely billy-goats.

My first sister was born at Kwa Maitho and was named according to custom after my *father's* mother, Nyambura. But she died soon after she was born. Then another sister was born, and, being the second girl, she was named after my *mother's* mother, Wanjiku. She lived and grew up with me. Father had been happy when I was born. Now Mother was very happy, for she had a daughter to help her with the planting of the crops, the cleaning of the house, the gathering of firewood, and the carrying of the water. My job as a boy was to take care of the sheep and goats.

Life in an African Forest

Many people in Europe and America think that Africa is one vast and large dense jungle. That is not so. Most of it is either desert or flat, grassy savannah land upon which the people herd cows and goats, or reap and sow; or where gazelles, giraffes, kudus, and lions roam in the deep grass that has not yet been put to the hoe or plough. The place where the Kikuyu live was once covered by a heavy forest. My people had cut and burned most of the trees by the time I was born in order to plant their crops. The elders knew that as the trees were cut the rain came less frequently, but as many more mouths had to be fed they kept on cutting. When the Europeans came they passed laws, setting aside certain areas as forest reserves. Trees could only be cut with permission, and some of them they attempted to care for and to turn into parks. For the work of caring for a forest reserve Africans were needed.

There was a forest reserve at Githara near Kwa Maitho about twenty miles south-west of Lumbwa Station, and when the 'Man Who Wore Glasses' killed himself and his Squatters were scattered, my father decided to take a job as a forester. We moved, therefore, to a clearing in the forest that had been provided for the African workers so that they could grow their own food. Mother cared for the crops; I cared for the sheep and goats; and Father worked among the trees. There were about thirty or forty of us living in the clearing. For me it was great fun, living among the big trees. For Father and the other men it was torture. They worked hard all day, but they got very little sleep at night. From dark till daybreak the night air was filled with the screeches and cries of forest animals—of baboons and hyenas and many more whose names we did not know. And there were the elephants. Our elders cowered in fear, as we did also, when we heard the mean little African bull elephants trumpeting in the night, and the men had to stay up at nights building fires to keep the elephants from crashing into the clearing upon our houses. The Kikuyu have never liked the forest. So, soon, in 1934, my father and the others decided to move into a village near the forest reserve where many more people lived—a village called Stoton. I was nine years old when we moved there. He was still working for the Forest Department earning eight shillings a month. I was ten when we left. I was both glad and sorry to leave the deep forest. I was frightened there, but there was also much fun.

Our homestead, like that of all other Kikuyu families, included two circular houses made of logs and with thatched roofs. One was for my mother and the young children and was called a 'nyumba'. One was for my father and the older boys and was called a 'thingira'. In the centre of both the *nyumba* and the *thingira* was a stone fireplace used for cooking. A log was always burning there, and it was considered very bad for a fire to ever go out in their house. If this ever happened, a ceremony was necessary to light a new fire.

A traditional Kikuyu house is not laid out in a haphazard fashion. Entering the door of the *nyumba* one will find that a screen faces him shutting off the inside of the house, a 'ruhirigo'. The centre of the floor is used for meals and sitting. At the back of the house directly opposite the door was my mother's bed. On one side of it was a little cupboard and shelf where things like knives, sticks for herding goats, and sometimes a spear or bow and arrow were kept. On the other side of my mother's bed was a kind of pantry for gourds and foods. Next to the pantry on the right were the beds reserved for the girls. Around the walls in the space not used for beds and storage we kept a space for goats and sheep, since the Kikuyu keep animals in the house like the peasants of Ireland and some parts of Europe are accustomed to do. Always there is a special spot called the 'Gichegu' for fattening a ram or two. Good mothers always kept the *nyumba* very clean. In general the men's house or *thingira* has the same equipment but not so much of it; custom does not demand that it be so precisely arranged.

When I was very small I slept in the *nyumba*. When I grew older I was very proud of being able to sleep in the *thingira* with the men.

It was at Stoton that I first began to learn Bible stories. One that impressed me very much was the story of David, the shepherd boy, for I, too, was a boy who had to care for my family's animals. Among the Kikuyu the young boys serve as shepherds and goat-herds. My father left at dawn for the forest, and soon after my mother would call me, or if I was sleeping too soundly would shake me gently. Sometimes when I was very hard to wake she would shout loudly: 'Wake up, Mugo! Stop sleeping so late like a European.'

When my mother woke me in the morning I was trained to run first outside to the wash place and then to come back for my breakfast, a delicious stew of corn and beans and vegetables. Some of this would be saved and wrapped in a leaf for my lunch. And then I was off to herd the sheep and goats.

Herding was, for us boys, great fun. We took the animals to the clearings in the forest and it was our job to see that they did not wander away and get lost, that no one stole them, and that no animals bothered them. We carried our 'ruthanju'—the stick for herding sheep and goats—and some of the animals had bells on them. All of us had heard tales in the men's houses of leopards who might attack the animals and of Kipsigis thieves who sometimes appeared suddenly with their spears and said roughly as they drove the stolen goats away: 'Go home and don't speak or we'll spear you.' I never met a leopard, but twice some of our goats were stolen by the Kipsigis while I was shouting for my father from a tree which I had climbed. But these were just scattered, unpleasant incidents. Usually it was great fun—trying to ride the big billy-goat like Europeans ride their horses, playing with the tame big black billy-goat, Kiumu, that followed me around; playing 'retrieve' with the sheep-dog named Simba, 'the lion'; or tussling with the other boys who were sometimes herding near by.

We boys were supposed to tend our animals and not to waste our time in playing. But we were like boys everywhere. When we saw a group of Kipsigis boys tending their goats in our area we would often gang up and rush upon them with our sticks and then the fight was on. Kipsigis boys were experts in wrestling.

Amongst ourselves we sometimes played a game by dividing up into two groups, each chanting riddles at the others to be answered, or singing challenges at each other: 'Goats are ours! Sheep are ours! Sky is ours! Sun is ours! Dare you to fight!' And nothing was more thrilling than a good fight between our dogs. Sometimes we whiled the time away by making bows and arrows tipped with porcupine quill, challenging each other to shoot birds; or sometimes we prepared ingenious bird traps. All of these activities were frowned upon by our fathers, and occasionally a father would come upon us delinquents, shouting: 'Why did you let those goats scatter?' and sometimes whipping

B

his youngster with a stick. There were times, too, when we went to sleep on a hot summer afternoon, and our fathers might come secretly upon us and box and cuff us.

When the sun was going down we turned our way homeward and in the dusk we could hear the goat-bells tinkling as we brought the animals home, tired and hungry. A warm supper of vegetables and, rarely, a bit of meat was always welcome. Sometimes we ate outside together and sometimes I ate in the men's house or the women's house. Food was always cooked in the women's house. Men did not cook in their houses. Supper over, the larger boys went to the men's house where, far into the night, riddles and stories would be told.

Father would let me go to sleep in the men's house even though the men were still discussing. Some of the other boys' fathers made them stay awake until all the male guests had left, saying: 'Your snoring will disturb us.' We learned much in the men's house—of legends and stories of the Kikuyu, of riddles, and of men's affairs. That was where we learned how to be men when we grew up.

Sometimes after the crops had been planted and, while Mother was waiting for them to grow large enough to cut or pull or dig, she would come to the fields where I was herding to bring me food or water. But usually she was too busy for that. Kikuyu women work very hard, cultivating their crops and carrying firewood or water. Sometimes they work together in groups, helping each other. Such groups have a name, *ngwatio*. Often I have heard a group of women working together and singing as they worked—making up songs about things that had happened, or boasting or joking through the words they sang, like this:

LEADER: Tuinire muciare kibura. (Let us sing for those who are
           born Ethaga.)
CHORUS: Huuh-hoo-aaae-aiya-ii-huuh-hioo. (Yes, it is so.)
LEADER: Look at me; I have a partner. Have you one?
CHORUS: No, she has not one. Huuh-hoo-aae . . .
LEADER: Maybe no partner because she is too ugly? (Sung jok-
           ingly.)
CHORUS: Huuh-hoo-aaae . . .

Sometimes Father joined in the hoeing when he did not have other work to do. Sometimes I helped too. Father, my

20

mother and my sisters and I would go down the line together. How Father loved to sing as he showed his strength:

> Put the hoe into the shaft—hauh!
> Like we did at Kwai Maitho—hauh!
> Or no calabash of gruel—hauh!
> Will you get when work is done—hauh!

Sometimes the line grew large with ten or fifteen people, and nobody wanting to admit that he was tired.

These were happy days, and still today I sometimes think with sadness of this life that I shall never know again, and that, now, my children will never know.

You must be Born Again

There are two great events in the life of every Kikuyu boy and girl which he or she can never forget. The first starts a person to thinking about being a man or a woman—'putting away childish things' as the Bible says—and the second *makes* him a man or a woman. The first ceremony is known as 'Njiarano' or the 'second birth'; the other is called 'irua' or 'Initiation'. I went through the first when I was eleven.

One day the men began to discuss me as they talked in the *thingira*, and the feeling grew that it was time that 'The Silent One' be born again. Even Mwando, my mother's brother, who was a Christian, felt that I should go through this very important ceremony. The men discussed it and decided on it, but the carrying out of it was women's business, and no men were allowed.

For many years the Kikuyu tried to keep this ceremony secret and the accounts of it which they gave to European anthropologists were not always true. As for us children, we knew nothing of what was going to happen to us on the day our mothers said: 'Tomorrow you will be born again.'

On the day that my second birth occurred the men and women of my clan, Ethaga, who lived in Stoton or near by gathered at our homestead. My father killed a fat ram, and the meat was cooked for the men to eat in the *thingira* while the women carried out the ceremony in the *nyumba*. They carefully took out the stomach and cleaned it, leaving the small intestine

21

attached. This was given to the women, who took it into the *nyumba*. I watched nervously, and then was called into the women's house.

Seated in a circle on the floor were my female kinspeople, some of whom I knew well and others who were unknown to me. My mother was in the centre. Everyone was quiet and very solemn. An old woman led me, frightened and almost shaking, to my mother and placed me in her lap facing away from her. I could tell by the motions they made and the feel of my mother that they were undressing her. They then took the stomach of the ram and wrapped me in it as though it were a cape, stretching it as they did so, and passed the small intestine backward between my legs. In after years, when the meaning of the ceremony was made clear to me by the older men, I knew that the ram stomach stood for my mother's womb and placenta, and the intestine was the umbilical cord.

I was pressed up close against my mother, and then one woman from the circle began to sing-song a prayer: 'On, Wamahindu, aaaririri ... ...' 'Our clan member, you who have died, bless this child that is being born.') Another woman called upon another of my ancestors, and, in turn, each of the women called upon others. They asked them to protect me, to make me prosperous, and to watch over me. In the meantime my mother was groaning as though she were in pain, and somehow, I have forgotten now whether an old woman told me to do it or not, I began to whimper and moan like a little baby. When all had called upon my ancestors to bless me my mother and I were laid on a mat, and I was told that for five days no men would enter the house, my mother would do no work, and that I was not to feed myself—that I must act as though I were a helpless baby. This I did with Mother feeding me soft foods, and occasionally I whimpered and cried. Nor could I leave the house.

At the end of the fifth day my mother arose and washed herself and me. She led me out of the house to the garden and showed me all of the tools she used in the garden and named the plants for me and told me: 'Mugo, you have been born again.' That was all, except that now I not only herded the goats but I was also supposed to pay attention to how men broke the earth and cleared a spot to grow things. My second birth had made me a full-fledged member of my clan, and had started me on the path to being a man instead of a boy. It was ten years later before I was initiated into the tribe, and of this important ceremony I shall tell later.

The 'Thahu' and the 'Purification'

My father, Gatheru, was over six feet tall and very strong. My grandfather, Mugo, and his wife, Njoki, were also very tall. My grandfather on my mother's side, Kuria-son-of-Nguuri, was as tall as my father was. My mother, Wambui, was only five feet six inches tall. My sister, Wanjiku, who was born after me, was taller than I was. The fact that I was not tall raised a serious thought in the minds of both my father and my grandfather, Kuria. 'What is wrong with Mugo?' Kuria asked, puzzled. 'My grandson is *mumu*, tough, but not tall,' he continued. 'Something must be done.'

Kuria, my grandfather, loved my mother dearly as she was the daughter of his favourite wife Wanjiku but, in general, he loathed short men. Fortunately for him, eleven of his thirteen sons were tall men. The other two of them he despised. He wondered whether the two short sons could stand a good fight in an emergency. My grandfather used to boast of how he fought in a skirmish between the Kikuyu Squatters and the Kipsigis at Kwa-Maitho. He was very strong, although his left arm had been amputated as a result of an injury he received during the First World War when the British battalion in which he was serving was heavily engaged by one of Paul von Lettow-Vorbeck's battalions. Lettow-Vorbeck was a very famous German general during the East Africa campaigns of 1914–18, and my grandfather has a high regard for his bravery.

Now, as Kuria was puzzled by my not growing tall, he asked my father to go and consult a Shaman, or medicine-man. He felt that somebody might have been casting bad *thahu* against me. My father agreed, and went to consult a medicine-man named Kanyita. Kanyita asked my father about my background, and how I was fed by my mother. He took his 'mwano', or sacred basket, and pulled out one of the gourds in which 'mbugu' were kept. (*Mbugu* are like beads, and have different colours. Some may be black or brown; there are also some which look like small, round, crystalline stones. A trained Shaman interprets the pattern after they have been thrown on a dried animal skin.) Kanyita spread a soft *rua* on the ground near his *thingira*. He then started throwing *mbugu* on the soft skin. He watched their movements carefully and asked my father to count them. This was done repeatedly. Ultimately Kanyita told my father that I, Mugo, was not growing tall, because, some time in the past, when my mother had been menstruating, she might have touched me with a hand or garment defiled by menstrual blood. This was tantamount to a *thahu*, or curse.

(In Kikuyu society menstruating women may not draw water used for brewing beer. Men may not have sexual play with them either. But, paradoxically, menstruating women can cook food for men to eat.)

Kanyita advised my father that Mugo should be cleansed or purified through a purification ritual called 'Kurutwo thahu'— 'cleansing out the *thahu*'. Kanyita himself would perform the purification. He asked my father to find a spotless brown ram for the ceremony.

Father told my mother and my grandfather, and Grandfather volunteered to bring a spotless ram right away. So on the following morning he brought *Ndurume Kimukuyu*, the brown ram. He left it in mother's hut and went to see Kanyita. Finally, the day on which purification was to take place was fixed being, I think, two days after the ram was brought.

When the time came, my grandfather came with one of my uncles, Ernest Kamara Kuria. In a short time Kanyita and his aide arrived. This was the first time I had seen Kanyita. He was a medium-sized old man with long hands and long fingernails and his hair was completely white. His eyes were red as though they had just been exposed to fire smoke, and he had a very heavy baritone voice. His looks would have frightened me to death if I had had to meet him alone.

After a short time my father went into the bush to cut some leaves, 'mathinjiro', on which the ram was to be strangled. According to Kikuyu custom, all animals, whether for sacrificial purposes or not, must be strangled rather than slaughtered. Father brought the leaves and spread them at the centre of our yard. They covered about six square yards. He then went into my mother's hut, and brought out the ram into the yard.

Kanyita's aide and my uncle Kamara helped Father to place the ram on the leaves, and so it was strangled. In the meantime Kanyita and my grandfather were enjoying some private conversation and did not approach the ram until it was dead. I was near my father all the time.

Finally, Kanyita and my grandfather approached the place where the animal was laid, and Kanyita ordered that when the ram was cut and all parts separated, the *taatha*, or the waste matter in both large and small intestines, should be saved in a calabash. His order was carried out by my father. Half of the meat was then roasted on a fire which was set in the yard just near the spot on which the ram was strangled. The other half was taken to my mother who was in the hut where my sister was cleaning the pots in which the meat was to be cooked. Custom forbids Kikuyu women from taking part in the strangling of animals, whether they be for sacrifices or not.

It was afternoon, the roasted meat was eaten and purification was to take place in the evening. In the meantime the men had a vigorous discussion in which my grandfather was so assertive that he appeared to dominate. He was, however, listening to Kanyita with particular interest.

When evening came Kanyita asked my father to bring the *taatha* which had been saved in the calabash. Kanyita took the calabash full of *taatha* and added a small amount of blood to it. He then took his medicine basket and pulled out two bundles of long leaves tied together. They looked like horse-tails.

Kanyita, his aide, my grandfather, father, and uncle, stood up. They formed a small circle, and called me inside the circle. Kanyita's aide was holding the calabash with the *taatha*. Kanyita dipped the two bundles of leaves into it and pulled them out wet with *taatha*. He sprinkled it on my head as if rain was falling on me. Everyone present was silent except Kanyita who was reciting various magical words as he sprinkled. Some of the words which I could hear went like this: 'I cleanse you of all the *thahu*, all the curse or defilement which you may have had in the past and present, and which might have been responsible for stopping your normal growth.' Quickly he asked his aide to smear my head with a lot of thick, wet *taatha* which looked like kneaded flour or wet clay. Kanyita then told

25

my father that I should not wash my head until two days had passed.

The purification was now over and Kanyita and his aide went away, but my grandfather, father, and my uncle were left in the yard enjoying the evening fire. I went to the hut with my mother and sister, my head covered with stinking wet *taatha*. The smell of the *taatha* was extremely offensive! After two days were over I washed my head, and it was not so easy to wash the *taatha* thoroughly from my head since it had dried in my hair. Now everybody in the family were certain that Mugo would grow tall. I am sure that Father was disappointed when I wrote to him in 1952 from Lincoln University in Pennsylvania that I was all right, but that I was only five feet and eight inches tall.

III

Youth in the Highlands

Father became a 'Doctor'

MY father had been born in the clan of Ethaga and of the line of
Mugo. This, the people believed, gave him supernatural
powers, though he would have to be trained to use them. But it
was his duty, after he had raised at least one son to the age of
initiation, to take his training and begin to practise as a
'medicine-man'. In areas such as the Land of the Strangers
where most were younger people seeking their fortunes, there
was constant discussion of the fact that there were not enough
'doctors'. Many felt that those born with the gift should perhaps
start their careers earlier. My father, however, was mainly
interested in getting more money and more sheep and goats.
Doctoring he would do when the time came. But his wish was
not to prevail—the 'call' same sooner, and he was compelled to
answer.

The sign came in this manner. A few months after my father
had built his *thingira* and *nyumba* at Stoton, and I was just over
nine years old, my mother went one day, as she did occasionally,
to the market, miles away at the Lumbwa railway station, with
several other Squatter women. They could not return the same
day, because they had to carry heavy loads of vegetables on
their backs and so they used to spend a night in a village about
five miles south of the station. On that occasion she had carried
a very big load of cabbages, peas, and cauliflowers.

She told me and my sister to sleep in the *nyumba*. My other
brother was to sleep in the *thingira* with my father. Very late
that night I heard a terrible noise as though someone was tearing

down our house. I jumped up and smelled smoke and saw fire. Some men rushed in and pulled me and my sister out, and began to try to move out some of our belongings before the *nyumba* burned to the ground. I started to the men's house and saw that it was a heap of ashes. I was told that a fire had broken out in the *thingira* and my father had awakened and run out with my brother calling: 'Fire! Fire! Fire!' Many people came and tried to help him to save some of his belongings. While they were helping to save the *thingira*, the *nyumba* in which my sister and I were sleeping caught fire also.

The next morning, as my mother returned from market, she was horrified, when still about half a mile away, to see that no houses were standing on our homestead spot. She started asking anxiously as she came: 'What has happened?' and then: 'How are my children? Are they safe? Were they burned?' But she felt happier when she arrived, for already our neighbours were at work building new houses for us as is the Kikuyu custom. When the houses were finished some of the 'doctors' in the area said to my father: 'The burning was a sign. You have been called to have yourself made a doctor. So it must be.' But my father still went about his business unheeding.

On the day that the houses were finished my father made ready to kill a goat and to ask Ngai to bless the new house and to purify the ashes of the old one. As he was preparing the head of the goat to cut off the horns, the knife slipped and he cut his hand. This was very serious, for during a Kikuyu purification ceremony no blood can be spilled other than that of the sacrificial animal. He went at once to a doctor so that he could now be purified. The doctor killed the goat, purified my father and the house, and then called him aside for a sober conference. 'Gatheru-son-of-Mugo,' he said, 'there have now been two signs. Become a doctor at once.' But Father was very busy with other matters and made no move.

Months passed. Certain family troubles arose which will be discussed later. And then my mother began to have a sickness of the throat. Father consulted a very famous doctor, one Ngubu who was known for miles around, about the misfortunes which seemed to be falling upon him. He told my father: 'There are two things to do. First you must become a doctor. You are avoiding the voice of Ngai. Second there are some who are not so prosperous as you and they have placed medicines in your house to do you harm. These must be removed. I shall do it for you. They are trying to destroy your family. Your wife may die. Your goats may die. You should consult another doctor and the two of us will remove the bad medicines.'

Father believed in the medicine-magic of his fathers, but he did not trust Ngubu. He knew that Ngubu was very famous and rich in goats. He suspected that he was using his fame to get new cases to get more goats. So he consulted a woman doctor. She told him the same thing. So now he decided to act.

Father went to a neighbouring farm where his sister—called The Beautiful One—was married to a prosperous Kikuyu. A weighty conference was held with some of the leading men there and they suggested that he consult a doctor they knew. This doctor consented to take out the bad magic from the house for a fat ram and a goat, and to make my father a Shaman for another very fat ram. The bargain was made, and it was arranged that the woman Shaman would assist him. My father's younger brother, who lived in our *thingira*, was also to assist in the ceremony.

The day of the cleansing of the house and the initiation of my father as a doctor finally arrived. A great crowd had gathered in our yard. The two doctors arrived, each carrying a *mwano*, or sacred basket, in which the powerful good medicines were kept. The male doctor put his basket down and took out of it a small gourd about the size of a teacup. He mixed some water and red powder in it and attached a long cord to it so that he could swing it like a censer. He called my father's brother to assist him and the cleansing began. He went to the centre of the yard and began to swing the gourd on the string backward and forward saying very solemnly: 'Eastern side, western side, northern side, southern side, show me where those poisons are.' Then he shook with a quick jerk and leaped toward the storehouse just beside my mother's *nyumba*. As he did so the gourd swung out like a pendulum toward the storehouse, and some of the red liquid spouted in that direction. In a very loud and authoritative voice the doctor cried out to my father's younger brother: 'There is one. Go take him!'

My little uncle ran to the storehouse, the doctor pointed out where to search, and he came forward with a piece of rolled up bark that had some white powder in it. The crowd cried out with astonishment and began to chatter to each other. The doctor then said very confidently: 'There are about six. We shall find them.' So the ritual was repeated five more times— the red liquid spurted toward the house of my mother near the door, to a place near my mother's bed, to a place near my sister's bed, and to two places in the *thingira*. The doctor ordered all the pieces of bark to be put in a pile together in the centre of the yard, and he stood over them and made a very solemn speech: 'I warn you, Gatheru-son-of-Mugo, in your home, your very home; one of your daughters was held tight like this by death (here he made a gesture). She could have died at once. Your wife, too, could have died at once had we not come to take out these evils things.' He then took another medicine gourd from his *mwano* and poured a liquid on the bad medicines to take their power from them, and ordered the people to burn them.

When the bad medicines had been burned my father was called to the centre of the yard. Around him were the two doctors who had performed the purification ceremony, and Ngubu, mightiest of Kikuyu doctors in the Land of the Strangers. It was they who would now make of my father one who could begin to practise. First they gave him five small gourds with medicine in them. These they took from their own *mwano* for, as they said: 'It is not good that a doctor begin his work with new ones. These are some old ones.' Then they took three small pieces of limestone, trimmed them neatly, and dug a small hole in the centre of each. Some very powerful medicine was put in each stone and they were sealed up. Three holes were dug at various parts of the yard and the stones were buried. My father was told that whenever he moved he was to dig up the stones, take them with him, and re-bury them at the new home site. They were his for ever to neutralize the evil magic that might be done to him.

Then something very important happened. The people began to demand that Ngubu, the mighty doctor, bless my father. It was thought that he did not like my father, and the people, therefore, insisted that Ngubu bless him publicly so that any evil he might have in his heart could not be used later against my father.

At this time my father was a fully fledged Mugo, but, before he could practise with confidence on his own, he had to undergo a period of further training with a more experienced medicine-man.

That same day I was given my 'githitu' and this is the way that it was done. During the ceremony a goat had been strangled for the doctors to eat at the setting of the sun. A piece of the meat was taken and powerful medicine was rubbed into it. Encased in a small stick, the whole thing was put in a leather band that was bound to my arm. This was my *githitu* which I would wear to protect myself from evil.

It was at Stoton that I first heard of Adam and Eve and the Garden of Eden—and that snake. As I look back on it now through the years, it was at Stoton where a snake entered *my* Eden. The snake that brought the trouble was in the form of a goat. Father was rich in goats; but goats were our undoing. Our *nyumba* and *thingira* were as popular as any in Stoton as a gathering place for children and their elders, for beer-drinking and story-telling far into the night. But the goats became too many, and the Government decreed that every man must reduce his herd to keep them from overgrazing in the forest clearings. Ask an Englishman or American to burn up his money or his best clothes—that was what it meant to tell my father to destroy his goats or sell them. What was a rich man without something to let people know he was rich? If father sold his goats for money he would get very little for them, and there was very little in Stoton to buy and very little that he wanted. Many were the discussions between the men, and between my father and my mother about what to do with the goats. A decision was finally made which may seem strange to European and American readers.

When I spoke of my mother's father at the beginning of my tale I said that he had nine wives. I used once to be ashamed to talk about this in front of Europeans and Americans. I am not ashamed any more, for now I know a little history and anthro-pology. I shall not be ashamed of my father for having many, nor even of some of my friends now living in Kenya who have several wives. I do not want polygamy for myself and I do not think that it is a custom that will last among my people in the modern world. But I know many good people, and wise people, and many happy people, too, who follow the custom of their fathers and are polygamists. Customs change, but not all people change at the same time.

So, rather than sell the goats he was not allowed to keep, Father and Mother decided to use the goats as 'ruracio', or a bride-gift, a dowry, to secure another wife. This, too, is a custom that many people have. Mother did not object for she, as a first wife, would now have another woman to help her with the garden and the household tasks. I did not object for now I could boast to the other boys that my father was becoming a *very* rich man—he had two wives. I would also have a 'maitu munyinyi', or 'small mother', in addition to my 'maitu', or real mother.

Many years before my father decided to take another wife, an English anthropologist named Routledge was visiting Chief Munge of the Kikuyu. His wife asked Munge's wife: 'What should I tell the women on my return to England about the women of the Kikuyu?' Munge's wife said: 'Tell them two things. One is that we never marry anyone we do not want to; and the other is that we like our husbands to have as many wives as possible.' It is still true today that Kikuyu women marry no one they do not wish to, but many girls now wish their husbands to have no other wives. My mother, however, had not learned Western ways, as they have; she was like Munge's wife.

My father took about fifty of his goats, and went home to the Kikuyu Reserve to find a bride. The usual custom is for the man to 'court' the girl, but sometimes, when taking a second or a third wife, a man would first make arrangements with her relatives who then would ask if she wanted to marry the young man. Father saw the girl he liked and began to discuss the amount of *ruracio* with her brother. But the girl knew her rights, and said she would never marry any man until she saw him and decided whether she would like him for a husband. My father was a strong and handsome man. She saw him and she liked him; so 'the goats were passed'.

I was very excited while waiting to see my *maitu munyinyi*. Mother was busy making arrangements to receive her, the woman that she would call *muiru wakwa*, 'One who is next to me'. When Father brought her home to the new *nyumba* that was built for her, all of us were pleased. Now I had a rich father, two mothers, and a sister. What more could a Kikuyu child ask for? I did a lot of boasting, and got into a lot of fights with the other herd boys.

But trouble in our household soon began. Word had spread among my new 'mother's' relatives back on the Reserve that she was married to a 'rich' man. One day a brother of hers arrived and was welcomed as a guest. He slept with us in the *thingira*. We slaughtered a goat to please him, and for all of us the taste of the meat was good in our mouths. But he stayed a very long time; in fact he did not leave. And then another brother came, and we slaughtered a goat for him, too. And more brothers came, and always for each the goat must be slaughtered. Now there were many mouths to feed from the two women's gardens. And the newcomers worked little, but ate much. My mother liked the new wife, for she was pleasant and obedient to her, and was a good worker, but my mother did not like the new wife's brothers who ate up the fruits of her labours. More important, she did not like to see goats continuously disappearing for their feasts and their sacrifices. After all, those goats could be used some day to get more wives to lighten her labour.

My mother is a strong woman and was never one to hold tight her tongue. She told the brothers how she felt. They resented the telling and began to insult my mother with the most cutting of insults to a Kikuyu woman: 'You bear children in number like the hatching of chickens' eggs.' My mother was very hurt. The hurt which first found expression in murmuring ended in bickering. Well do I remember what my father said, an easy-going man he was, when she first mentioned it to him: 'Oh, leave that matter!' And well do I remember what he *did* when once he saw the two women arguing and shouting at one another. He cuffed them both, and told them they should get along with each other better; that they were bringing dishonour to the house of a respected man, a 'doctor', Gatheru-son-of-Mugo.

But he did not ask his second wife's brothers to leave the *thingira*.

My *maitu munyinyi* tried to solve the problem by going back home to her parents in the Reserve. My father went to ask her to come back to live with us. Her brothers, now that they saw the trouble they had made, offered to return the bride-gift of goats and to take their sister home to stay. But Father's prestige

33

was at stake, for should not a real man be able to keep peace among his wives and not admit defeat? He would not agree to a divorce by the returning of the goats. And so my second mother came back from the Reserve again to Stoton to live with us. And the brothers stayed on, too. My mother and little mother then began to quarrel again.

I was very unhappy about this trouble in my family. I thought much of it when I was herding our stock alone, for I loved both my mother and my father, and I liked my little mother too.

Father tried to be patient throughout the dispute between his two wives, although he sometimes lost his temper. That he did not lose it more often, or have occasion to lose it more often, was due to Mwando. Mwando and my father were of 'rikar-imwe', which means that they were age-mates, that they had been initiated into manhood together. Among the Kikuyu being circumcised together is a bond that binds men to one another and to each other's children even closer than to their own brothers. For when you have squatted on the earth together waiting for the circumciser's knife to cut you, and have danced together after you have shown yourself brave while all the girls are looking on with admiration, how can you ever forget? Mwando and my father liked each other so much that when Mwando came to Stoton to work my father asked him to live in his *thingira* with him. So it was they shared our men's house together. Each liked the other. Each respected the other. But they were very different. Father was a *Mugo* practising the medicine-magic of his ancestors. Mwando was a Christian, converted by the Church of Scotland. It was Mwando who tried to calm the two women, and who counselled my father to be wise and patient—and Christianlike. Father listened to the advice about wisdom and patience—and ignored the admonition about Christianity.

Mwando believed in two things—Christianity and education. His one great passion was to see a church and school at Stoton. For this he begged money from the Church Missionary Society, from the Church of Scotland mission, and from anybody else that he could get to listen. Stoton got its church and school. Mwando raised the money, but he could not teach. Kimani did that, for he had had a primary school education and was

34

something of a learned man, well-fitted to preach and teach. Kimani had high status, too, for he was an important overseer on the farm.

The school was equivalent to what would be in England an infant and primary school combined, but its facilities were very, very poor indeed, and although the standard was pretty low, infants, juniors, and grown-up persons attended this school. Ages did not matter. The emphasis was put on simple arithmetic, writing, and reading. Those who were able to read the Bible felt as if they were very *profound* or *learned*.

As Kimani was an overseer, and couldn't therefore conduct the classes during the week-days from Monday to Friday, he held classes in the evening for the grown-ups and certain young persons, and reserved Saturday classes for the infants and juniors. Later on a regular teacher from Kikuyuland, named Kamau, who was also related to Kimani, was employed to become a regular teacher for the school so that Kimani could concentrate on his responsible job as an overseer. Kamau was educated in the Church of Scotland mission and was a good teacher. He introduced soccer to Stoton, and the young men enthusiastically played it on Saturdays and Sundays. Squatters in the Forest Department were much freer than their brothers on the European farms.

I started to attend the church and wanted very much to go to school. Father made no strong objection to either, but I was ashamed to go to school. On my arm I proudly wore my *githitu* which showed that I was protected from being poisoned. I had vowed to wear it until I had been through the ceremony that would make me a 'doctor' like my grandfather and my father. The goat boys who were not Christians admired my *githitu*, while the Christians teased me about it and suggested that I cast it off. When herding goats I was surrounded by boys, most of whom were not Christians, but I was not ashamed and fought back with words and sticks. At school, however, it was different, for most of the boys who went there were Christians. I wanted an education. Should I become a Christian so as to get it without having trouble with my classmates? I did not know. I wanted to go to school, but I wanted to be a 'medicine-man' some day, too.

Most of the young Kikuyu I knew went to church. The

children of my age liked to hear the singing and the preaching. The older boys liked to look at the girls who flocked there in their clean, straight, white dresses and pretty kerchiefs tied on their well-oiled hair. Very few of us were seeking the truth. We were looking for fun, good singing, story telling, and excitement.

I did not know then that most of the hymns that were sung so lustily were written in England and America. I remember particularly how we sang and pattered our feet over the Kikuyu words that mean in English: 'There is a Fountain filled with Blood drawn from Emmanuel's veins; and sinners plunged beneath that blood lose all their guilty stains'.

Mwando was always urging my father to put me in the school, saying: 'Gatheru, why not send him to a Church of Scotland mission school back in Kikuyuland, if he does not feel happy here?' Sometimes my father was on the point of agreeing, for he, too, wanted me to get an education. But he was so busy with family affairs that he never made up his mind. Both Mwando and Kimani were Christians, but the arguments they used on my father were secular. 'Important people are those who are educated,' they would say; or 'Let Mugo get an education and he will become very important—an overseer perhaps, or even a postmaster.' I listened to it all. I wanted to be important, maybe even a postmaster—but I wanted to be like my father, too, casting the *mbugu* out, the *mwano* to see what Ngai had in store for people. For, although I had very high regard for Christians and education, I still thought that the Kikuyu medicine-men had power to communicate with Ngai, which power the Christians did not possess.

On several occasions Mwando and Kimani stressed how Jesus the Son of God was able to heal the sick, and how important it was for the non-Christians to join the church. Naturally, I was puzzled by all this idea of healing because the very famous Kikuyu medicine-men who lived at Stoton like Ngubu were also healing the sick. Yet Christians like Mwando and Kimani could not heal the sick at Stoton! Nevertheless Mwando's and Kimani's reputation was very great. This was true of Kimani, especially since he was also an overseer or a head of the entire community at Stoton.

Neither Mwando nor Kimani limited their preaching to the

36

teachings of Jesus only. They stressed the need for self-improvement, honesty, and education.

And then the Stoton school was closed after a period of one year. The forestry department may have felt that the Kikuyu Independent Schools Movement was trying to interfere with the school, which would stir up the Squatters politically. The church was not closed, and also it was argued that the school was taking boys from work. But the Kikuyu were determined that their children should learn the mysteries that come in books. They organized themselves to pay one shilling for each adult and fifty cents (sixpence) for each child so that they could organize night classes in a home near by, a home on the farm of a European who was called 'Kibogoro', 'One who is bow-legged'. For personal reasons Kamau joined the Forest Department and was no longer a teacher. The evening classes at 'Kibogoro's' were conducted by yet another young man called Mbuthia who was also educated at the Church of Scotland mission school in Kikuyu Country. Kibogoro Farm was located on the north-west of Stoton about seven miles away. It was decided people should not talk about these evening classes publicly lest Kibogoro might get to know about them and order the classes to be discontinued. I attended these classes. Most of the people from Stoton who were attending them were adults, and although they were conducted in Mbuthia's home-*thingira*, we used to refer to his home as 'school'. From Stoton to Kibogoro Farm we travelled on foot. There was a very dense forest in between. We carried paraffin lamps with us. Young men carried some knives and sticks for protection in case of sudden attacks by leopards. Small boys like myself were put in the middle of the line as we walked through the forest. Some young men would sing out loudly in order to scare out the wild animals. Some carried fire, too, as it was said that wild animals are usually afraid of smelling fire.

There were fifteen students from Stoton, and several more from Kibogoro Farm. The standard of education was not higher than that of the previous school at Stoton. We were all taught together on the same blackboard, but older students were taught much more 'advanced' arithmetic than the young ones. All were to go to school until each learned to read and write a letter in our native tongue, for the missionaries had written

37

grammar and books in Kikuyu and we dreamed of writing our own books some day. The elders learned some English, too, and we children listened as they learned, and like little parrots would say words although we did not know what they meant: 'This is a man.' 'I am a man.' One thing we learned to say quite fast and learnedly: 'All that you do, do with your might. Things done by halves are never done right.' We learned a little about how to count and add and subtract, too. The school did not last long. Mbuthia became interested in one of the attractive girl students and married her. His romance interfered with our night classes with the result that we had to discontinue our studies after three months.

At that time one of my uncles, Aaran Wainaina Kuria, was working on the farm of a European named Tennett about fourteen miles south-west of Lumbwa Station, and about eighteen miles north-west of Stoton. He was living with two of his young brothers, my grandmother Wanjiku, and my aunt on my mother's side. When they heard that I had to discontinue my night classes, they asked my parents whether I could go and stay with them because the Kikuyu who were working for Bwana Tennett had also organized night classes for the adults, the young girls, and the young boys. They had employed another one of my uncles, Peter Wainaina Kuria, who had obtained his education from the Church of Scotland mission, Kikuyu, as a teacher. (My grandfather, Kuria-son-of-Nguuri, on my mother's side, had sons and daughters by his nine wives. I referred to all these sons and daughters as my uncles and aunts.)

My parents agreed and, at the age of ten, I left Stoton for Bwana Tennett's farm. They received me very warmly, and after two days I started night classes along with the rest of the students. The classes were very large and better organized than those which Kimani and Mbuthia had conducted at Stoton and Kibogoro Farm. They were held in a big *thingira* which belonged to Peter, the teacher. The only trouble with these night classes was that they were regarded as a meeting-ground for young men and young women. Sometimes Peter was very much annoyed by this kind of thing. But the romance among the young people continued! To my surprise I found out later on that even Peter himself was interested in one of the girls who was so pretty that the boys had nicknamed her 'Tukere tweru', meaning 'Girl with pretty legs'. Peter married her eventually.

Unfortunately for us Peter and his wife, Tukere tweru, decided to move to another more distant farm called 'Kwa Njoroge' Farm.

We were dismayed, but there was nothing that we could do. Our night classes were, therefore, discontinued after two months since there was no one to replace Peter as a teacher. It appeared to me as if there was a mutual streak of weakness in Mbuthia of Kibogoro Farm and Peter of Gwa Tennett—romantically speaking!

My progress in these classes was very satisfactory. I could read, write, do some simple arithmetic, and was also beginning to read some Swahili and English sentences.

When this news reached my parents at Stoton, they asked me to return home since our night classes were discontinued. I felt as if my chances of ever getting an education were now very remote indeed. So I returned to Stoton thoroughly discouraged.

From this time on I began to beg my father to send me to his father back in Kikuyuland so that I could continue in school. His answer was: 'I fear to send you, son. All Kikuyu both fear and respect those of the Ethaga clan, but fear is stronger than respect for the first sons of doctors. There have been those who poisoned the first son who had not yet been made a doctor and did not know how to protect himself. Stay here with me.' He was my father, so I stayed and herded sheep.

The men who worked so hard to start the schools among the Kikuyu believed that if their people knew the truth, the truth would set them free. One kind of truth was that which one got from one's fathers. Another kind of truth was that which one got from the white man's books. This my father believed. But there were other Kikuyu who believed that there was also truth to be learned by worshipping the white man's God. Father did not believe this, but he made no objection to my learning about the white man's God. Some of my earliest memories are those of Mwando sitting in our men's house reading his Bible aloud and singing hymns in Kikuyu. How he loved to read from Revelations—all about the beasts and the Four Horsemen, and the pearly gates, and about John being taken up in the Spirit. I liked to hear him read it, too. And, I liked to go to church.

Among the Kikuyu those who speak well have always been highly honoured, and the very word 'chief' means 'good talker'. As I look back on it now, two kinds of sermon texts seemed very popular. First, there were the ones that carried a point that you could not make any other way without fear of losing your job or your place as a Squatter. The story of Baalaam and the ass that spoke was a great favourite. When the preacher repeated the words of the donkey: 'Why do you beat me so hard?' I am sure now that it had some meanings that Baalaam's ass did not put into it. Another favourite was the story of how Jesus fed five thousand people with just a few pieces of bread and fish. Another text was used, so it seems now, to criticize both the Europeans and some of the Kikuyu—the one about it being easier for a camel to get through the eye of a needle than for a rich man to enter heaven. I remember that at the end of this one the preacher would sometimes shout: 'O people of Kikuyu, come to God!' The other kinds of sermons were the ones about how to live right. The Ten Commandments were talked about very much, as well as the words of Jesus on how he would come and tell the people that 'When I was hungry you did not feed me; when I was in jail you did not visit me'. They preached often about Daniel in the lion's den and the Hebrew children in the fiery furnace. Revelations, too, they liked. I still remember how they scared us with the fire of Hell and with the story of that man Ananias, who told a lie and fell down dead.

The Christians sometimes looked at my *githitu* and said: 'Mugo, you'd better throw that thing away and go to church and stay with the church.' But I did not. There was one thing about what the Christians said that both worried me and fascinated me—the end of the world. Sometimes I became frightened. Having read or heard a passage about what people should do 'in the time of the end', I found myself praying as I herded goats: 'Oh, Jesus, let it not come in a cold season.' But so confused was I about these matters that when I was praying for a sign or a vision I would sometimes ask God to let Gabriel blow that big horn I heard about as a sign. I was not thinking that that would bring the world to an end!

I have often wondered why I did not become a Christian then, for Father was not offering any objection, Mbuthia was encouraging me to do so, and I was very fond of my young

Christian playmates. I think one reason was the matter of the eating of the meat. My father was a 'Man of God'. His fees were paid to him in the form of goats, and whenever he made a sacrifice for someone or for himself we ate the meat of goats. The Christians would not let their members eat meat which they said 'had been sacrificed to idols'. I did not like the idea that I could not eat meat prepared by my father.

But I was seeking—in a random way—truth, some kind of truth to set me and the Kikuyu free. To get that truth I felt I had to go to school. But where? And could I do so without giving up the ways of my fathers which I did not want to give up? The answer came sooner than I expected, and it is tied up with the story of Karanja and the 'Good European'.

This is the story of Karanja upon whom fortune smiled, and who then smiled on me. But I cannot tell it until I tell first of my father's sister—The Beautiful One. She had married a Squatter on the farm of a very wealthy Englishman whose place was about twenty miles from ours. The Englishman was a kind man and one who wanted to see Kikuyu live a life of peace, plenty, and happiness in their own land. Unlike some settlers he allowed an independent school upon his farm. The head teacher of that school knew my mother, for he had been initiated in the same age-grade with her. They were, therefore, very close in heart. He wanted to see me educated and he thought of a plan. He asked my father's sister, The Beautiful One, to invite me to stay with her for Christmas in 1935. Mother brought the message and my father said I could go.

It was a very merry Christmas. My parents permitted me to cast off my goat skin that I had worn all my life, and they bought me a fine white sheet. So my mother and I both went, she, too, in her clean white sheet. We travelled on foot through a forest of seven miles and long plains extending from Kibogoro Farm to the farm of the 'Good European'. Vegetation was very green and beautiful, and we could see antelopes and impala eating grass in the plains. There was no fear of leopards there. The sun was shining brightly when we arrived. My aunt was an expert in the making of 'chapatties'—a special kind of Kikuyu and Swahili bread, and she had plenty of it. Never had I eaten so much, and fat meat, too. We had much discussion with the head master, who took a liking to me. He said: 'Let us educate

Mugo and some day he will be a head master, too. Let us train him to read well and to write well, and some day he may even be an overseer on a European's farm. All Europeans will respect him, and he will be able to do much good for the Kikuyu.' I was impressed by all this and was very sure that I could be both a good head master and a good overseer. Mother and I were very happy, and when Christmas was over we left for Stoton loaded down with goodies to take to my father.

Since the school at Stoton was closed, I now had the hope that I could go to live with my father's sister on the Good European's farm and go to the school there. But there was trouble in this aunt's house even as there was in ours. Her husband, being an overseer, had much wealth in goats and money. My aunt was a second wife, and the first wife did not get along well with her. My aunt longed to leave and return to her father's people in the Reserve. My father, who had brought her from the Reserve to Stoton, urged her to stay. But she was unhappy, and one day she disappeared. Rumours spread very fast that she—The Beautiful One—was back in Kikuyuland and doing very bad things. Friends of her husband began to say: 'He lost nothing when he lost her. She had no children. She could never have them. She was barren.' That she had no children had always been one of the things that caused a strain between her and the first wife, although her husband loved her. All of this hurt me very much for I loved my father's sister; she had been very kind to me. It hurt my father, too, for she was his favourite sister. And now I could never go to the Good European's farm to go to school.

One day my mother, as was her custom, had gone to the market at Lumbwa Station. On the way she passed a man whose name we all knew but whom she had never met— Karanja Njai Kamau. Everyone knew about Karanja. He was the trusted servant of the Good European, Mr Sydney Carlin, who admired him for his quick intelligence and his honesty. It was thought by many that Karanja did much for the Africans on the farm—that it was the European's liking for him that had made the *Good* European become good. Karanja gave my mother some tea and some sugar. He spoke pleasantly to her and told her a secret to tell my father. He, Karanja, had been sorry for my father's sister—The Beautiful One—and he had come to love her, too. He was the one who had sent her to the land of the Kikuyu, and she was even now arranging for a divorce, so that some day she could become *his* second wife. He would make her happy and treat her well. And he would send me to school.

One day Karanja gave my mother a gift of five shillings when he met her at the market. He was being friendly with us for he would have to ask my father's permission when he decided to marry my aunt, my father's sister. Father was very pleased to think that a big man like Karanja with power, and influence, and wealth was going to marry into our family. And then one day it seemed as if tragedy had struck. Word circulated fast that the Good European had sold his farm to his brother-in-law and was going to retire to England. It was a very real tragedy for us because we heard that the Good European liked Karanja so well that he was going to take him to England with him as his servant. Now he would never marry my aunt. Father would not get the goats which were to be passed for *ruracio*, and I would not get my education.

But fortune smiled on Karanja, and through him on me. The Good European decided not to take him to England, but to give him the enormous gift of 2000 shillings and to pay his fare back to the Reserve to the land of his fathers. My father was jubilant, and so was I. Father invited Karanja to our homestead for a big beer party to which many people would come and where much *njohi* would be drunk, and where there would be laughter and feasting and dancing. On the night that Karanja came to our homestead he told us all another secret. My father's sister— The Beautiful One—was going to have a child—she that the gossipmongers said could never bear.

Father was deeply impressed when he heard that his sister would soon have a child. 'It must be those great Fort Hall medicine-men,' he said. 'They are mighty men, being close to Mt Kenya and Ngai. It was their medicine that made it so that my sister will bear a child. It is with those doctors that my son Mugo-wa-Gatheru, must study. He will be among the greatest of them, a very great and mighty man of God, weighty in knowing what Ngai is saying through the *mbugu*.' I was over-joyed, for now I knew that if Karanja and my aunt asked him to let me live with them, Father would let me go.

43

But I was frightened and confused, too. I wanted to be a mighty doctor, yes! But I also wanted to study in a school and learn the things that were in the white man's books. And while I prayed to Ngai, I prayed also to God and Christ—all three. I did not brood overmuch about this, but it did worry me. I wanted to ask Karanja to take me with him, but one does not ask of an elder. And then one day Karanja came, and he said to my father: 'Gatheru-son-of-Mugo, your sister is to be my wife. Cannot your son be also my son? Let me take him to the land of his fathers. I have much wealth. I shall make him an educated man. For me, I can only write my own name, yet I have made many shillings working for the Good European. But when our children are men, the writing of the name will not be enough.'

I stood trembling and almost crying. Karanja was too honest to say what I had hoped. Why did he not just say: 'Give me Mugo. I will have him made a mighty medicine-man.' I knew that Father would then let me go. I myself would study to be *both* a doctor and an educated man. Now Father might refuse. My father sat and pondered long. I sat in fear. And then at last Father arose and said: 'So let it be.' I went to the Kikuyu Reserve to be educated.

IV

Becoming a Kikuyu

The Native's Return

THE day was bright and the sun was shining brilliantly that August day in 1936 when Karanja, his second wife Wambui, and I left Lumbwa Station bound for Fort Hall in the Kikuyu Country. I was going 'home'. My mother and sister were there to see us off. Happiness, excitement, and sadness were in my heart. Happiness because I was going to Fort Hall to get educated. Excitement because this was the first time I had travelled in a train. Sadness because I was leaving my family.

As we entered the train I saw my mother crying and laughing at the same time. I think she and I must have been having the same feelings. I started crying, too, but I tried hard to conceal it for I did not want Karanja and Wambui to see me crying. The pressure of sadness bothered me especially when I pictured my mother and sister walking thirty miles back home from Lumbwa Station to Stoton without me. People used small narrow paths through the forests, hills, and valleys. Most 'Squatters' travelled this distance on foot for there were no trains into the back country. They carried their products on their backs to sell them at the market in Lumbwa township—peas, beans, cabbages, cauliflowers, carrots, with potatoes, and maize. It was only a few well-to-do 'Squatters' who had donkeys. My family had none. I cried again when all of this came into my mind. And then I slept.

When I awoke the next morning we were in Nairobi, the capital city of Kenya. I had seen nothing like it before. It was so

45

big, so confusing, but so interesting. I wondered how I could ever find my way if I were left alone in a place like this for even a very few minutes.

Never before had I seen so many Europeans and Indians. Buildings were very tall and big. Everybody was looking busy. Life was really very fast for me.

Karanja hired a rickshaw to take us from the Nairobi rail station to Kariokor, a section of Nairobi. It was also the first time I had travelled in a rickshaw. On our arrival at Kariokor, Karanja called on his friend who was expecting us and in whose house we were to stay overnight. He was very kind. We washed ourselves in his house, ate breakfast, and rested ourselves very comfortably.

The next morning we took a motor bus in Nairobi for Fort Hall, a distance of about fifty-eight miles to the north. Thence it would take us to Karanja's home at Githiga, about thirty miles west of Fort Hall at the edge of the Aberdare Range. The motor bus was to take us on to Githiga, too, from Fort Hall Station.

It was in Fort Hall township that I started noticing differences between the Kikuyu living in the Kikuyu Country and those who were living as 'Squatters' on the European farms, or as 'Squatters' of the Forest Department. There were not very many fundamental differences, except for dress and figures of speech. The physical features and climate of the country were different. For example, the soil was almost red everywhere except in the western part of Fort Hall. There were many hills, and also numerous streams which came from the hills. This was quite a new kind of country for me.

Apart from the differences in dress and figures of speech I found out, too, that the Kikuyu people who lived in the Kikuyu-land were less afraid of the so called 'witch-doctors' and 'magic' than were the Kikuyu 'Squatters' in the European settled areas. For example, the Kikuyu in the settled areas were much more afraid of seeing or looking at the dead body of a person than the Kikuyu in the Kikuyuland. Kikuyu 'Squatters' were much more 'superstitious' than their brothers in the Kikuyu Country.

We arrived in Githiga on the evening of August 7th 1936. We were met by some of Karanja's relatives, but my aunt, The Beautiful One, was not there to meet us.

Karanja had a small retail department store at Githiga in partnership with Mr William Wanjama. Soon after our arrival at Githiga I observed that Karanja was a very well respected man in his community. He was also considered as a middle-class man by Kikuyu standards of the 'thirties. For example, he had many cows, sheep, goats, three wives with several children (the Kikuyu don't like the idea of counting the number of their children), he had also a nice home, land, and the department store.

From Githiga we went to Karanja's home about two miles away from the River Kayahwe. On our arrival I was amazed at the number of children who were there. Karanja's father was a polygamist. He had many sons beside Karanja, who were also married. It was really a big homestead, with many huts surrounded by a fence. At the centre of this homestead there was a yard with a big fire. There were women and children surrounding the fire. Karanja's father was also there. Many bananas, yams, and sweet potatoes were being roasted. I, too, was invited to sit near the fire, but I was very shy. Everything looked different to me even though I also was a Kikuyu. I was also sad because my aunt had not yet arrived home from her garden. Everybody kept on looking at me, and this made me exceedingly shy and frightened. I was longing for my aunt to come soon and take me to her house!

When my aunt arrived she noticed me before I saw her. She avoided coming to me directly because as soon as she saw me she started crying. I, too, started crying when I saw her and heard her shouting: 'Mugo! Mugo!' I tried to stop crying because all the boys, girls, and women were looking at me, but I could not help it.

After about fifteen minutes my aunt came and took me into her house. Then we both stopped crying. She started asking me about home, and about our journey from Lumbwa to Nairobi, Fort Hall Station, and to Githiga. She cooked tea and a delicious stew of chicken, yams, and bananas for me. I felt at home completely. I was no longer homesick or shy. My aunt loved me so much that I could not really tell the difference between her and my own mother. I was very happy.

Near the end of my first month at Githiga I entered the Kahuti Elementary School run by the Church Missionary

47

Society. Its standards were as those of a junior primary school in Great Britain. It had about seventy-five students ranging from five to eleven years of age. This was the first time I had any formal schooling. It was also the time I became a Christian, christened 'Reuel John'. The name Reuel was suggested to me by my mother, even though she was not a Christian herself. It so happened that one of the overseers at Chepsion Farm was a Christian called Reuel. This man was very polite, clean, intelligent, and easy to get along with. So my mother liked him very much. The result was that his Christian name Reuel became a symbol to my mother of someone with these qualities. The name 'John' was of my own choice after I had read about John the Baptist in the Bible. So I became Reuel John Mugo Gatheru.

My school teacher was alert, active, physically strong, and forthright. He taught me the basic rules of numbers—arithmetic, writing, reading, geography, and general knowledge. These subjects were taught in both Kikuyu and Swahili. At that time English was not taught in the mission schools to Africans below the age of twelve to sixteen years. On the other hand, the Kikuyu independent schools encouraged the teaching of the English language to all children from seven to sixteen years, though facilities for teaching English were not too good in the independent schools until much later in 1940.

Besides ordinary class work we, as students, were also supposed to do some practical work on a school farm. We were also required to do drilling. 'Turn right'—'Turn left'—'Turn about'—'By the left—quick march'. To be~ n with I was not too good at drill or in planting beans, peas and maize, but later on I developed some skill. I resented drilling very much because the headmaster, who conducted it, was very rough on those of us who made mistakes. The headmaster was very arrogant and had violent disagreements with my teacher and the entire school. He used to discipline the boys and girls so severely that their parents complained bitterly against him. As public pressure grew he was forced to resign.

Out of school hours I used to help Karanja's father tend cows, goats and sheep, along with other boys of Karanja's family. We also did a lot of swimming in the River Kayahwe when the animals were resting. Other boys from neighbouring locations would join us and we would even play football and do some wrestling.

Life at Karanja's home was a very happy one. I was treated like any child in the family, if not better. As a Christian I was not supposed to eat meat of any animal offered for a sacrifice, so whenever there was a sacrifice which would involve the killing of goat or sheep Karanja would buy a big chicken for me and his young brother so that we, too, could enjoy meat when the non-Christian members of the family were eating the meat of the animal offered for a sacrifice. I should add that Karanja was, and still is, living like a Western oriented Christian, but at the same time he maintains some tribal practices and beliefs too. He never became a Christian, but he encouraged his children to be Christians. I believe he did this because it was through Christianity that his children could get an education, and he wanted them to be educated. But he himself and his wives did not need education and therefore there was no use in their becoming Christians. Perhaps I misjudge him, but this is what I believe. He had a lot of influential friends who were Christians, but I never knew why they did not bother to persuade him to become one.

I attended Kahuti Elementary School for about two years. Then, in 1939 when I was about fourteen, I was transferred to Weithaga Sector School of the Church Missionary Society which had higher grades than Kahuti. Weithaga was about ten miles from Karanja's home, and I used to walk this distance five days a week. It was pretty rough, too, especially during the rainy seasons.

Life was different to that at Kahuti and, although I remained at Weithaga from 1939 to 1940, I did not like the school too much. For one thing, it was thought at Weithaga that Kahuti people had used arbitrary pressure to force out their headmaster who had been punishing the children too severely and, as some of the teachers at Weithaga had been classmates of his, they naturally sympathized with him. There was, however, something more important.

As I have already hinted, the best education was to be had at the mission schools of which Weithaga was the most important in the area, a sort of clearing house for some 350 pupils from different locations on their way to primary schools. At Weithaga

49

I had my first lesson in English but it was here also I first experienced Christian snobbery. Most of the Christian pupils despised the few from non-Christian families, who therefore found it difficult to make friends. The ones who suffered most were those with tribal marks on their faces, of which they had once been proud.

Children can be thoughtless and therefore cruel, but the teachers who were also guilty cannot be so easily excused. Their behaviour did not reflect on Christianity but now illustrates for me the dangers of a privileged system, however well-intentioned.

Working for Wages

Early in 1940 before I completed my studies at Weithaga, several boys near Karanja's home decided to go to the Rift Valley Province during the school holiday and try to work on European farms picking pyrethrum flowers from which insecticide is made. There was a rumour in circulation that one could earn a lot of shillings by doing so. I made up my mind to join this group so that I might have some few shillings before the school reopened. I did not need money very badly, but sheer curiosity pressed me much, and I told Karanja and my aunt about it. They did not object, but they advised that I return before the school reopened.

So we set off for the Rift Valley Province. Fortunately for us, a group of eight boys, there were other boys from our neighbourhood working in the Rift Valley. We knew where they were. From Karanja's home to the Rift Valley Province we travelled on foot, walking through the Aberdare Range. The forest of the Aberdare Range was very dense. As we entered deep into the forest we couldn't hear any human voice, only the birds and the monkeys climbing bamboo trees.

As we penetrated a distance of about ten miles in the forest we saw footprints of elephants which had just moved. We also saw their droppings which looked warm. We thought that the elephants must be close by. We were frightened, but we decided not to get ourselves into a panic. We walked hurriedly and didn't feel really safe until we reached a place called Njabiini which was in the savannah a few miles away from the Aberdare

Range. There were many people, and the town had the atmosphere of a prairie town in North America. There were also quite a number of Kikuyu owning shops, butchers, and small restaurants. It had very beautiful scenery.

We spent a night there and on the following day moved to our destination, 'Kamiruri' Farm—'The farm of one who whistles'. We arrived in the evening, and found many boys and men from Fort Hall District there. On the following morning we were taken to the office of 'Kamiruri's' wife, so that we could be issued with cards necessary for timing, etc. We were now ready to work.

'Kamiruri' himself was in the British Army. He had left his farm in the care of his wife. Now she was about thirty-six years old, and so arrogant and cruel that she was called 'Nyakang'a' by her Kikuyu labourers. 'Nyakang'a' refers to a woman who talks too violently and would even dare to strike a man. She would punish any one of her labourers by making him carry a very heavy log to and fro for as much as two hours. She really did not have any mercy. She seemed to hate the Kikuyu bitterly; but she also needed them very much as capable labourers.

Our pay was four shillings a month! In addition we were given rations of posho, a cornflour from which a kind of porridge is made. My friends and I worked for two months. It was a wonderful experience, and one which I shall never fail to remember. After a day of hard labour we uncircumcised boys often had a hard time with men who were already circumcised. They would harass us to death. If any one of us touched or stepped on a circumcised fellow's leg we would be punished collectively. They were really tyrannical! We were also forced to eat after the circumcised ones had eaten. I was really learning what age-grading among the Kikuyu meant. I knew that I would never feel like a man until I had been circumcised. This experience began to turn my mind towards that important Kikuyu event.

After the school vacation was over I returned to Githiga with six shillings in my pocket. My aunt and Karanja did not think I looked any better for my experiences, and did not see any importance in such an 'expedition'. However, they did not talk about it for long. They took my six shillings and bought me a sheep.

51

The sheep was not for a feast. It was bought because of the Kikuyu belief that the first money of one's own earnings should buy something like a sheep, goat, or cow, something associated with wealth so that in the future one would accumulate more wealth. Call it superstition if you will, but we did.

Father has Bad Luck again

I completed my studies at Weithaga in 1940, and in 1941 I entered the Kambui Primary School near the capital city of Nairobi. This school was attended by children from fourteen to eighteen years of age. Its standard was as those of a secondary modern school in England. English and Swahili were taught. I was sixteen years old by this time and I could read and write Kikuyu and Swahili fluently. I could speak some English, too, and handle arithmetic. I was also beginning to learn something about the great world outside Kenya. I knew a war was on. Things were beginning to change in many ways in Kenya. I wanted to learn all I could about this world. But I was also sad. I knew that when I went to Kambui I would be leaving Karanja and my aunt, The Beautiful One. And I would be leaving the new friends I had made. Before starting in primary school I decided to return to the Rift Valley Province to see my parents. They had often sent word that they missed me very much.

My parents had moved again. There was no settled life in one place for them. They left Stoton and moved to Londiani about forty miles away. My father continued his work in the Forest Department. One of the major reasons why they had to leave Stoton was that after I had gone to Fort Hall with Karanja a large number of Kikuyu Squatters moved to Stoton from other parts of the Rift Valley Province.

Among the newcomers there was a large number of sorcerers who practised black magic and who were suspected of poisoning a lot of people, particularly young children. In Kikuyu society it was always assumed that when a healthy man died suddenly, without a previous illness, his death was caused by witchcraft.

Meetings were held and both Mwando and Kimani appealed to the entire Stoton community to try to find out who were these sorcerers. The community was larger than it used to be, so the appeal went unheeded and the deaths continued. People were especially horrified when Gacanja died. His father, Ngubu, was the most famous medicine-man in Stoton and it was felt that if he was powerless to protect his family then no one could be safe from these evil men.

I remember Gacanja's death particularly well because he was the first dead man I ever saw. The Kikuyu do not like their children to see dead bodies and I was dragged away quickly by my mother—however, I saw his mother raise his head which so frightened me that even today I feel the same fear rise in me when I pass a cemetery.

People continued dying and Kimani and Mwando suggested that something should be done to catch the sorcerers red-handed. The practice was that dead bodies were not buried. They were taken from the village into a deep bush or forest where wild dogs and hyenas would eat them. In fact, one could hear horrible wild cries and fighting by the wild dogs and the hyenas in the area where the dead bodies were taken to in Stoton. It was very frightening.

The fact that the Kikuyu did not bury their dead does not mean that they did not revere them. On the contrary, the Kikuyu believed in the continued existence of the spirits or 'ngoma' of the dead. The body might be destroyed by fire or eaten by wild dogs, but the spirit did not perish. Only the spirit of a man was important after his death, and in fact if a body was not eaten up by the animals it was assumed that the dead man had not been a good-natured person. It was therefore said that sorcerers would not be eaten by the hyenas who are themselves scavengers and the lowest of animals, as even they would recognize the evil in these men and reject their bodies although their spirits had left them.

It was also believed that whenever a sorcerer had killed a man by his witchcraft he would follow the relatives of the dead person into the bush, taking infinite care that they did not discover his presence. After the relatives had left, the sorcerer would go immediately to the body, before the animals had time to discover it, and would cut a piece of flesh from the dead one. He would then burn the flesh and mix the ashes with his poison to add more 'power' to his poison.

Punishments inflicted upon the sorcerers when captured were very severe. When one was caught he was brought into the village near the main street (King'ang'a-ini). A horn would then be blown so that the people could come and see the captured sorcerer. He would then be taken around the main streets in the village, his hands tied together by strong leather rope, 'Mukwa'. Children and women were not allowed to touch him. They were considered delicate and might be harmed or influenced by one who had been handling poison and poisonous objects. In fact, even those men who handled the sorcerers could not go to their homes directly before they were purified.

After the procession through the village dry banana leaves or dry grass were tied around his body and then set on fire. Young men armed with swords and spears would watch him writhing, screaming with agony until he was entirely burnt up.

Occasionally the villagers would decide not to burn him. Instead they would find a big beehive, put the sorcerer inside it alive, cover it, and then roll it down the slope of a very high hill like a tyre or wheel. By the time the beehive reached the bottom of the hill the sorcerer would be dead.

Relatives of the sorcerers were looked down upon with unspeakable contempt. They were not punished or harmed, but were shunned by the rest of the village community. They could not marry or be married in the village and nobody would speak to them and often they were asked to leave the village.

One day a boy of one of our friends in Stoton died suddenly in the evening hours. Mwando and Kimani were called at once. They suggested that the boy's body should not be sent into the bush right away, but that it should be kept at a distance of about one mile from the village. The plan was that a group of young men armed with pangas should accompany Mwando, Kimani, and the boy's relatives to the spot where the dead boy's body was so that they could sit there under the bush and see whether they could catch the sorcerer. They also hoped that they would bring the dead boy home alive! This sounds pretty fantastic, but the rumour had it that before a sorcerer cuts a piece of flesh from his victim he first of all has to bring the dead person to life again, ask him or her several questions such as: 'Who brought you here?' 'Would you like to curse your people?' and then order: 'Do not look at me.' The sorcerer would then re-poison the person, cut some flesh, and go away.

They thought that they would wait until the sorcerer brought the boy back to life and when questioning started, capture him instantly. Mwando, Kimani, and the rest of the young men sat down silently as if they were soldiers near the enemy line. Unfortunately, no sorcerer appeared. They sat there for hours, and at about three in the morning they went home leaving the dead body behind. At about eleven in the morning some young men went there to see the boy's body. On their arrival at the place they found the dead boy's body had been cut! This accelerated the fear among people tremendously. Many people decided to leave Stoton for some neighbouring farms.

In addition to the panic created by the sorcerers there was a well surrounded by a forest of bamboo trees from which people drew some water. The well brought water from a deep hole and the water squirted out as if it was being pumped by a powerful motor. In the village young girls and women in general started having goitres. The commonly accepted explanation for this was that a big snake was inside the hole and was urinating, which in turn polluted the drinking water. No one could say why the men were not affected. As I look back it is curious to me to remember that Mwando and Kimani believed in those rumours, although they were such staunch Christians.

There was no settled life for my family in another sense, too. The quarrelling between my mother and father was still at a high peak. I had heard that my father was always taking sides with his second wife—the young one. I did not like this. I was annoyed. I did not want to leave my mother and her six children under these circumstances. I decided to go home, at least for a short time, to see how things were before going on to Kambui.

My deep sympathies were with my mother, but I also felt sorry for the bad luck that trailed my father too. This time the bad luck may have helped to lift a burden from Father's shoulders. As I have said before, he was very divided in his mind about being a Mugo. It had its privileges, but it had its dangers and responsibilities too. Something happened that made Father drop his doctoring. The story of this I shall tell.

Shortly after my mother and father moved from Stoton to Londiani a forest fire swept through the Squatters' area and once more our two houses were burned. My father's *mwano* (medicine basket), with all its contents, was burned. He should have felt this as a great disaster. But apparently it was not so. He did not even suggest inviting other medicine-men to help him make another one. I think, too, that he had been associated with people who had Christian influence, and they may have discouraged him by telling him not to continue as a medicine-man. They would say: 'Look here, Gatheru, son of Mugo, you have a son getting an education. Why should you go on with ideas like these?' My father would then be confused. He would nevertheless think of the 'spirits' of the dead ones that might be angry with him if he decided to throw his *mwano* away. Yet it was a disturbing thing, especially during the time of moving from one place to another because no one was supposed to eat food or anything else while carrying *mwano*. Hence it was a great burden on his shoulders. So that when the forest fire came accidentally and burnt it, then he did not seem worried about it. Now it was gone.

I was very happy to see my parents again. My father strangled a very fat ram for me. He also listened to me with keen interest.

Everyone in that neighbourhood was new to us. However, my parents managed to make friends with their neighbours. I did not meet my old friends, since they were still at Stoton.

After staying for one week with my parents at Londiani, I started getting to know various young people around. They were very friendly to me. I should admit, however, that I felt too profound for them. They were not educated as I was. I did not regard them as my equals. A sort of snobbishness? Probably.

In the evening the young people would come to our house to visit me. My mother would then give us some food. In this Kikuyu society boys and girls could eat at other people's houses. It was rude not to give food to a child who came. One would be ashamed if a child went away and said: 'Parents of Mugo did not give me food.'

A lot of boys continued to come to our house. They asked me numerous questions on my experiences in the Kikuyu Country, and opportunities for education.

I stayed with my family for three weeks. I enjoyed them very much, and would have liked to stay longer but I had to return to Kikuyuland for education. So I set off for Fort Hall to be initiated or circumcised before I proceeded further with my primary school education.

The Day the Knife Bit Me

No Kikuyu is a man until he has been circumcised, until he has been 'bitten' by the knife, Kahiu, until the ceremony of *irua* has been held. The Kikuyu do not circumcise at birth as do the Jews. They do it at puberty as do so many other tribal peoples throughout the world. Circumcision is the sign that now a child has become a man. It is an important ceremony for every Kikuyu. The Kikuyu also practise what is sometimes called 'female circumcision', a ceremony to make women out of girls. Much has been written on this custom which anthropologists call 'cliterodectomy'. My fellow countryman, Jomo Kenyatta, has described both ceremonies in a book called *Facing Mount Kenya*.

I was now sixteen years old. Unlike girls, boys could go through this ceremony between fifteen and nineteen years of age, in the Kikuyu society. Girls were circumcised earlier so that they did not menstruate before the circumcision. It was considered a bad *thahu* for a girl to menstruate before the initiation ceremony, and should that happen a *Mugo* was consulted so that she could be purified.

Usually boys entering primary schools uncircumcised had a hard time with the men who were circumcised. They were harassed in the same way that 'freshmen' are in American colleges or new 'Fraternity Brothers'. Hence six of us in my neighbourhood decided to get circumcised. I had attended many circumcision ceremonies in Fort Hall during the course of my stay at Karanja's home. They were festive occasions, full of excitement. I should say that I enjoyed them very much. The fact that I was a Christian did not prevent me from enjoying these ceremonies. For after joining the Church in 1936 I discovered that there were many things which the Kikuyu were practising in their society that resembled what the Christians believed and practised. For instance, sacrifices, the importance of the seventh day, some ideas in the Ten Commandments, and the fact that a dead man's spirit is not perishable. I got the idea that if the Christians could drop their insistence on the existence of the devil, and of Jesus as magnified in their religion, Christianity would not be too strange to the Kikuyu. Perhaps I may digress for a moment. As I have already indicated elsewhere in

57

this book, the Kikuyu did not know anything about devils and Jesus. They believed in one Ngai who lived everywhere, and principally on the mountain like Mt Kenya. They recognized the spirits of the dead ones. There were bad and good spirits. Bad spirits would be equivalent to what Christians referred to as 'devil'. The difference is that in the Kikuyu society bad spirits could be made *good* by means of *appeasement*—that is by sacrificial offerings. I did not think that the Christians could appease a devil or compromise with him. Bad spirits were brought about by one's own relatives who had died and before their death had grievances against certain members in the family. In other words, if a man was treated unfairly by members of his family his spirit could retaliate for him after his death—if he died before he had forgiven the wrong done.

Retaliation took the form of bringing sickness into the family of those who had angered the dead one. Spirits were also classified according to the clans and, in fact, no one could be affected by spirits of another clan which was not his own—unless there was some connection through marriage or adoption. However, strangers' spirits could affect anyone in this way: if one's home was near a public road and one refused to feed a hungry person travelling on the road he could curse the person concerned, and if he died of hunger his spirits could disturb the family of one who refused him some food or water. Hence it was a custom in the Kikuyu society not to refuse food or water to strangers passing along the public roads.

But to return to *irua*. Now my turn was coming. I was both happy and excited—and a little bit afraid. Five boys of my age were circumcised on Friday, August 16th 1940. Their homes were near Kahuti Elementary School. I was circumcised on Wednesday, August 21st 1940, near Karanja's home. I remember the date very well. Our circumcision rituals were not complicated because being Christian boys we were not supposed to go through those very complicated processes to which the 'primitive' or 'un-Christian' boys were subjected. Although there was an established ceremony Christians were exempted and, therefore, could depart from it without being looked down upon by the non-Christian Kikuyu. In fact *transculturation* which was taking place in the Kikuyu society seemed to have been accepted without serious resistance although bitter misunderstanding

58

had previously occurred on account of female circumcision. The Kikuyu had high regard for their Christian brothers, particularly because of their education. Whether directly or indirectly, Christian Kikuyu might have acted as agents in introducing *transculturation* in the Kikuyu society, though the principal transmitters of this process of *cultural trade* were the European missionaries.

Circumcision is a painful thing, but a candidate is not supposed to show any feeling of pain while his foreskin is being cut off. He is also not supposed to watch the circumciser. A crowd of men and women gather around the candidate or candidates. Women stand in front of the candidates, while the men stand at the back. People joke and say that the women take an interest in watching boys' penises! When boys and girls are being circumcised on the same field or spot, the boys usually line up on the upper side, while the girls line up in front of the boys.

Each candidate has a helper or an aide who held his cloak in the old days, or a sheet nowadays. These aides are like the best men or maidens in weddings. Candidates are clothed after they are circumcised. Boys' aides do not come near until circumcision is over. The theory is that boys should not be supported. They should be able to demonstrate their bravery by relying on themselves even in the painful process of circumcision. On the other hand girls must be supported by two aides since they are considered delicate and may perhaps collapse if they are left alone like boys.

As far as I was concerned my ceremony was to be very simple. Yet, on the night of August 20th 1940, I did not sleep at all. I lay there wondering how a circumciser's knife would feel upon my delicate flesh. One of Karanja's brothers was to be my aide. He went out at 5 a.m. to get a circumciser named Macharia wa Muriu to come and circumcise me. At about 6 a.m. I saw my aide and Macharia coming across Kayahwe River. I felt like a soldier just before he is given his orders and is ready to go to the front to face the enemy!

After they had arrived at Karanja's home I was asked to go and wash myself in the Itare River on the western side of Karanja's home about half a mile away. It is usual for candidates to wash their bodies, and especially the penis, that there may be no offensive dirt thereon. It is also considered a bad thing if one should engage in sexual relations before the day of circumcision. So Muchaba, my aide, followed me to the river. Along with him were fifteen or twenty women and girls. I did not want to be followed by a large number of people like that who might later on see me naked! However, I could not help it. I was very embarrassed.

After I had washed myself Muchaba advised me not to wear anything again. So we walked back near Karanja's home where I was to be circumcised. I was naked and followed by a large number of women who were happy—singing, dancing, and shrilling. I felt even more embarrassed.

These songs were consolation, advice, and encouragement to dispel any fear that I might have had. They told me that 'We of the Ethaga clan have never cried, do not cry, and shall never cry when we are initiated, or show any sign of fear. Those who may do so are only the children whose mothers were not wedded when they had them, but were wedded afterwards.

'Be firm, our Mugo, be firm and brave, so that you may encourage the young ones who will be circumcised after you. Be firm.'

As we approached Karanja's home I saw Karanja with a crowd of people forming a circle and waiting for me.

The circumciser was in the crowd. As soon as I arrived I was told to go to the centre of the crowd. Muchaba, my aide, was very close beside me. My heart was pumping fast! I sat down in the centre of the crowd. But now I was completely fearless. Muchaba was about nine feet from me holding a white sheet which was to be put on me after circumcision. Beside him was Karanja holding a fried chicken and a kettle of chicken soup to be given to me after circumcision.

The crowd was very silent, waiting perhaps to detect whether I would show a sense or feeling of fear. I was aware of them and their expectations. After I had sat down I folded my two fists like a boxer and put them on the right side of my neck. I then turned my face towards the Aberdare Mountain on the western side of the Kikuyu Country. I was now ready for the knife!

In a few seconds I heard the circumciser approaching me from the right side. I was not supposed to look at him so I kept on looking on the left side. He held my penis, pulled the foreskin back and cut it off. It was very, very painful! But I did not

60

show any feeling of fear or even act as if I were being cut. No medical aid was applied first or later, and this made it extremely painful.

Just before the circumciser cut me for the second time I heard Karanja's voice ordering the circumciser *not* to leave a 'small skin' hanging under my penis. That is called 'Ngwati', which was to be fixed immediately after the second cut. The reason Karanja cried out was that Christian boys were against this 'small skin' being left. It must be appreciated that it was a very old and strong Kikuyu custom to leave that 'small skin' hanging. I think that *Ngwati* served as an identification of the Kikuyu, Embu, and Meru people from the rest of the Kenya tribes who also practised circumcision, but did not have *Ngwati*. I think, too, that *Ngwati* was a proof among the Kikuyu showing that so-and-so actually went through the Kikuyu ceremony of *irua* or initiation ritualistically. The reason given by Kenyatta in Chapter VIII of *Facing Mount Kenya* for this custom seems to me, if only on biological grounds, extremely dubious. It would have been a sign that I was a 'primitive' Kikuyu. This I did not want to be. I think I rather detested the idea of *Ngwati*, anyway.

The cutting was over. I was now a grown-up Christian Kikuyu, circumcised but without *Ngwati*. I was a man. Muchaba, my aide, came to me and put a sheet around me. I was now allowed to look down at the handiwork of the circumciser and see what had been done to me. Blood was streaming from me like water from a pipe. Thank God I did not faint for I would have been disgraced! The crowd was glad because I had shown courage. They dispersed singing and happy that another Kikuyu child had been brave and had become a man. They sang out: 'He is brave.' (Arikuma!) Muchaba showed me how to hold the sheet around me so that it would not become soiled with blood, and he proceeded to guide me home.

Muchaba, Muchaba, I think of him now! He who stood beside me when the circumciser's knife bit into me, and laid the sheet upon me and led me away! Karanja informed me in 1954 that Muchaba was killed during the Mau Mau crisis in 1953.

My aunt was looking very serious as I approached the house, but also very happy. She did not come to the circumcision because she thought she might be scared when the circumciser laid the knife on me. She did not want to show this fear in public because people in the entire community would have talked about her if she had shown fear at the circumcision of the first-born child of her brother. People who show fear at circumcision ceremonies have a very bad reputation among the Kikuyu. This is true of both men and women. Men who show fear may go a long, long time without getting a girl friend.

My aunt's fear was not just of the knife and the blood. The real fear was that I would show fear. This would have embarrassed her for life. It would also have been socially fatal for me. When a group of, say, thirty candidates are circumcised on one spot, if one of them gets scared and shows a sense of fear the rest will spit on him or her after circumcision is over. They sometimes form a procession to do this. I witnessed this once in 1936 when I went to Fort Hall. Hence my aunt's fear was fully justified. She was waiting anxiously to hear from someone as quickly as possible whether I had been scared. I think that the word was passed on to her very soon that I was extremely firm and brave. She was very happy indeed!

Muchaba took me to my little house. He made me sit down on banana leaves. This was the usual custom in circumcisions. The theory was that if I slept or became unconscious my penis would touch the banana leaves and not stick on them as it would do on sheets or blankets. The banana leaves were very cold in the night, but I had no choice.

News of my circumcision spread widely to the other newly circumcised boys. I was now a very proud circumcised Kikuyu man. I was also gladdened by the fact that I would now be able to mix with all the beautiful girls in the neighbourhood. Customarily uncircumcised boys cannot speak, date, or mix with circumcised girls. They must not use bad language in the presence of circumcised people, especially if those words are connected with sexual intercourse. If they did in the old days they would be beaten to death. They could only do such things when they were alone. However, newly circumcised boys, 'mumo', cannot speak to previously circumcised girls for a year! This was especially true in the old days. The reason is hard to understand and this boycott and many other customs are losing their hold very rapidly.

After three weeks I started feeling better and I got in touch with the five boys who had been circumcised on August 16th 1940. When we met we talked of our experience. As newly circumcised boys who were not yet completely healed we were not supposed to meet any old women in the paths, streets, or roads. We were supposed to avoid meeting them by passing through the bushes when ever we saw them. Custom required this. At the same time no uncircumcised boy or boys could come near us, or talk or use bad language before us. We were now mightily jealous of our newly acquired status!

After we had healed completely we started acting like the other circumcised men. For instance we would walk with great confidence, stay out as much as we could, and take responsibilities that are assumed only by the circumcised ones in Kikuyu society.

I become a Member of the Age Grade '40'

Those of us everywhere in Kikuyuland who were circumcised in 1940 were referred to as *rika ria forty*, an age-grade of 1940. I was proud to be of the 'Forty Group'.

The age-grades and clan systems were vitally important in the Kikuyu society. They had strengthened the Kikuyu very strongly. In fact, I venture to say that the age-grades and the clan system could be regarded as two of the roots of the Kikuyu spirit. They not only strengthened society but also encouraged 'competition' and advancement in any enterprise. They were not static things or things that could be laughed and scoffed at as 'primitive'.

The age-grades did not create an atmosphere of a rigid social stratification. Each age-grade was like an independent unit whose members were just like other members of the previous age-grade. Undoubtedly if certain members of a certain age-grade failed to represent their age-grade responsibly they would find themselves being slighted or perhaps despised. But this sort of thing would not have constituted social stratification. There were, however, some kinds of social stratification in Kikuyu society, but they were very flexible indeed. For instance, there were meetings in which young men could not be allowed to participate unless they paid certain dues, just like the fraternities and sororities in the United States. In fact, the age-grades

63

could be regarded as 'records' in the earlier Kikuyu society since the Kikuyu did not have a written record. The age-grades were based on happenings. For example, an age-grade which took place during the time of an epidemic would be called 'rika ria muthiro, or 'age-grade of epidemic disease'. Any age-grade which took place during the time when the white men brought the aeroplane into Kenya was called 'rika ria ndege' or 'age-grade of the aeroplanes'. These age-grades were stored in the Kikuyu language and therefore could not be forgotten. They were like a network or web. In addition the Kikuyu language itself was like a written record. It was built up in a network of numerous proverbs, legends, riddles, and fables that were easily transmittable from generation to generation, as in early English society, and in some parts of Europe today.

Commenting on the Kikuyu language in his book, *The Akikuyu*, Father C. Cagnolo observes:

> The inherited wisdom of the Kikuyu is best revealed in his language, proverbs, legends, and fables. The Akikuyu do not possess books on ethics, psychology or other high-flown theories of modern science, but they possess a rich inheritance of common sense which is handed down in oral tradition from father to son, told by grandfathers to the young people in the evenings when the moon is shining, in the form of endless proverbs, parables and stories which were so popular among Eastern peoples.

V

The Discovery of my People

The Search for Education

I WAS now sixteen and circumcised. I was a fully fledged Kikuyu. And we who had been cut together were men and could now make our own choices. Circumcised men and women are supposed to be free from parental discipline as long as they observe tribal norms. Some of the circumcised ones went into the city of Nairobi to look for work. Some joined the armed forces. But some of us were determined to get an education and we began to scatter about searching for schools which could take us. There were no public elementary schools in Kenya in the 1940s—only mission schools and the independent schools run by the Africans themselves, plus a few schools run by estate owners.

I decided to try to enter a Catholic primary school called Kabaa in the district of Wakamba, east of Fort Hall, because I knew a young man near Karanja's home who had attended there and he had been telling me how good the school was.

I travelled first by bus to a town called Thika. For the trip from Thika to Kabaa three buses had been reserved by the Kabaa school authorities for students from Kikuyu, Nairobi, and Nyanza Province. I stayed at Kabaa for seven days during the registration period but there were more students than places and finally the principal told us that priority had to go to Catholics. He sent the non-Catholics away to find other schools.

Many of the thirty who were turned down did not have means of transportation all the way back home from Kabaa, and I was one of these. So we had to walk many miles westward from Kabaa to get a bus to Thika. It took us many hours to make it with all our luggage. We were sure we were in danger all the way from Wakamba witches who, we superstitiously believed even though we were Christians, could use their witchery to do us harm. We had to ask Wakamba women to sell us milk along the way. It was none too clean.

One leader, Washington Mwangi Njuguna, was very smart, six feet tall, husky, and resembled John Wayne, the American movie actor. His resourcefulness got us through many difficulties. For example, in that barren part of Ukamba water was not easy to get. Washington would dig a hole about three feet deep in the ground with a stick. We would then wait for a few minutes for some water to come out. It was dirty water, but we drank it anyway! We needed it. We found a Wakamba market where the food was good but costly. We refused to pay the high price. We might have been killed, but, despite this, Washington insisted that we would not pay because he thought that the Wakamba had fixed an extra high price on food for us just because we were 'foreigners'. He felt confident that since there were thirty of us we could eat the food and then throw a few shillings to the food owners. Should they raise any trouble we could beat them up. It appeared quite incredible to most of us that we should actually be able to stand off the entire township if all the Wakamba should decide to oppose us, so one of Washington's best friends acted like a good counsel. Largely due to his diplomacy, we were able to avoid trouble. He persuaded Washington that we should leave the market forthwith. Finally we found an Indian merchant's shop where food was not so expensive, and then we managed to get a motor bus the rest of the way back to Thika. Here we found good food and felt at home for there were many Kikuyu.

Our group broke up at Thika, some going one way and some another in search of an education. John, a good friend of mine, and I decided to try to find a place at Githunguri school. This school had been founded by Mbiyu Koinange, the first Kenya African ever to get a degree. We would go and see the great Mbiyu Koinange and study at his school. But we decided to go to Nairobi first where John had relatives.

We met one of John's brothers in Nairobi and John decided

to stay there and not go to school at all. I decided to go on to Githunguri, about twenty-five miles away. So I took a bus from Nairobi to Kiambu and there found that I had missed the last bus to Githunguri. As I knew nobody in Kiambu I decided to walk on to Githunguri that night. By chance I met a postman who had come to Kiambu to pick up the mail for Githunguri. He had also missed the bus. We started out together about 6.30 in the evening and walked for three hours. Then the postman suggested that we stop and spend the night at the home of a friend of his who was doing some accountancy for Githunguri. This friend was very kind to us.

When I arrived at Githunguri school the next day I met with a great disappointment. The school was open and full! They would not accept me! So I decided to go on to Kambui Primary School.

There I found two more latecomers. The principal told us that we were all late, but that he would admit us if we passed a maths examination set in English. One of us failed. I passed second in the examination, and the other student was first.

I started attending classes in January 1941. Kambui mission was under the direction of two American missionaries from Brooklyn, New York. The primary school itself was headed by a very pleasant Englishman from Wolverhampton named Edward Lindley. There were many students from all over Kikuyu Country, Embu, Meru, Ukamba, and three or four from the Rift Valley Province, and I made several friends among them.

Instruction covered subjects like geography, history, mathematics, agriculture, carpentry, biology, hygiene, and English, with two hours a week for practical work on the school farm of about thirty-five acres. Sports were also encouraged. I took an interest in playing soccer as my extra-curricular activity. For the first time I was really studying English grammar and composition extensively; English—the language that was to open many doors to me and which was to be, for me, my third language along with Swahili and Kikuyu.

Among other things I enjoyed history, geography, English, and biology. On the campus during the intervals, students often discussed school subjects. Those who knew mathematics best were called 'mathematicians'; those who knew history, 'historians'; Swahili experts were 'Swahilists'; English experts, significantly, perhaps, 'grammarians', etc. We often discussed the war, and many of the boys who had left this school in order to enlist in the armed forces. There was a school programme on the radio every Friday discussing the war and the Allied success against the Axis Powers. I liked to listen to the war news very much. In fact, I did not think that the war was a bad thing. I wanted it to continue so that I could hear more about Allied bombing. I think I must have been naive about the war.

In 1943 my attitude changed. Instead of regarding the war as amusing I came to appreciate its horror. One of my uncles, whom I loved very much, and two of my best friends from Fort Hall were killed in action in North Africa, and several others that I knew well were torpedoed on their way from Mombasa to Burma.

Most boys at school regarded the war as I did. In other words, I regarded war like sport, an exciting game in which I cheered the house team and did not worry too much about the successes of the other side. There was no reason why I should have felt any more involved than this but, obviously, the death of my uncle and friends made the war real to me; and it came to pass that I became very frightened about it—especially when I pictured in my mind that I should no longer see my beloved uncle and my friends. Each time I looked at the picture of my uncle which he had sent me I became more horrified.

The boys at school were also scared lest they should be drafted into the armed forces and they were worried about their relatives and friends who were fighting in North Africa and in South-East Asia. There was also general fear that if the Allies were pushed back, the entire country would be in danger, too.

When I saw some Italian prisoners of war passing by train through Nairobi to the Rift Valley Province I wondered why they were to be spared. I hated them because of what had happened to my uncle and other friends. I wanted to see these prisoners exterminated.

There was an acute shortage of food all over Kenya as most of the foodstuff was sent to the armed forces. Ironically, however, some people became very rich overnight because of black marketeering. Not only in Kenya, I believe.

As many Europeans were inducted or drafted into the armed forces, including, of course, some of the Kenya settlers, a considerable number of Africans replaced them and were therefore doing the jobs which the Europeans had been doing. For example, one of my uncles (I have more than twenty) was left in charge of a large European farm near Lumbwa Station— managing the farm and supervising over three hundred labourers.

This revolutionary change, however temporary, could have taken several scores of years to come about if there had been no war. Many Africans liked their new high positions and they did their jobs most efficiently.

Some Africans whom I met regarded war as a European war. In fact, I heard one man complaining that he did not like the idea of his son going to fight for 'Mzungu'—'European'. However, I did hear also, though I was not mature enough to appreciate the situation, some Africans saying that they were ready to fight for the Allies.

An incident which had impressed them all and which they remembered concerned the famous American Negro sprinter, Jesse Owen, who represented his country internationally many times.

In 1936 at the Olympic Games in Berlin Hitler met all the competitors and shook hands with all of them—all, that is, except Jesse Owen who was black, saying that he could not shake hands with an ape. This contemptuous public insult impressed the Kenya Africans far more than all the military splendour of the mighty German Army, and indeed it is now clear to the world that they were right.

Remembering Jesse Owen, the Kenya Africans feared what would happen to them if Hitler should win the war. There were songs, especially in the Kikuyu Country, which were sung warning people about the impending danger if Hitler won the war. One of these songs which I remember in Kikuyu went like this: 'Riria Hitler agatua mikwa tukohwo njoki ta cia ng'ombe … ' meaning 'Should Hitler win the war and come marching towards Kenya, we shall be tied by our necks with yokes, thus carrying and pulling carts like oxen'.

The impression created by these songs against Hitler was very effective in that it made most Africans realize that the war was for everybody and that Hitler was as much an enemy for the black men as he was for the Allies. This impression was also strengthened by the memories of the Italian invasion and occupation of Ethiopia.

Kambui being far from Fort Hall where Karanja's home was I had to live on the campus. Living conditions were not very attractive at Kambui at that time, and I could go to Fort Hall only when the school term was over, by bus and by train. My aunt and Karanja used to miss me a lot during term, so occasional visitors and letters told me. Karanja had many educated friends who could write letters for him.

In 1942 Mr Lindley left Kambui for Maseno in Nyanza Province and was replaced by Mr Robert Macpherson, a Scotsman, whose manners I admired very much. I studied the English language under the guidance of his wife. They were very nice people whom I greatly liked. I stayed at this school until 1944. The little English I knew I learned through the patience of Mrs Macpherson.

In 1944 I took the Kenya Primary examination, and then in December of that year I went again to visit my family. They had moved again from Londiani to a farm called Chepsion. The family rift between Mother and Father was still not resolved, and I felt awfully sorry about this. My mother explained the situation to me. I also talked to my father, and finally went to see my uncle who was living at Londiani about thirty miles from Lumbwa. We held a family conference, and we all agreed that separation was the only logical thing. My mother now had seven children and my father threatened not to support them at all. One of my sisters had got married that year to a man my father did not like. My mother thought he was the right man for my sister and I agreed. In January 1945 my mother and her children left Chepsion Farm for Londiani to live with my uncle. I had been in favour of this and it made me happy, for I realized that now my mother was finally out of her terrible agony. I was glad to have played a man's part in settling the matter.

About this time some of my family and friends advised me to try and get the job as telephone operator at Kericho, twenty-two miles from Lumbwa Station, so I started out for the interview. I didn't know whether I had passed my school exams or not and I therefore decided to return to Kambui to find out. I *had* passed. I was overjoyed. I forgot all about telephone switchboards but I had no money to go further in school since Karanja had many responsibilities and could no longer help me.

On the way home from Kambui I decided to stop in Nairobi to see a friend of mine who was working in the Medical Department. We were very happy to see each other and we went visiting girls and dancing and had a really good time. He was in a Medical Department uniform. I thought it looked very good. He said to me; 'Mugo, join the Medical Department. You will make much money, and you will learn something useful. There is much respect given us, too. And the uniforms make the girls like us, you know.' He laughed. I decided to join right away. There were no examinations of any kind, but we were under Civil Service rules, and were supposed to stay out of politics.

So it was that on February 5th 1945, I joined the Medical Research Laboratory in Nairobi to train as a laboratory technician. There were people of many tribes there—Luo, Kipsigis, Nandi, Teita, Kikuyu. We got along pretty well together. I liked some of the doctors. One of them whom we liked very much was a government senior bacteriologist. He was quite unlike the missionaries. He said to us: 'Believe in science. That leads you to truth. There is no God like they tell you.' This was a new idea to us—startling but fascinating. Which white men were right?

Life in Nairobi City

Nairobi has today a population of about 210,000, but when I joined the Medical Department there were only 118,976. It was a very beautiful modern city with all the conveniences of life.

The Medical Department had a training school up-town west of the city in which laboratory and hospital technicians were trained. I was one of these trainees, and we lived in dormitories built and roofed with corrugated iron as if we were on a college campus.

Like the dormitory, the hospital was also built and roofed with corrugated iron. Both were old, greyish-looking buildings which were not only antiquated but were temporary and built like army barracks. In fact, we were told that they were used as

71

the army centre during the Great War, 1914–18. But the laboratory building was a beautiful, modern building with large and broad windows. The grey stone walls, which grew blinding white with distance, were shadowed by the dark blue of the tiled roof. The windows were many and at a distance they looked like many cars lined or parked together at a show—especially when the sun was shining. A neatly cut fence surrounded the building and there was a very beautiful garden with flowers and green grass.

Inside it was divided into several sections: biology, bacteriology, pathology, biochemistry, and entomology. It was the headquarters of the East African Medical Research Laboratories. Both the hospital and laboratory were being financed by the Kenya Government.

We were given food, uniform, books, and fifteen shillings per month as pocket money. I was getting twenty shillings because I was one of the prefects at school. We were not allowed to go into Nairobi city except on Saturdays and Sundays. I liked my work and had it not been for politics perhaps I would have carried it on successfully as a career.

On Saturdays and Sundays some students would go to the movies or dances in social halls down town. I never liked to go to the movies in Nairobi because, at that time, the Africans were required to have passes in order to buy tickets. These passes were given by the managers who owned the cinemas. The system was very irritating. For example, before an African was given a pass or passes, depending on how many people he wanted to take to the movie, he was advised as follows:

It is desirable to go to the cinema house properly dressed and clean, and when you see something funny on the screen don't laugh loudly with your mouth open as most of the 'natives' do. Finally, don't turn your head about observing other customers, or go about touching other people with your shoulders...

These instructions made me feel that the Africans were being regarded as small children who did not know how to behave in a public place.

City life was very peculiar to me. It was fast, impersonal, insecure. Everybody was busy, aggressive, and for himself. Later on I found out that to get along in the city I had to act as the city dwellers did. Did I imitate them unconsciously or as a means to an end? The answer is perhaps a combination of the two.

Psychologically, I felt a changed man. My language and way of viewing things were very different from what they used to be when I was tending goats and sheep, and, of course, very different from my school life.

I tried very hard to adjust myself to this crazy urban world. It was, I thought, very spectacular. The more I lived in it, the more I found new, fascinating, and challenging things to overcome. It was a *dynamic* world.

In it I first became aware of the injustices which my people suffered, and experienced most of them myself now I was exposed to them.

The city of Nairobi was divided into several different locations according to the different races which were living in it. The Europeans occupied the best sections known as Kilimani Ngong, Karen, Kileleshwa, Muthaiga, Upper and Lower Kabete. The Asians occupied the second best: Parkland, Pangani, City Park, Easleigh, and Ngaara Road area. The Africans occupied the poor third: Kariokor, Nziwani, Starehe, Majengo, Pumwani, Shauri Moyo, Kaloleni, and Makongeni.

In the African locations there were poor lights on the streets. Library facilities and social halls were ill-equipped. Public lavatories were very, very dirty. Some of them did not have running water. Instead, they had hard tins like dustbins in which people 'eased' themselves. There was an inescapable offensive smell when these bins were full of faeces, and especially when the municipal workers who removed them were late (as they always were). One public lavatory was used by over a thousand people.

Those public lavatories which had running water were constructed in a peculiar manner. There was a large narrow trench inside them which was about one foot deep and the water ran in it as if in a small canal. The water flushed automatically but the capacity of one lavatory was not sufficient for the number of people who wanted to use it. Consequently, the water system was always defective and the faeces, therefore, could not be flushed away. Having no alternative, people would then continue 'easing' themselves until the trench was full up.

73

They would then be forced to use every inch of the floor until it became impossible to get inside—this became increasingly difficult to gauge since there were not enough lights within.

The tins and floors were a sickening sight, and there were flies everywhere. One could see long threads or rings of tapeworms on the faeces dropped by people who were suffering from them, an inevitable disease amongst those forced to live in such circumstances.

In the African houses there were no lights, water supplies, or gas for cooking. The Africans used paraffin or kerosene oil lamps, charcoal fires for cooking, and water drawn in tins or emptied oil drums.

In each African location there was a water tap where long queues of people lined up with their tins and drums. If you wanted to cook a quick meal it was impossible unless you had some spare water in the house.

Like public lavatories, one water centre served about one thousand people and was open only three times a day. You could see three or four columns of queues around one centre. Some people had to line up with their tins and drums about fifteen minutes to six in the morning. The last hour of closing the centre was seven in the evening. The water was supplied by one pipe.

In every African location, except Majengo and Shauri Moyo, the houses were built of stone and tile-roofed. In Shauri Moyo the houses were built of concrete and roofed with corrugated iron. In Majengo the houses were much more poorly built— square with walls made from wooden frames packed with mud, and roofed with corrugated iron, or even metal sheets beaten out of ordinary empty tins.

In all houses in every African location, rooms were very small and overcrowded. Some people would sleep on the floor without mattresses except for a few blankets and sheets. Old sacks once used for sugar or flour were used as mattresses. There were no nurseries for the African children and no secondary schools.

The only government primary school for Africans in the entire city, although we formed more than half of the city's population, was not well equipped. For example, there were no library and no laboratory for experiments, although pupils did not leave until the ages of fifteen or sixteen; tools in the carpentry shop were inadequate; classes were overcrowded. Sport facilities were insufficient with only two footballs *for the whole school*. There were only one globe and one map for the geography classes, and these were kept in the office of the headmaster and were given out only when demanded by the geography teachers. Above all—the school was under-staffed.

Playgrounds and cinemas for the African children were non-existent.

Roads and streets were dirty, muddy, and during the dry seasons extremely dusty. In the city there were beautiful restaurants, hotels, and bars, but for use by the Europeans only. The Asians had their own, too, but, on the whole, Africans were not welcome there, although, outwardly, the Asians sympathized with the lot of the Africans. Africans were not allowed to buy hard liquor or European beer. In fact, there was only one drinking place for Africans in all Nairobi. It was situated in one of the African locations and, however far away he lived, any African wanting a drink had to travel there for the privilege of buying the local Nairobi Corporation brew especially for Africans.

The Africans, therefore, were always complaining about their life in the city. I found myself deeply involved and asked myself the cause of this universal misery, and why something could not be done to satisfy the grievances of my people. Why were the Africans always treated in such a humiliating and degrading fashion and always accorded the last place in what was after all, their own country? I asked many people and, depending on the race of the person to whom I was talking, I learnt the various stock explanations.

For example, many young Indians, perhaps because they felt their own position in society to be insecure, suggested that ignorance and lack of education among the Africans was the root of the problem. The Europeans would agree with the Indians but would add, somewhat mysteriously: 'Rome was not built in a day,' which was no great comfort to the Indians. Others, of course, offered colour or racial prejudice as the cause. I listened to all these theories. They sounded interesting but I found them all unsatisfactory: if the problem was so easily expounded, why was it so difficult to resolve?

One of the most obvious, and indeed one of the most important, reasons for the poor living conditions of the Africans was the
curious disparity in the rates of pay between the races, which in
itself is a good example of the tyranny exercised by the European employers over the African labour force. I found that the
Africans working in the city, whether clerks or labourers, skilled
or unskilled, were getting less wages and salaries than their
European and Asian counterparts. I discovered to my utter
amazement and horror that an African with a first class
Bachelor of Science degree was getting about £15 per month,
while an Asian with a senior Cambridge school certificate
equivalent to the present Ordinary Level of the General Certificate of Education, was getting £30 per month, and a European
with a London University matriculation certificate was getting
from £45 to £50 per month. Educationally, I could not understand why the very few educated Africans in the Medical Department were not getting equal pay for equal work with the
other races who were working along with them. I thought that
perhaps the Europeans and the Asians who were working with
us might have had superior teachers in their schools, and that
was the reason why they got more money and respect than we
did. But, on the other hand, we all performed various identical
experiments in the laboratory.

In my laboratory experiments and tests I found we Africans
were as fully qualified as the Europeans and the Asians. It's
true. The Africans, however, received lower wages and
salaries.

Poor rates of pay meant that Africans were unable to buy
their own houses or improve those which they rented. In this
context it should be remembered that each African, whether
he was employed or not, had to pay a 'poll' tax, and was liable
to arrest and imprisonment if he was found in Nairobi looking
for a job without paying this tax. Yet without the job, he could
not pay the tax! A confusingly vicious circle.

The city government, like any European corporation, was
responsible for: roads, water supply, sewers, fire services, street
cleansing, lighting, conservancy, refuse collection, housing, and
public health services. It obtained its finances from grants (i.e.
the Colonial Development Corporation), revenue, from fees,
and charges, and the balance was obtained by local taxation.

I spent so many Saturdays and Sundays talking politics with African politicians that I found myself increasingly less interested in my laboratory work, although I had seen a great future in it as a career when I joined the Medical Department.

In the course of my training I decided to take some correspondence courses from South Africa and Britain in order to improve my English and to try to get a higher school certificate.

Often I started feeling a 'calling'—a vocation that I should join my people in their agitation for political, economic, educational, and social reforms. The more I saw of those dirty and filthy lavatories in the African locations of Nairobi, the more I felt that I should take up the challenge. The more I noted that most of the Europeans and the Asians in the city had owned or hired private houses which were built of stone or concrete, tile-roofed, surrounded by beautifully cut fences, lawns of green grasses, trees, and flowers, in cool and healthy sections of the city—the more I became embittered.

Apart from my friends in the Medical Department I made a lot of friends in Nairobi city. I was also well known to important African politicians.

VI

The Making of a 'Subversive'

A Brush with the Kenya Law

EVERY day during 1945 and 1946 I washed the test tubes and ran the blood tests at the Medical Research Laboratory. In the evenings I took my correspondence course and I read much. I was learning more and more about the troubles of my people. My blood was boiling inside me. I felt I was wasting my time doing this kind of work. I wanted to get an education as soon as possible to do something to help my people. I felt cramped and hamstrung. As a civil servant I could not participate in politics. Yet, I was thoroughly disturbed by many of the things that were happening—especially by the editorials and comments in *The Kenya Weekly News*, a newspaper which expressed the most extreme views of the settler community. What I read there was bitterly annoying, and I began to feel that the aim of the European settlers in Kenya was to keep the Africans down-trodden for ever. There was nothing that aroused my feelings so much as those editorials in *The Kenya Weekly News* between 1945 and 1947. I wanted to fight back by answering all these attacks on my people. After much thinking I decided to write some letters to the editor. Some of my letters were published. Others were not.

The Africans at the Medical Department liked my letters very much, but some of them advised me not to sign my name but to use a pseudonym in case I found myself in trouble with the Government. I did not listen to all this advice. I am afraid I liked to see my name beneath my letters and articles! Writing these letters made me a 'subversive'.

Soon, everyone in the Medical Department was talking about my articles which had been noticed also by officials of the department and even by the police. However, I was encouraged by several leading Africans in the department even though they feared that my articles might end my career as a laboratory technician. One of them even used to help me draft some of the articles. He was not, however, so eager to see his name appear in the newspapers. As a keen politician, he valued his career and was ready to use me.

On one occasion he drafted an article for publication in one of the European papers which was so seditious that even I wondered whether we dare submit it. Finally, I decided to sign a pseudonym and sent it to the editor. When the editor of this extremely conservative paper read the article he sent it at once to the Criminal Investigation Department.

In a sense I enjoyed seeing my name in the press and hearing the people praise me. However, I was unique in the Medical Department in that only I had the courage to write these articles and letters; many of the other Africans would have liked to imitate me but, as government employees, they did not dare to take the risk in case they should lose their jobs and bring hardship on themselves and their families. Of course, as a young bachelor, I had far less to lose. They were in a very frustrating position. For example, there were six senior African laboratory technicians at the Medical Research Laboratory who had joined the service fifteen to twenty years before. They were so highly qualified that they even acted as instructors to the new recruits to the department. They even taught the Asians and Europeans. But surprisingly, the Asian and European trainees were always paid more than their African instructors.

The African uniform was also different from that worn by Asians and Europeans. The latter had white overalls and the Africans' were khaki. The African overalls had M.R.L. (Medical Research Laboratory) marked in red across the chest. The overalls worn by the Europeans and Asians were plain.

It was obvious to me that the Africans in the Medical Department harboured a deep resentment against the restrictive social conditions in which they lived and worked. It was therefore only natural that they should support me whole-heartedly in my political writing.

From the point of view of the Kenya settlers I had become 'a politician' and therefore, according to their logic, 'dangerous'. Something should be done about it. I was told that it was against the law to write all these articles. The Criminal Investigation Division asked the Medical Service why all these articles were appearing in the papers. They wanted to know why a government servant was allowed to act this way. The Senior Medical Officer called me in one day and said: 'Now, you know as a government servant you aren't supposed to take any part in politics. I'll try to protect you. But stop!' I stopped for a while. Then another Kikuyu friend wrote articles using my name. The C.I.D. started investigating again. In August two officers went to see the Senior Medical Officer again. He was very embarrassed. He told them that some action would be taken against me immediately; and it came to pass that I was fired straight away. I went to a municipal councillor and asked him what to do. He said: 'Write a plea. Say you did foolishly and ask for pardon.' He drafted the letter for me. The apology was accepted. I told my friend not to use my name any more. But I thought that I would find it difficult to stop writing letters to the newspapers. Subconsciously I felt guilty in having said that what I had done in writing letters to the editor was foolish. Was I not fighting for the rights of my people? I wrote more articles!

One morning about eleven o'clock in December 1946 I heard an assistant pathologist of the Medical Research Laboratory talking on the phone. In his conversation my name was mentioned. He was talking to the Senior Medical Officer in charge who had been contacted by the C.I.D. to warn me against writing any more articles since I was a government civil servant. The assistant pathologist advised that I go and see the Senior Medical Officer again.

When I entered his office, accompanied by a sergeant-major, the Medical Officer looked at me very seriously. Then he shouted: 'You foolish young man! If it were not for my efforts they would have taken you and put you in jail. This is a very serious thing, do you understand?'

'Yes, sir,' I replied.

He told me two police officials had been sent to see who I was. They had also made a formal complaint to the medical authorities about a government civil servant being allowed to participate actively in politics. However, he told them that I was a very foolish young man who did not realize what he was doing.

After a long talk full of friendly advice he asked me to return to work, and to write no more articles. I said I wouldn't write any more. But my heart kept on burning within me whenever I read the editorials in *The Kenya Weekly News*.

After three weeks of silence I could not resist replying to one of the letters to the editor of *The Kenya Weekly News*. The editor inserted his footnote to my letter: 'The above letter was printed to illustrate the mentality of an instructed African, R. Mugo Gatheru, employed by the Kenya Government ... ' This was really an accusation for it attracted the attention of the Government. It was the root of many troubles which were to confront me later on.

After the letter was printed a letter was sent to the Senior Medical Officer by a government press officer. I was again called into the office for further warning. The Senior Medical Officer told me that if I did not stop 'that nonsense' I should have to leave. He seemed, however, to be sympathetic. I now began to feel the gravity of the whole situation. I talked about it to my friend, Eliud Wambu Mathu, who had been introduced to me by one of my friends who was also working at the Medical Research Laboratory. I know Mathu thought I was something of a youthful 'hothead' and that he knew I was heading for trouble. But he felt there was a place for me where I could write as much as I liked and say what I wanted. So he spoke to the officials of the Kenya African Union and asked them if they could let me have a job working with the English-Swahili language newspaper of the organization, *Sauti Ya Mwafrika*, *The African Voice*. They agreed on condition that my appointment was confirmed by Jomo Kenyatta. Mathu made an appointment with Kenyatta for an interview in Mathu's office, and it came to pass that there Kenyatta and I met. Mathu said:

'Mzee, this is Mr Gatheru from Fort Hall who has been working as a trainee in the Medical Department and would like to join the union as an assistant editor.'

81

'Fine, fine,' Kenyatta said.

'He's a really good man, and widely read,' Mathu emphasized to Kenyatta.

Kenyatta looked at me and asked:

'Are you ready? Are you ready?'

'Yes, I'm ready, Mzee,' I said.

'All right. You may start your job as soon as possible,' he said.

'Thank you, Mzee,' I said.

The interview was over. Mathu saw me to the door, while Kenyatta was reading a newspaper.

On the following day I tendered my resignation to the superintendent of the Medical Research Laboratory. The superintendent accepted my resignation 'with regret'. He told me that it was his feeling that many of the articles or letters to the editor that had not been published had been turned over to the Criminal Investigation Department for attention.

In March 1947 I took my new job as an assistant editor of *The African Voice*, the official organ of the Kenya African Union. The union had been formed in 1944 as soon as Mathu was nominated as the first African member in the Kenya Legislative Council. Its immediate aims were: to unite the African people, to fight for improved social, economic, political and educational betterment, and for independence.

At first, it was called the Kenya African Study Union and in 1946 the name was changed to Kenya African Union. The office of *The African Voice* was at that time two tables in a large room about thirty feet square which it shared with all the other departments of the union. It was located right in the centre of the city in one of the busiest roads in Nairobi—the government road—and was actually an extension of an old office belonging to an Indian barrister who was sympathetic to the African cause for freedom.

There were three of us working for *The African Voice*, the executive officer, his clerk, and myself. There was only one light in the entire room and our 'office', in addition to its two tables, had six chairs, one typewriting machine for three of us, and a shelf for the files. The red walls of the room were peeling. The office was on the fourth floor of the building surrounded by barristers' offices, and on the fifth and top floor just above us there was a dance hall for the Seychelleses. The sound of the music was often deafening.

Financially the union was not doing too well, for it owed several hundred pounds. Its income depended on the money raised during big political meetings held all over Kenya, but this was insufficient.

Outwardly the union as a propaganda machine was effective and appeared strong, but inwardly it was weak. Although Jomo Kenyatta was newly elected president, he was very busy with money-raising and the management of an important African independent school which Mbiyu Koinange had founded at Githunguri.

It was often several weeks before Kenyatta could come to the office and sometimes our salaries were in arrears for as long as four weeks. We also had a lot of trouble with the publishers who printed *The African Voice* because the union did not have enough money, and often they refused to release the paper for sale until their bills had been paid.

If one remembers that KAU had been founded only three years before the time of which I speak, and also the extreme hostility of the Kenya settlers towards its continued existence, it is not hard to understand why the organization of the union was still so elementary. It was a difficult struggle for all of us (my colleagues and I were dead broke all the time) but, although no individual can be criticized, it seemed to me that considerable reorganization was necessary.

The executive officer of the KAU and I did all the clerical work, editing, and soliciting advertisements for the paper. Our clerk helped us in typing, posting, and collecting letters. Many people from all walks of life came to the office. They had various grievances and wanted us to help them. We did what we could and those whom we could not help, or whose cases were too complicated, we sent to Mathu's office as he was in a strong position to present grievances directly to the Legislative Council.

Every day we worked hard from 8.30 a.m. to 5.30 p.m. from Monday to Friday, planning the general strategy of the Kenya African Union, writing stinging editorials in *The African Voice* and discussing the colour bar in Nairobi.

Our clerk was a very discouraged young man. The economic,

political, and social conditions of the Africans often made him sorry that he was one of them. For example, one rainy afternoon he told me:

'You know, Mugo, this town is getting more rotten every day.'

'Why?' I asked.

'At lunch time I had a terrible experience. I went to buy a pair of trousers in a shop just off the corner of the Government Road and the European saleswoman turned me out. She told me: "You dirty damn fool, can't you see your shoes are messing up my floor?" Everyone else had mud on their shoes but, although I said I was sorry, she still threw me out.'

'Don't you worry, things will be better one day,' I said.

'When we are dead?' he asked.

'No, in our lifetime.'

'You're optimistic,' he said.

'Remember there was a time when there was no African member in the Kenya Legislative Council. Today we have two; and tomorrow we shall have three or four.'

'Yes, but how long are we going to endure all this?' he asked sadly.

'Until we're well organized,' I replied.

'If my skin were a little bit lighter I would opt out of our society and become a Seychellese,' he said. 'We suffer too much.'

'Don't be a fool. It seems to me the woman who insulted you was right in calling you a damn fool, though for different reasons. You're selfish. All you want is privilege for yourself. You forget your own people.'

'I know, but ... ' he said.

'But what?' By now I was angry. 'What about your mother, father, brothers, and sisters? Are you ready to leave them?'

Eventually we dropped the argument and went on working. Sad experiences such as this were commonplace in Nairobi. At the time there seemed to be no immediate end to them and it can be understood that sometimes a man was driven so far that, in his despair, he would commit suicide or even attempt to revenge himself on those who were responsible, sometimes with tragic results.

84

In the evening after office hours were over I always had to take papers home with me to work on for the following day. I was living at Kaloleni—one of the African locations. I shared two rooms with a friend of mine who had been my classmate at Kambui Primary School and also in the Medical Department. He had resigned from the Medical Department because of inadequate pay and was now working as a clerk for the East Africa Meteorological Service. He, too, was interested in politics.

Our two rooms were poorly furnished. We had no lights and instead we used a kerosene oil-lamp with a charcoal fire for cooking and heating. We queued for our drinking water fifty yards away from the house and we shared the lavatory with four other people—a separate building fifteen yards away from the house. There was no running water in the lavatory—only a tin in which we 'let' our faeces. Sometimes the place smelt offensively. The tin in the lavatory was often full of faeces as the municipal workmen were always late in emptying the tins. There was no light in the lavatory. We had to use our kerosene oil-lamps, or matches, and if the tin was full of faeces one's leg was easily soiled with it.

Despite these disadvantages, Kaloleni was considered to be one of the most modern of the African locations and one of the best in which to live.

Our house, like most houses in that location, was built of stone and roofed with tiles. Each of our two rooms had three windows and our total furniture consisted of a table, two chairs, and two beds. The nearest shops were about a quarter of a mile away.

The little leisure which we had was spent in discussing politics and our hopes for higher education. We read history and political literature dealing with the Indian struggle for independence. We read Gandhi, Nehru, and M. A. Jinah pretty thoroughly. There was little social life for us.

As an assistant editor of *The African Voice* I wrote many articles protesting against the pass laws, colour bar, and deplorable wages and housing, and demanded the opening up of the Kenya Highlands for the Africans.

The Kenya African Union is no more. It was declared 'subversive' in 1953 and banned. The authorities were very careful to point out that they did *not* mean that the Kenya African Union was Communist or even under Communist influence. They meant that it was stirring up trouble in Kenya and was therefore 'subverting good order there'.

Most people spoke of the organization as KAU ('cow'). It was centred in Nairobi, but in the rural areas and various small towns across the country the Kenya African Union was decentralized; there were fifty-three branches all over Kenya. There were also a president, secretary, and treasurer in every district; however, they were supposed to submit their progress reports to the head office in Nairobi.

Practically all the African chiefs were bitterly opposed to the Kenya African Union. Many of them frequently threatened to arrest the leaders of the union in their respective districts if they should hold a political meeting without prior authorization from the District Commissioner. This was especially true of the Kikuyu-Embu-Meru districts. The chiefs were government servants and, of course, feared the Kenya African Union as a threat to their prestige and control over the populace.

One of the major criticisms against the chiefs by the Kenya African Union was that they were instruments of oppression in that they only received orders from their superiors and did not take trouble to interpret the African demands to the Government. In the African understanding or sense of the word 'chief', it meant a leader of his people. A genuine leader who was also a source of suggestions towards progress and inspiration. He was not a 'carrier of orders' given to him by somebody else.

As a counterpart of the Kenya African Union there was the European Electors' Union. All European settlers were members of this organization. Among other things, the organization stated that the European leadership must not only be maintained permanently in Kenya, but that self-government, eventually coming to the country, would also be controlled by the Europeans (as in Southern Rhodesia), enabling them to create a 'white dominion'.

Actually the Kenya Government, the British Colonial Office, and the white settlers of Kenya seemed to have disregarded the previous British policy on Kenya. For instance, a Kenya White Paper of July 1923 states:

The interests of the African natives must be paramount and that if, and when, those interests, and the interests of the immigrant races (European and Asiatics) should conflict, the former should prevail ...

The British Government's official policy in Kenya changed tremendously in later years. African interests were not *equally* considered, much less paramount. To substantiate this fact I shall refer to one of the many skirmishes in Kenya's political conflict.

In 1947 the then Colonial Secretary, Arthur Creech Jones, issued a White Paper, 191, which proposed that the European, Asian, and African races should each have equal representation in a new East African Central Assembly. Considering that Kenya had 30,000 Europeans, 100,000 Indians, and 5,500,000 Africans this was still a long way from democratic equality of representation. But the white settlers in Kenya so frantically harassed the Colonial Office with protests to even this slight concession to African interests, that White Paper 191 was withdrawn and replaced by another which accepted the principle of majority representation for the whites.

VII

I am Hit by a Truncheon

EARLIER I mentioned the 'tyranny' of the European employer and the use of such a word needs justification. It might, therefore, be convenient to explain here the 'Kipande' or pass system as it was applied in Kenya and how it affected me personally.

The Kenya Africans were sick and tired of insulting, humiliating, and discriminatory passes and the laws which had instituted these passes. The most hated pass of them all was called the Kipande which was like a registration certificate and which the Africans had to carry on their person at all times. An American friend of mine who saw this pass remarked to me that it was based on the assumption that a large number or proportion of the Africans were inherently dishonest.

What was the Kipande System?

The Kipande system was officially introduced in Kenya in 1921. Every male African above sixteen years of age had to be registered, finger-printed, and issued with a registration certificate—Kipande. Kipande was different from the passport, the birth certificate, the identity cards in Britain, or social security numbers in the United States of America.

In Kenya a policeman could stop an African on the road or in the street and demand that he produce his Kipande—regardless of whether the African concerned was as wise as Socrates, as holy as St Francis, or as piratical as Sir Francis Drake.

Kipande was also used to prevent the African labourer escaping distasteful employment or from unjust employers who had power to have him arrested and then fined, imprisoned, or both. When Kenyatta took over the leadership of the Kenya African Union from James Gichuru he announced publicly that the Africans had carried 'Vipande' (plural for Kipande) long enough and that they should burn them if the Kenya Government refused to repeal the ordinance which had instituted the system. The alternative, Kenyatta explained, was for the Kenya Government to issue Vipande to all the races of Kenya—the Europeans, the Asians, and the Africans. The Africans, at that time, were seriously prepared to take action, illegal if necessary, to abolish Vipande whether the Government liked it or not. Mass meetings were held all over Kenya at which a lot of money was collected to buy wood for a big fire at the centre of Nairobi city on which all the Africans would burn their Vipande. This was to be an historic fire!

Quickly and wisely the Kenya Government promised the African leaders that the Kipande system would be repealed forthwith and that a system of identity cards for all the races in Kenya would replace it.

The Africans welcomed the government promise and in 1950 the Kipande system was abolished. But the scars of Kipande remained. In the thirty years of its existence Kipande caused great humiliation and hardship and was a constant grievance among my people. It cannot be said that the British Government knew nothing of this: when sending Kenyatta to England on various occasions from 1929 onwards the Africans instructed him to speak not only about the thorny problems of land but also to protest about Kipande.

A well-known missionary, and one of the few well-wishers of the Kenya Africans among the Europeans there, complained in a letter to the London *Times* of June 1938 that not less than 50,000 Africans in Kenya had been jailed since 1920 for failure to produce Vipande—an average of 5000 Africans per year!

When the Kenya Government announced officially in 1948 that the Kipande system would be abolished the Kenya settlers, as was expected, resisted strongly. The instrument which they had used so long in keeping the African labourers in a state of serfdom was now being lifted. They accused the Government of yielding to 'African agitators' and 'irresponsible demagogues'! The settlers did not stop to ask themselves what would be the effect of the frustrated anger of the Kenya Africans. They did not understand that no human being, of whatever nationality, can keep on indefinitely without breaking through such frustration. After all, the Kenya Africans had carried their Vipande on their persons from 1921 to 1950, and yet the Kipande was only one of innumerable grievances.

The Europeans and the Asians were free from having Vipande. The psychological effect of the Kipande system was equal to that of an African calling a European 'Bwana' instead of 'Mr', or of a European calling a seventy-year-old African 'boy', or referring to 'natives' without a capital 'N', or 'native locations' in the city instead of 'African sections'.

The Africans were constantly worried by these passes. I remember full well that, whenever my father mislaid his Kipande he was as much worried and unhappy as if he had been an important government official accused of accepting a vicuna coat from a private citizen!

There were also numerous other passes which were equally insulting, and principally the so-called 'The Red-Book' issued by the Labour Exchange and which every African domestic servant was required to carry. In the Red-Book the character of the African concerned, the amount of pay he was receiving, and the cause of dismissal were to be recorded.

I remember well one afternoon when I was walking with Muchaba who had been my chief aide during my *irua* or circumcision ceremony. We were in Pangani, one of the sections of Nairobi, when we heard a voice far away call 'Simama' or 'Halt!' We did not pay too much attention since we were discussing family matters. Suddenly, we heard another voice shouting loudly: 'You! Stop there!' We looked back and saw two policemen hurrying towards us. We suddenly had butterflies in our stomachs. We stopped and waited for them and, as they were approaching us, I whispered to Muchaba:

'Do you have your Kipande with you?'

'No, I don't have it,' he replied.

'I don't have mine either.'

'We'll catch hell now,' Muchaba said.

The two policemen came up to us.

'Why didn't you stop at once when we called you?' the first one asked. And the second one, sarcastically:

'Who do you think you are?' even before we had a chance to reply.

'At first we didn't know you were calling to us, sirs,' Muchaba said. 'We are very sorry.'

'No, you look like law breakers, like most of the Kikuyu,' one policeman said.

'Show us your Kipande quickly!' the second one demanded.

'I don't have mine. I have just forgotten it,' Muchaba replied.

'Where?'

'Where I work,' Muchaba said.

'Where and for whom do you work?' asked the policeman.

'I work for a European lady just near the Fair View Hotel.'

'What do you do?'

'I am a cook,' Muchaba replied.

'Do you have any other pass as an identification?' asked the policeman.

'No. But I can give you my employer's address and the telephone number if you like,' Muchaba said.

'Idiot!' shouted the policeman. 'How stupid can you get? Do you expect us to make telephone calls for all criminals we arrest without their Vipande? We are not your telephone operators.'

'What can I do then?' asked Muchaba.

'Carry your Kipande with you,' replied the policeman. 'Incidentally, who is this fellow here with his arms folded like a great bwana. Do you have your Kipande?' They turned to me.

'No, I don't have it. I have never had a formal Kipande,' I said.

'What!' they both exclaimed thunderously.

'When I joined the Medical Department in 1945 the Senior Medical Officer sent me to the Labour Exchange to obtain my Kipande but I found out that the copies of the formal Kipande were exhausted. I was given an emergency certificate and told to get a formal Kipande later on,' I explained.

'Are you still in the Medical Department?' they asked.

'No, I am working for the Kenya African Union as an assistant editor,' I said.

'Where do you live?' they asked.

'Kaloleni,' I replied.

'Just because you are working for that trouble-making KAU you think you don't have to carry Kipande?'

'No, that is not the reason. I just forgot my emergency certificate. I don't think that KAU is trouble making. We fight for the rights of everyone in Kenya, including the police,' I said.

They looked at each other, confused.

'Do you have any other papers as identification?' they asked.

'I have some papers with the letter-heading of the Kenya African Union.'

'We are not interested in letter-heads. We want official documents. Any fool can produce letter-heads.'

This comedy finally ended and they decided to take us to the police station.

We walked in front of them and they followed us. As we were walking I tried to get a handkerchief from my pocket to blow my nose. One policeman thought that I was insulting him by putting my hands in my pocket like a big bwana and hit me on my shoulder with his truncheon. He hit me hard. I tried to explain to him that my nose was running but I saw he was ready to hit me again, and so I kept quiet. Muchaba said nothing.

As we approached the police station I heard somebody calling: 'Hey you, that's Mr Mathu's man. What did he do?'

Muchaba and I were afraid to look back in case we should be hit again. The two policemen answered the call and then suddenly told us to stop. We turned round and saw two other policemen coming towards us. I recognized one of them. He was my classmate at Kambui Primary School and he knew both Muchaba and I full well. We were relieved and happy! The four policemen conferred together and the one who knew us explained to his colleagues that we must have been telling the truth, and that we should not be arrested. Two of them agreed but the third still wanted to go to the police station.

At last they let us go but by then Muchaba was very late in returning to his work. His employer was very, very angry, as her dinner was late. Muchaba had not telephoned and she had no idea where to find him.

I advised Muchaba to take a taxi but there was none in sight. It was getting too late. Finally he took a bus and, when he arrived at his employer's home, he found her waiting near the gate holding a pen.

'Bring your Red-Book right away. You have no job now. You are entirely unreliable, a lazy, untrustworthy African. I hate you bloody niggers,' she said.

Muchaba had no chance to explain anything. He was told to pack up his belongings and leave at once. He had some heavy luggage and couldn't move it all at once and so he took it bit by bit to the nearest street. Finally he took a taxi and came to my place. I took a chance and let him stay with me for the night! If the police had knocked me up in the night and found him with me, both of us would have been in trouble.

That evening, as he had never learnt to read or write English, Muchaba asked me to tell him what had been written in his Red-Book. I knew Muchaba very well to be a sensitive and intelligent man and was sickened to read: 'He is quick in his work; he likes sweet things and may steal sugar if he has a chance; sometimes his thinking is like that of an eleven-year-old child.' When Muchaba heard this he was so angry that he burnt the book. I cannot blame him for this but it put him in serious difficulty as no one would give him another job unless he produced the book, even this one with its permanent defamatory record. It was more than a month before the Labour Exchange agreed to issue Muchaba with a new book (I can only liken the process to that when one loses a passport), and then he was able to get another job working as a cook for a wealthy Indian businessman.

Muchaba's story can also illustrate the considerable licence allowed by their superiors to the ordinary police force, at that time largely illiterate, which in itself contributed to the atmosphere of European superiority and power which sapped the resistance of the unorganized African population.

In the evenings the police could knock on the door of any African in the African locations and demand to know how many people were sleeping there, how many had Kipande, and proof of where they were working. This could have happened to any African rooming place, and almost always the police called about eleven o'clock or midnight.

In some cases, a man and his wife might be sleeping peacefully but they had to open the door quickly. Police would then ask the man to produce Kipande and to say where he was working. They would search everywhere with their flash-lights and, if they were satisfied, would leave the place without even saying sorry to the couple they had awakened.

I remember full well when the police knocked up one of my uncles at about 12.45 a.m. When three policemen entered the room my uncle and his wife were trying to fix their pyjamas. One of the policemen shouted:

'How many people do you have in this room, eh?'

'Only my wife and myself, sir.'

'How many people do you usually accommodate?' the second policeman demanded.

'None at all except my wife.'

'My wife, my wife,' the third policeman shouted. 'How do we know she isn't just a prostitute from Manjengo, eh?'

'No! No! You have it all wrong. This is my own legal wife and if you insist on disagreeing with me please take me to the police station,' Uncle protested vehemently. His pride and dignity were badly shaken. Utterly hurt.

The three policemen left. They had caused great upset and inconvenience to my uncle and his wife but he had no remedy. He could not sue the Police Department which could always say 'They did this in the course of their duty to uproot undesirable natives': an excuse invariably accepted by their superiors.

I would illustrate the general attitude of their superiors to the police by quoting from *The Report on the Committee on Police Terms of Service*, 1942, which among other things says:

> The evidence submitted to us indicates that, in general, the illiterate African makes a better policeman than a literate African. The latter is less amenable to discipline and is reluctant to undertake the menial tasks which sometimes fall to the lot of ordinary constables. That being so, it seems to us that the policy of recruiting literates should be pursued with great caution, and that no special inducements by way of salary are necessary. In fact, we venture to go so far as to recommend the abolition of literacy allowance for new entrants.

In the rural area it was difficult for me to realize that the Africans were always accorded the last treatment. The city life taught me this.

It could well be asked why the Africans submit to the unjust domination of the police and the system of Kipande. For once the answer is quite simple: lack of good organization, one virtue of their civilization which the Europeans were not eager to pass on, and the determination of the Europeans to preserve their privileged system at any price. Thus, in 1945, there was only one African representative in the Kenya Legislative Council, none in the Executive Council, and in 1946 two were nominated in the City Council with no real voice in civic affairs. There was no effective organization to correlate the grievances of the Africans and present them with any force. Certainly neither the European settlers nor the British Colonial Government felt any inclination to remedy the appalling and obvious defects in the system which they had created, for which they were responsible, and which only they were strong enough to change.

Forced to live in such conditions of physical and moral degradation it is not surprising that there was psychological confusion or ambivalence among my people. In fact, there appeared to be two groups of them in the city. One group regarded the city as a place for making money. These people thought that Nairobi was a city belonging to some other people —the Asians and the Europeans—and that a 'true' African could not regard himself as a part of Nairobi. Real home was in the rural area. Nairobi was, therefore, identified with the immigrant races and by the Africans only as a means to an end.

The result was that after working for a considerable number of years in Nairobi these people would eventually return to the rural area with some money, returning to the city only to replenish their income. Some would continue working for a long time but their feelings and security were always in the country where they might have owned a small piece of land. Some men had left their wives working on their small holdings in the Reserves while they were working in Nairobi.

The reasons for this ambivalence were innumerable: for instance, lack of economic mobility for the Africans in the city, insecurity in all types of occupations, appalling housing situation, and pass laws. The number of Africans who could afford to buy or own permanent homes or property in the city was extremely small.

There were also sociological implications. A man worked in

the city for many months and years without seeing his wife and children and this made life somewhat one-sided. Most Africans, especially those who were working for the Europeans as domestic servants, were not allowed to live with their wives in Nairobi. The European employers usually provided small houses which looked like garages near their homes for the African domestic workers. These small 'houses' were called 'quarters' and no African was allowed to have his wife visit him in his given quarter. However, most domestic workers had their wives visit them secretly at night. But, if a European had a dog in his home it was more difficult. The dogs would bark!

After a man's wife had visited him in his quarter, she usually stayed in that quarter at all times. She couldn't come out in the open lest she be seen by the boss. She was like a prisoner.

Many European employers did not permit the police to visit or to knock up these quarters in the night—unless an employer suspected that his servants were allowing visitors to spend a night in these 'little houses'. Hence, a wife could visit and stay indefinitely provided she remained in the house at all times and came out only when the boss and his wife had gone out.

Of course, as in every situation, there were certain exceptions in that some European employers allowed their domestic servants to have visitors of either sex for a limited period. But the number of these 'good Europeans' was very small.

I knew a lot of people who saw their wives twice or three times a year. Sometimes their wives would come to Nairobi to get pregnant and return to the Reserves after a month or so. Some people did not see their children from one Christmas to the next.

The second group of Nairobi Africans consisted of people who were working as simple clerks, factory helpers, and city labourers. These people did not want to have anything to do with the rural area. They detested working on the small plots of African land, in the country, disregarding the fact that the city and country were so interrelated that, even if, for the sake of argument, there were enough industries to absorb them in the city, those industries would still be dependent upon the produce from the farms in the rural area.

The people who were in the second group did not appear to

have reasonable alternatives. They did not have property or any amenities in the city but were working for some £2 to £3 per month—a hand-to-mouth existence!

There were, therefore, no permanent African families residing in Nairobi as their real home. This created another important social problem. The men working in the city had little social life. For example, if a man wanted to go to a dance in one of the African social halls there was no girl to take with him—unless he had asked his girl friend in the Reserve to come for the occasion, which would have involved a long trip from the country to Nairobi and perhaps the inconvenience of returning home in time. Moreover, very few parents would have allowed their daughters to go to the city for social events. On the other hand, there were no African girls working in the offices as clerks. There were only a few nurses working in the Medical Department, but their hours of work were irregular. There were, however, a large number of African women who had left their husbands in the rural area because of various matrimonial causes, such as barrenness, adultery, their husbands' polygamy or unfaithfulness with loose women in the city while they themselves were working hard in the Reserves, infidelity to which they felt forced to retaliate.

These women were working in the city as 'ayahs'—taking care of children or baby-sitting for the Europeans generally and for some Asians. One might call many of them prostitutes. As a result men in the city could call upon them and invite them to a dance or evening out. Some of these women were wealthy and, in fact, wealthier than many men in the city and they owned some mud-built houses in one of the African locations called Majengo.

They rented their houses to anybody who needed a place to stay while working in the city. Some of their tenants were respectable people who had left their families in the countryside. Other tenants were ordinary women in the city who were not fortunate enough to have sufficient money to have their own houses as their colleagues had. The rooms in these houses were very small—about six feet by eight feet—and their dividing walls were very thin so that one tenant could hear practically all of what was going on in the next room. This was highly frustrating if, for instance, a wife had come to the city from the country to visit her husband who was a tenant in one of the houses, and his neighbour was one of the city prostitutes!

I had a chance of talking to some of these women to find out their problems and how they liked the city; for as an editor.I tried to learn everything I could about practically everything. Some of them appeared to have legitimate reasons for leaving their husbands. For instance, one hot day I went to talk to one who owned a big square mud-built house roofed with corrugated iron. There were six tenants in the house, each occupying a small room. Its walls were polished by white clay soil called 'Lami' which shone as white as chalk.

I knocked on the main door and it was opened almost at once by one of the tenants who directed me to a green door. I knocked and the lady opened the door. She appeared excited, but friendly and co-operative. She was in a white velvet dress, beautifully made, white pointed shoes, and no stockings. She had long curly hair, and two long ear-rings. I think she might have been between thirty-six and forty years of age.

'Have a seat,' she said.

'Thanks,' I said. 'I would like to know what problems you usually experience in this location as I am interested in all problems affecting our people in this country, you know,' I added.

'All right, what do you want to know particularly?' she asked.

'Perhaps this may sound too personal to you and I'm sorry if it does, but can you tell me how you happened to come to this city?'

'Oh! It's a long story, but I don't mind telling it to you briefly,' she said. 'Incidentally, do you want a cup of tea?' she interjected quickly.

'Yes, I do, and thank you for your willingness to tell me about yourself,' I answered.

She started making tea in what was called the 'Indian style' whereby the water, sugar, tea, and milk were put in a pot and boiled together. It was then strained in a kettle. It was very strong and nice. When the tea was ready she poured two cups, and handed one to me. I was reading a copy of *The East African Standard* while the tea was being made.

'May we continue?' she asked.

'If you please,' I replied.

'I was married fifteen years ago in Kabete. My husband and I loved each other very much. We had a little piece of land on which we grew various types of vegetables, and we had a few goats and sheep, and eventually two sons and a daughter. We worked very hard during the earlier part of our marriage. But, later on, my husband turned into an alcoholic. He used to drink hard and came home very late in the night. He would then start arguing with me violently, and if I tried to say a word he would beat me severely. Yet, I had been taking care of our children, animals, and everything else at home while he was busy drinking.'

'Did you try to speak to his parents about it to see whether or not they could talk to him and persuade him to stop drinking?' I asked.

'Yes, I did. But he did not listen to them. Whenever I did that he would beat me more and more saying that I was exposing his dignity to his family,' she said. 'I planned many, many times to run away from him but each time I tried I remembered our children and then I would stop. It was horrible,' she said.

'Were beating and drinking the only things which made you leave him?' I asked.

'No. They were only a part of a very complicated problem. For example, he used to complain that every member of his age-grade had more than one wife and that I did not work hard enough so that we could have enough wealth which would, in turn, enable him to pay the dowry for another wife. Yet he was drinking whatever little money I made. For instance, if I went to the market with a big load of bananas for sale, when I came home in the evening he would take all the money I had earned during the day, and buy sugar and honey to make some drink, and in this way we could hardly have enough for him to have other wives. What could I have done?' she asked.

'So you left him finally?' I asked.

'Yes. My daughter, who was our eldest child, acted as the mother of our two sons. Life was also very difficult for her. After her circumcision she ran away from her father, too. She went to Nakuru to work for a European as an ayah. I felt very bad about her as I wished for her to get married and have her own

99

home with her husband. But I can understand why she did what she did.'

'Are you consciously or unconsciously sorry that you left him?' I asked.

'No, I'm not. It was the only just course which was left open for me,' she said.

'What happened to your husband and the two sons?'

'Well, my husband kept on drinking. He then sold all our animals, and our two sons were desperate. They came to see me often. But whenever they returned home they were beaten badly by their father because they had gone to Nairobi to see their prostitute mother. Finally, I was able to put them in a mission school to get educated, and today one is a successful artisan in Mombasa, and the other one is a clerk in Nairobi. I saved them from that tyrannical man!' she said. 'Incidentally, I heard recently that my husband was last seen at Naivasha working as a labourer, looking very poor and worn,' she added.

'Would you help him in any way if you found him in difficulties?' I asked.

'It all depends on what kind of difficulties. I wouldn't mind buying him a cup of tea. But I think he's too self-centred to accept anything from me. For, to him, I'm just a brutal prostitute,' she said.

'Would you say that most of the women in the city might have had, generally speaking, an experience such as yours in the past?'

'Yes, I do, especially those who came to Nairobi in the 'twenties and early 'thirties. But most of the later arrivals had the impression that there was an easier life in the city than there was in the Reserves. But you realize that there are numerous reasons for matrimonial troubles everywhere,' she said.

'Do the police do something about checking on these women?' I asked.

'Yes. They knock on their doors in the night to find out who are the men with them. Sometimes they arrest and beat the men but they don't bother the women as much,' she said.

'How is it that they don't bother the women?'

'Because the policemen, like any other African men in the city, do not live with their wives here in Nairobi all the time.

Their wives are also in the Reserves. Consequently these women in the city "help" the policemen, too,' she said.

'Help the policemen!' I exclaimed.

'Of course!' she said. 'Are they not men?' she asked slyly.

'I see. Would you say that this is a form of bribery?'

'Not exactly. But I shall leave it for you to decide,' she concluded.

There was no need to try to exaggerate the pathetic economic, political, and social life which confronted the Kenya Africans in Nairobi. All one needed was to go to any of the African locations and see for oneself various problems openly displayed.

In the evening some Africans would be found playing cards and draughts. Others would be drinking some stinking municipally brewed drink—'Tembo'—at Pumwani as an outlet for their handicapped life.

The Dream of the Warrior

Day after day, as I lived and worked in Nairobi, my mind would drift into 'The Dream of the Warrior', a fable I made up in which the main character was a Kikuyu boy named Gambuguatheru, a disguised form of my own name. My dream was, to me, also a kind of 'revelation', in which it was 'revealed' to me that it is wrong to think that heroism can be displayed in warfare only, though many people cling to that idea. A true hero may also display his mettle in fighting against the wrong deeds or ideas of those around him, just as much as in actual warfare. And so I kept on dreaming.

Gambuguatheru, of my dream, was a boy when the white men came. He became so curious to know who they were and what they wanted in his country that he was determined to go and question a European. One evening he told his father of his intent, and his father was so astonished at his son's daring that he would not allow him to sleep alone in his room for fear he might escape and go out to accomplish this dangerous mission. Next morning his father, still determined to dissuade Gambuguatheru, told him how the white men could shoot black men at a great distance and how they could make a box (gramophone) speak, but Gambuguatheru was still determined.

At noon he went to a certain missionary station and there he found an English missionary. He was told by the missionary that the sole aim of the white men was to preach the gospel. After receiving several presents he returned to his home. The whole family was amazed to hear of the boy's adventure since he was the first among them to talk to a white man. And he had returned unharmed.

In spite of his father's opposition to any more contact between his son and the missionary and the latter's plan to spread the new gospel, Gambuguatheru decided to take the leadership of his people so that their ignorance of the foreigners might not cause them loss in trade or menace their control of their country. How to do that was a serious problem. People began to fear him for his queer behaviour, but his personality was such that once he began talking people gathered round him to listen. In this way he was able to make most of the people trust him.

During this time there was a belief that if one wrote a letter trying to contact a European, or if one invented something like a machine, one's hands would be cut off by the white men. Gambuguatheru wanted to prove the truth or falsity of this belief so that he could rid his country of apprehension if it was false. 'But what shall I write about?' he wondered. At last an idea struck him. He saw that the country was desperately in need of education and he wanted men and women to come who would concentrate only on educating his people. After much thinking and hesitation he wrote the letter and gave it to the missionary, who posted it for him to England. After a year he got a reply which promised him that he would get the men he wanted in a few months' time. And nothing was said about cutting off his hands for having written the letter.

Gambuguatheru then decided to turn to matters concerning the administration of his country. Already some administrative centres had been established in different parts of the country. He learned that the Europeans staying in these centres were called District Commissioners. They had already begun giving orders to the people around them. He very well knew that these District Commissioners would not agree to train him so that he could become a District Commissioner too since he would be trying to be their equal. So taking his spear and club he went out to go to the Governor to demand such training.

At the Governor's gate he was stopped from entering by gate-keepers. He was so dusty that they could not believe that such a man was entitled to talk to the Governor. Fortunately, the Governor happened to be walking round his garden and saw him. Gambuguatheru at once left the gate-keepers and ran to the nearest side of the garden. Then, speaking the bad English he had picked up from the missionaries, he shouted to the Governor. It was a wonder to hear an African talking to the Governor on such a subject in so loud and peremptory a manner!

Although he was the dirtiest man the Governor had ever seen, Gambuguatheru was admitted. It was arranged that he should be trained as a District Commissioner. The training took two years, after which he returned to his home and was made a D.C. He found that his people had abandoned all their old customs and copied the foreign ones. He was not impressed by all this. Within six months he had made his people see the mistake of giving up all their customs, so that it was easy for him to introduce subjects like African pottery, painting, the blacksmith's craft, and carving in the schools. Later, he established a school teaching only old things and trying to improve them by applying foreign methods where necessary.

The results of this school were so successful that years afterwards it was one of the biggest and most liked in Kikuyuland. After Gambuguatheru's death his statue was placed at the gate of the school, and the following words written on it:

A HERO HE WAS INDEED! IN BOTH THOUGHT
AND DEED. HE NEVER LEFT ANYTHING
UNDONE IF HE KNEW IT SHOULD BE DONE.

Now that I have had a college education I recognize that in this daydream, which I used to imagine at the age of twenty, my unconscious mind had condensed and disguised all sorts of ideas and images that I was getting from my reading and from the new experiences I was having in the big city of Nairobi. Now, for the first time in my life I was beginning to get interested in 'politics'—those serious affairs that were affecting all Kenya Africans. My image of myself and of what the country needed was not yet clear. The vision of myself in the dream was a sort of combined image of 'The Educated Ones'—that very small group of Kenya Africans who had been away to colleges and universities overseas and who were the acknowledged leaders among the Africans. Of these, three stood out above all the rest, Jomo Kenyatta, Mbiyu Koinange, and Eliud Wambu Mathu. To understand my dream, one needs to understand them.

VIII

Jomo Kenyatta—The African Messiah

EVERYBODY, everywhere, who reads newspapers or listens to the radio has heard of Jomo Kenyatta, the man the American newspapers called 'The Burning Spear', who in 1953 was sentenced to seven years' hard labour on a charge of having organized and led 'the dreaded Mau Mau rebellion' in Kenya. In 1945, when I first began to awaken to the meaning of politics, Jomo was only a legend to me, for he was in a far-away land, in England, and had been there for seventeen years.

Every young African knew something of Kenyatta's story. We all knew that our fathers and their fathers in the years soon after the First World War had formed an organization called the *Kikuyu Central Association*. They did so because the British Government had decided to give large tracts of their land away to ex-soldiers from England. And we knew that in 1928, a young mission-educated Kikuyu named Johnstone Kamau had become Secretary-General of the KCA and under the name of Kenyatta had begun to edit its newspaper called *Muiguithania* (meaning literally 'One who makes people agree and compromise'). All of us knew that Jomo had gone to Britain in 1929 to protest about the taking of the land and that he had started to study there at the London School of Economics with the great anthropologist, Malinowski, and that he had written a book about the Kikuyu people called *Facing Mount Kenya*. There were a lot of other things we had heard about but of which we were not so sure: that he had journeyed into the land of the Russians and stayed there for some time; that he had married

105

an English woman and had had a child by her; that he was known to all the powerful politicians in Britain; that he had many friends in the Labour Party which took power in 1945.

We had all given our pennies and shillings at rallies to be sent to England to help Kenyatta to represent us there. We believed that some day he would return and bring new hope and perhaps new laws about the land. And we believed that all settlers feared nothing more than a return of Jomo Kenyatta to Kenya. And some of the illiterate people had put all of this hope and admiration into songs which were sung in the Kikuyu Country.

The Kikuyu Central Association was banned in 1940 as a 'subversive organization' because it kept agitating for the return of the African lands and for equal rights. The Europeans feared that KCA would hurt the war effort in Kenya. In 1944 the Government allowed the Africans to start another organization, called the Kenya African Union. One African newspaperman began to publish a newspaper in Kikuyu which agitated all the time for the return of Kenyatta to Kenya. Then one day in 1946, after Labour had won the election in England, Kenyatta came home. At last we young people saw him. We liked him and his bold, loud, challenging voice, and we liked his programme.

To most Africans of the generation of my father and my father's father, Jomo's name has been associated with the fight about land—not with political matters as representation in the legislature or who shall or shall not be the first prime minister of Kenya. They sent Kenyatta to London in the year of the beginning of the Great Depression to protest about the land.

As Kenyatta lived and travelled in Europe, he began to see the Kenya problem not just in terms of petitioning the British Government to rectify past injustices with regard to the land. He saw the problem as one of teaching Africans how to get enough political power to control their own affairs in Kenya.

Although to the older people Kenyatta was the man who would restore the land, to the young people of Kenya in 1946 he was an African Messiah who would now lead them towards self-government just as Azikiwe in Nigeria and Nkrumah in the Gold Coast were doing. In 1947 they elected him president of the Kenya African Union. Now, in 1964, he is, at last, Prime Minister of Kenya!

'*Mr Mbiyu*'—*The Man of Gethunguri*

In 1945, Jomo Kenyatta was only a legend to us, but there was another educated Kikuyu who was with us in the flesh, and for whom all of we young people had great admiration. He, too, had spent many years overseas, but not in Britain. He had gone away, even before Jomo Kenyatta went to England. He had stayed so many years that many people thought he was lost and would never return. And then, one day in 1939, he came home again. He came wearing a long black gown and a flat hat with a tassel on it. He had stopped in Britain on the way home and studied there for a while and had diplomas from schools there, too. This was Peter Mbiyu Koinange, son of a senior chief of the Kikuyu.

Mbiyu's father had sent him away in 1927 to the Hampton Institute in Virginia, U.S.A., the same school which had trained Booker T. Washington who wrote *Up from Slavery*. He had heard about this school from the Phelps Stokes Commission which had toured East Africa studying educational problems at the request of the Colonial Office. Mbiyu's father had told him to train himself to serve his people. Mbiyu spent four years at Hampton preparing for college entry. I have heard that he was very popular there and was a first-class football player, as well as a good student.

He then went to Ohio Wesleyan College (now University), where after four years he took his B.A. Years later when another Kenya African student attended this school, Mbiyu's teachers and friends in neighbouring towns spoke with great pleasure of having known him and of how he taught them to play the African game called 'Giuthi'.

Finally, he took his M.A. at the Columbia University Faculty of Education there. When he left America he decided to stop in England to take some lectures in anthropology at Cambridge and to get a diploma from the Institute of Education in London. And then he came home in the year 1939. I was about fourteen years old then.

'Mr Mbiyu' decided to form a school to train teachers for the Africans' 'independent schools' and so a school at Gethunguri came into existence. It was attended by over 800 students ranging from seven to twenty-one years of age. Its standard was equivalent to the Ordinary level of the General Certificate of Education. The idea was to make it a University College of Kenya from which people could obtain their teaching diplomas, trade certificates, and degrees. It lasted nearly thirteen years until it was closed down by the Government during the Emergency. It was flourishing in 1941 when I tried to enter it after my circumcision—a story I have already told. It was only natural that my friends and I should have headed for Gethunguri. Mr Mbiyu and his school represented to us the brave, independent Kikuyu spirit. We knew the main outlines of Mr Mbiyu's story, and of how the school at Gethunguri was founded, just as we knew the story of Jomo Kenyatta.

When Kenyatta came home in 1946, he and Koinange began to co-operate together in the building up of the Kenya African Union. They also attempted to found an organization for bringing Europeans, Indians, and Africans together in peaceful, friendly relations. Mr Mbiyu was very keen on what might be described as 'grass-roots diplomacy'.

In 1947, Mr Mbiyu went to London to represent the Kenya African Union there for two years, and then was invited to India by Prime Minister Nehru. Later he went back to England to represent Kenya Africans and was there when Mau Mau broke out. He was in effect exiled all through the Emergency but was allowed to return home for three days to visit his aged and very sick father who had been arrested. When Mr Mbiyu became the model of inspiration to us he was an educator. We watched him grow into a political leader, and we young people were proud of him.

I suspect the fact that Mr Mbiyu had studied in America and that the first Kenyan to get a master's degree had been educated in that country, was one of the things that influenced me to want to go to America to study some day. The second Kenya African to go to America to study was Julius Gikonyo who left in 1948 and came back home in 1957 with a Ph.D. degree in Political Science. I was the third student to go to America. Since we went, over eight hundred Kenya students have gone there. Mr Mbiyu pioneered the way for us. Now, he is Minister of Pan-African Affairs in Kenya.

To the young Kikuyu of 1945 Kenyatta was the promised Messiah, but there was also an Elijah who had come before him. This was Eliud Wambu Mathu who, in 1944, became the first African to sit in Kenya's Legislative Council. Due to pressure from the Africans it was decided that they would be permitted to have *one* representative in the Kenya Legislative Council—ONE. He was to be appointed by the Governor, although the Europeans had elected members. It was inevitable that Eliud Wambu Mathu would be that one. He was educated, mild mannered, and moderate.

Mathu's father was a medicine-man who lived in a place called Waithaka. Young Mathu went to the Church of Scotland mission near the town of Kikuyu, and when he finished he became a school teacher. In 1937 he started educating himself by correspondence through the University of South Africa, and managed to pass the very difficult matriculation examination of the University of South Africa. He then began to study for the external degree offered by the same university. By this time he was teaching at the Alliance High School, Kikuyu, the headmaster of which was Mr Greaves. Mr Greaves liked him and gave him much assistance and Mathu successfully passed his examinations in political science, history, and psychology, and received his B.A. degree. He then went on to South Africa itself for higher studies and from there to Balliol College, Oxford, where he spent two years. He returned to Kenya in 1940 to become a teacher again at Alliance High School, Kikuyu.

Soon after Mathu's return, his friend, Mr Greaves, was replaced by another European. Mathu did not get along too well under the new regime, so he left to establish his own school at his birthplace—Waithaka. His school progressed very well.

After Mathu was appointed to the Legislative Council he also went into business and was very successful. Although he was an *appointed* representative, he represented African interests very well. He was a fluent and fiery speaker like the American Adlai Stevenson or the British Aneurin Bevan. The Africans liked the way he talked. The Europeans respected him.

Immediately after his nomination, Mathu stressed the importance of having a country-wide African political organization to advise on various problems in the central and local governments. He thus stimulated the formation of what became the Kenya African Study Union and later on the Kenya African Union (KAU). I still remember his first letter to the editor of the *East African Standard* in Nairobi on this subject, in 1944. The idea was to unite all Africans in Kenya irrespective of tribe. All of us young Africans were proud of this man of our people who spoke not only for the Kikuyu, but for all Africans in the Kenya Legislative Council. Many of us wanted to be like him some day.

Although I admired both Kenyatta and Koinange, I think it was Mathu's speeches, in those days before Kenyatta came home, that first stirred my heart most thoroughly. Mr Mbiyu was quietly working away day by day building up his school. Kenyatta was far away overseas. But Mathu was acting in a drama on a stage where all could see him and hear him—in the Legislative Council—and his speeches were reported regularly in the *East African Standard*. I went sometimes to the Legislative Council to hear him in the flesh, and it was thrilling. Mathu's example made many young Kenyans yearn for a higher education. On my part, I began to see the salvation of Africans through education. I dreamed of playing some part in Kenya's public affairs myself when I became educated. And it came to pass that Mr Mathu was eventually responsible for something that changed the whole course of my life.

The name Mathu means 'pawns'. The name Wambu means 'one who shouts loudly'. There are many who feel that these two names actually characterize Mathu's personality. He first came to power as an appointed representative of the African people, not an elected one, and this put him in a very difficult position. During the Emergency between 1952 and 1955, 'Mathuism' meant trying to 'stay in the middle'. At that time Mathu found himself in a position worse than that of the Frenchman Talleyrand. He made mistakes, but his successes were enormous, too.

In 1956, when the Kenya Africans were allowed to vote for their representatives to the Legislative Council for the first time, Mathu stood for office, but he lost the election. He lost again in

1958, this time to the young American-educated Julius Gikonyo Kiano. So he retired to his farm in Kyanugu. It is too early to say what Mathu will do eventually politically. It may be that he will be like the Roman Cincinnatus.

Mathu is like the American Al Smith, 'A self-made leader'. He is an energetic man, forthright and well educated, and he has shown that he can be tough. He always comes up on his feet. In 1961, he served in the Congo as Deputy Director of the United Nations operation there.

Kikuyu Domination or Myth?

There have been serious charges against my people. For example, that they are natural-born 'agitators', 'bush-lawyers', and that they organized Mau Mau in 1952 in an attempt to drive out the Europeans from Kenya, and consequently establish the Kikuyu dictatorship over the rest of the Kenya tribes, followed by a return to barbarism and darkness. I am tempted to say something about this problem—without involving myself in an unnecessary controversy.

Most of the Kikuyu live on what is called a 'Reserve', or the 'Kikuyu land unit'. They were put there in the same way that the Navaho, and Fox, and Menominee Indians were put on reservations in the United States. A group of people from Europe came after the First World War and fell in love with our land. They liked its fine climate and its fertile fields, so they began to settle there. At first my people accepted them as guests. When they began to abuse our hospitality we and the other Africans— the Masai, the Suk, the Wakamba, and the Nandi—fought against them. But bows and arrows were useless against guns. As the Masai were our enemies of the past they sometimes fought alongside the Europeans against us. Other Africans were later used to help fight the Masai. There were many more of us than there were American Indians and many fewer Europeans. Yet, for the last sixty years the country was dominated by about 60,000 Europeans and the 7,000,000 Africans were largely confined to Reserves.

Not all white people who came were interested in taking the land. The missionaries came to tell us of a new God and brought with them schools and modern medicine. Traders came to sell us many products we had never seen before. And people from India came to work in building railroads and later settled as traders. There are 250,000 of them now. Against these there has been some resentment, but not real bitterness. That has been reserved for those who took our land from us.

By 1920 there were enough Europeans in our country growing sugar, coffee, tea, and sisal products to make agriculture a profitable business. Then gold was discovered. Kenya was declared a Crown Colony under English rule. Many of my people protested as they saw more and more of our land being taken, and in 1923 the British Government made a strong statement to the effect that the rights of the Africans must be respected as the land was ours. 'The settlers', many of whom were retired soldiers, threatened to revolt and set up an independent state. The British Government sometimes tried to take our part, but it felt that it must also not go too much against the opinions of the settlers, their own kinsmen who came out to Kenya from England.

In 1934 something occurred that hurt us much. About 17,000 square miles of the best land in Kenya was declared open *to white settlers only*. It was called 'The White Highlands' and both Africans and Indians were barred from settling on it. This created a strong and deep feeling among my people that they had not been treated right. How can there be an exclusive 'White Highlands' in the Black Man's country?

The coming of the Europeans also created the 'Squatter'. As great farms came into being in the 'White Highlands' growing crops and cattle for the market, it was necessary to secure labour. Most of the Africans lived in their own villages and were not interested in working for wages. But some were, and besides it was becoming harder to secure a living for many people as the amount of land for Africans grew smaller. So, as I have related, the custom arose of Africans settling on Europeans' farms. The African and his family would be given a plot of land to till, and in return he gave most of his labour to the European farmer. Sometimes he got a small wage, too. Often he did not. He was called a Squatter and his position was something like that of a share-cropper in the American South. By 1950 over one-third of the Kikuyu were Squatters. To a Squatter, the European farm was just a work place. The Reserve was really 'Home'.

As a son of the Kikuyu people I find myself living in two worlds, and in the telling of my story I am telling the story of my people who are also caught between two worlds. I do not tell this story as a tribalist or a chauvinist. I do not believe the Kikuyu were born to rule or oppress others, or that they are superior to other Kenyans or Africans. I tell it because I am proud of the people which gave me birth and because I feel they have been misunderstood by many.

Mau Mau is over. A new Kenya is in the making—a Kenya of many tribes and several races. New leaders are emerging— young men who, while proud of their own tribal groups, think of themselves first as Kenya citizens and who work together forgetting all about their tribal origins. I should re-emphasize the fact that my people have no plans or intentions of establishing dictatorship in any form over anybody in Kenya. The more we know about each other's customs and history, however, the better we shall understand each other.

IX

I Discover 'Canutism'

DURING 1946, the year before I became Associate Editor of *The African Voice*, I 'discovered' America. I began to think about Mr Mbiyu and how he had become the first Kenya African to win an American college degree. In fact, we often discussed America, Americans and particularly American Negroes. I was always one to take up my pen and write and I therefore wrote to the American Consul in Nairobi and asked him to send me the names and addresses of the leading American Negro newspapers, magazines, and colleges in the United States. He sent me several addresses.

So, even before I became associated with *The African Voice*, I began to write to various people in the United States and I sent a number of my articles to the Associated Negro Press in Chicago. An American Negro who was greatly interested in Africa, George Francis McCray, read them and we began to correspond with each other. He told me gently that they were not quite up to the ANP standard, and none of them ever saw the light of day. But George McCray became my friend and that friendship changed the whole direction of my life.

In the meanwhile I decided to write Tuskegee Institute in Alabama asking both for admission and a scholarship. I did not realize that without a high school training I stood very little chance of being accepted. The president wrote to say that no scholarship was available but admission was possible. He indicated that the tuition fee would be $600 per year. I had nothing, but I was determined to go to America for higher education, especially to obtain the B.A. degree in History and

Politics which would enable me to contribute something to Kenya's advancement. I was interested in seeing and meeting American Negroes, and Red Indians. Particularly, I had a tremendous curiosity about the Negroes and their progress in the United States. I am certain, even now, that this curiosity is being shared by many Africans in Kenya and in East Africa in general.

I planned a campaign to reach my goal. I sat down and wrote a letter to one of the Negro newspapers in Chicago, care of the Associated Negro Press. I appealed for donations in the hope that I would receive enough money to finance my study at Tuskegee. I also pointed out that I was interested in corresponding with Americans interested in discussing social, economic, and political affairs. I almost wrote to Joe Louis for a scholarship!

Replies were not very favourable. I received only about twenty-five dollars. As for the pen friends, two people replied saying that they would be interested in corresponding with me. These were Mr George Francis McCray in Chicago, who headed an organization called the Afro-World Fellowship and Mr Julius C. Graham of Ohio.

I expressed to them my deep interest in pursuing higher education in the United States. Their replies were encouraging. For instance, Mr McCray passed on one of my letters to Professor St Clair Drake at Roosevelt University in Chicago. They discussed the possibilities of my going to the United States and attending Roosevelt University on a foreign student scholarship. All arrangements for the scholarship at Roosevelt University were completed. Professor St Clair Drake had even volunteered to be my sponsor for coming to the United States, and for my eventual repatriation to Kenya.

My correspondence with McCray and Graham continued on as usual. Mr McCray told me that chances of my getting a scholarship were very good, and that I should start planning my trip to the United States. He said the Afro-World Fellowship would also assist me. I therefore started appealing to various people for my fare to the United States. Response to my appeals was favourable, but slow.

About two months after I became an editor of KAU I received a letter of admission from the registrar of Roosevelt

University. In addition, Professor Drake sent me three forms indicating that he would be responsible for me financially in the United States, and for eventual repatriation to Kenya.

With these documents in my possession, I then actively appealed to the Kenya people for funds. I appealed to the Africans, Indians, and Europeans—everybody!

My relatives gave many tea parties and sold land to raise money. Over in the Rift Valley Province, my Uncle Ernest Kamara Kuria was also raising money for me.

In the meantime, I took my letter of admission to Mr Mathu who telephoned the American Consul immediately. The Consul asked Mr Mathu to send me to him right away. I decided to approach the American Consul through Mr Mathu because certain persons from the Criminal Investigation Bureau had mentioned to me casually that the CID might not be willing to recommend my visa to the United States.

After reading over my letter of admission to Roosevelt University and the three forms, the Consul said he had no objection to my going to the United States for an American education. He only asked me to get another letter from the registrar of Roosevelt stating whether the scholarship was for one year and whether it could be extended. The registrar replied promptly saying that the scholarship was for one year, and that it could be extended. I took this letter to the American Consul. He demanded two further documents necessary for a student visa to the United States. These were: a police record indicating that I had never been convicted of any criminal offence in Kenya Colony; the other was also a 'police record' to be issued by the Criminal Investigation Department, indicating that there was nothing against me in Kenya *politically*! I was shocked.

By 1947 I had heard of many 'isms'—Fascism, Absolutism, Nazism, etc. I wasn't clear about what most of these 'isms' really meant. But there was one kind of 'ism' I understood, the kind that meant 'keep Kenya Africans down'. I felt this very personally and I gave to it the name I used for any man who balked and frustrated me in his effort to 'protect' the white settlers of Kenya from criticism. He had much in common with the English-Danish king who commanded the tide on the shore but had no power to control it! I called it 'Canutism'.

Following the advice given by the American Consul, I went to the CID office in the Secretariat building in Nairobi. The officer in charge directed me to his subordinates, who issued me the first document. I took it to the American Consul. He told me to get the other one at once, from the Criminal Investigation Department—Special Branch. This was headed by a certain 'Canute'. I went to Canute's office, and on my arrival showed him a letter which was written to me by Mr McCray about my scholarship at Roosevelt University. Canute read the letter very carefully and at the same time started taking notes. After he had finished reading it he said to me coldly:

'Mugo, I can't give you the document needed.'

'Why, sir?'

'I just can't, that's all,' he said.

'Now, sir, eh ... eh ... '

He silenced me with a wave of his right hand. 'No, I'm sorry, Mugo,' he continued. He did not even refer to me as Mr Gatheru. He did not tell me the reasons and as he was talking to me he started walking around the office as if he was bored by my presence.

'What can Mugo do now?' I asked myself. I walked out of his office. He did not say anything to me as I was closing the door.

Highly mortified, frustrated, and dejected, I went directly to Mr Mathu's office and told him of my experience with Canute, and Mathu got in touch with the Chief Native Commissioner. Canute sent a letter to Mathu informing him that he 'could not issue a certificate or good conduct in respect of R. Mugo Gatheru ... ' Mr Mathu contacted the Chief Native Commissioner again and the Chief Native Commissioner advised him to desist. I became very much disturbed and frustrated and stayed awake all night long.

In the night I talked to myself like a madman:

'Are the rest of the -isms like this one?' I asked myself. 'If so, I can now appreciate the bitter experiences of those who are suffering from these -isms. Woe is me!'

I was now learning the hard and personal way. I heard the voices of two Mugos. The first voice asked:

'Why do you seem to hate Canutism and yet there are certain things in it which you seem to uphold?'

'I do admire some things in Canutism, but I hate that Canutism which prevents me from being like Canute.'

'Mugo, are you not African?' the first voice asked.

'I am; why?'

'Are you not contradicting yourself?'

'Well, under the African Canutism, I assume that the wise men will counsel that two wrongs never make a right,' the second voice answered.

'Very well, you are a real Christian.'

'No, I don't think that one has to be a Christian to understand that!' the second voice retorted.

'What!' the first voice exclaimed.

'I'm not egocentric, but is it not only too human to understand that two wrongs never make a right?'

'Yes, I know what you mean, but ... but what can you do now?' the first voice asked.

'Never mind. Remember the Kikuyu proverb, "Muheria ngia ndagiragia gukie"—no one can stop the working of Nature,' the second voice concluded.

After much thinking, I decided I should not put all my eggs in one basket. I wrote to one school in India for admission, and to another one in South Africa. They both admitted me. My idea was to get out of Kenya and try to obtain a U.S. visa without anybody's interference. I thought that my best bet would be South Africa but I had to obtain a South African visa in order to go there.

I wrote in vain to the South African High Commissioner in Nairobi for a South African visa. I again went to Mr Mathu, but there was not much he could do for me now. I was on my own.

I wrote to the Governor of Kenya through the Chief Secretary, with copies to the American Consul, Mr Mathu, Roosevelt University, Canute, and the Chief Native Commissioner. The Governor did not bother to reply to my letter. I sent him a second letter. No reply.

Later on, I thought I should take the matter right up to the Colonial office and so I wrote a letter to the Secretary of State for the Colonies, with copies to the Governor of Kenya, Mr Mathu, Canute, the American Consul, Roosevelt University, and the Associated Negro Press. At this time I thought that my best bet was to go to India. But would Canute interfere again?

There were also two or three more Kenya students who had been offered scholarships in the United States and were refused recommendation for visas. As a protest to these arbitrary refusals, several letters appeared in the *East African Standard*, the most popular and influential newspaper in Kenya and East Africa. The letters on behalf of the students were answered by an editorial of January 26th 1949, which read, in part, as follows:

> There is plenty of evidence to show that African undergraduates have fallen victims to influences which operate neither for their benefit as individuals nor for the ultimate advantage of the countries from which they come—the British Government and the Governments of the East African territories have a clear and indivisible responsibility not only to protect the individual African—but what is more important, to protect the public of all races from the exploitation of this human material.
>
> It matters much less whether a few Africans have to be deprived for some time of the opportunity these scholarships seem to them to present, than that some should be turned into agents of forces abroad today with the express purposes of destroying democracy in general and the British Commonwealth and Empire in particular, and then return to spread evil doctrines and unrest among ignorant elements in the population.

This editorial appeared as if it were a government reply to me and other students who had been denied a chance to avail themselves of the scholarships given by American colleges and universities.

X

Brown Man's World

The true realist is the man who sees things both as they are and as they can be. In every situation there is the possibility of improvement, in every life the hidden capacity for something beter. True realism involves a dual vision, both sight and insight. To see only half the situation, either the actual or the possible, is to be not a realist but in blinkers. Of the two visions, the latter is the rarer, and the more important. But to be whole, and to be effective, we need both...

LESTER B. PEARSON
(Prime Minister of Canada 1963) discussing
'Democracy in World Politics', 1956.

SINCE all my plans to go to the United States or to South Africa seemed doomed to failure, I started making arrangements with St Joseph's School in Allahabad, India. It seemed logical to go there and study while waiting for some change in the situation, and if I was not successful in my attempts to go to the United States from India, I could continue my higher education in India.

I continued appealing for money from various individuals and organizations. The Africans in Nairobi contributed generously to my educational fund. I found that the less educated Africans were much more willing to contribute than the more educated, and yet the less educated were earning so much less than the educated! I also began to penetrate the Brown Man's World.

One Friday evening I went to appeal to a wealthy Arab who

was operating a successful restaurant business in Nairobi. He was a bald, heavy-set man, well dressed, and he talked like a professor of ancient history. On my arrival in his beautifully decorated restaurant he said:

'Hullo, young man, what can I do for you?'

'Quite a lot please,' I answered.

He pulled up two chairs and invited me to a cup of coffee. We sat in the corner of the tea room. He appeared most kind and receptive. This was the first time I had seen an Arab interested in an African, though I had heard it said that they were generous and friendly to the Africans who believed in Islam.

'Continue,' he said.

'My name is R. Mugo Gatheru of Fort Hall District, and I work for the Kenya African Union as an assistant of the *African Voice*, its official organ. Now, an American college in Chicago has offered me a scholarship to study higher education in the United States. All arrangements were completed, but I could not secure a so-called "certificate of political good conduct" from the authorities concerned. Hence, I could not apply for the U.S. visa or for South Africa. Now, I am planning to go to India. Would you, therefore, be interested in contributing whatever you may so wish towards my further education?'

'Well, young man, I can understand your problem,' he said. 'May I see your letter of admission from the college in America and also from India? You see, there have been some people coming to appeal to us for financial aid under false pretences, and I must be very careful about all this.'

I pulled out the two letters of admission, and handed them over to him. He read them very attentively, handed them back and said:

'I'm in complete agreement with your desire for higher education. Usually, I do not contribute my money in this way. I like to help people through organizations. However, since your case is very urgent I shall give you one hundred shillings now, and refer the matter to the Kenya African Union later on.' He pulled out his wallet and handed me a note. He also asked the waiter to bring us two more cups of coffee.

'Thank you very much,' I said.

'Don't mention it,' he replied. The waiter brought us two

cups of coffee. As the Arab gentleman was stirring his coffee, he continued:

'You could have applied to go to Baghdad University. It's a very fine institution. I believe that the entire history of the east coast of Africa dating from about 2673 or 2661 B.C. is stored in the University of Baghdad and Al Azhar University in Egypt. Have you ever thought of that?' he asked.

'Yes I have,' I answered quickly, 'but I think that I would have to be a post-graduate student to benefit by those universities. I must complete my undergraduate studies first.'

'That's a good idea,' he said. 'You Africans need business men, educationists, and politicians, and you must produce these people very fast. The tempo of the present world's situation is moving very fast indeed.'

'That's painfully true,' I replied.

He wished me good luck in my studies, and asked me to remember him when I got to India.

As I have said previously, this was the first time that I had actually seen an Arab being interested in African affairs. A political novice, I was grateful for his disinterested kindness. Like the Indians, whom I shall describe later in this chapter, the Arabs contribute to the existence of what is known as a 'Plural Society' in Kenya. Their importance in Kenya politics is, therefore, worth noting.

It is reported that the actual colonization in East Africa began with the Arabs from Oman in the eighth century A.D. Travelling Arab dhows plied their trade up and down the east coast of Africa for centuries before the coming of the white man. The Arab's chief centres have been Mombasa, and especially Zanzibar. Zanzibar had a bad reputation when its slave market was one of the largest in the world, and so the great part that its Arab and local inhabitants—the Swahilis—played in the opening up of East-Central Africa was overlooked or unknown. The slave trade, although important, was only one of the many activities of the merchants who made Zanzibar their head-quarters, and leaders of trading caravans thought little of going half-way across the continent at a time when the white man's map of East and Central Africa was almost blank.

Because of this daring spirit, the language of Zanzibar (Swahili) became the trading language of an enormous area.

Swahili is now widely spoken in Kenya, Tanganyika, Uganda, and to a certain extent in the Congo and the now independent territories of Ruanda and Burundi.

The Swahili people came into being as a result of racial admixture amongst the Arabs and the East African local inhabitants. After Kenya was declared a Crown Colony of Great Britain, the Arabs, like the Indians, were allowed to move into the interior and carry on their businesses as they wished. The Arabs have not been able to match the Indians commercially. Nevertheless, their effect on the East African people through their religion is of great importance. A considerable number of East Africans have been converted to Islam.

My quest for a higher education brought me into contact with people of many different nationalities who made me realize that politics of a so-called 'Plural Society' like Kenya were very complicated. But I remained firmly hopeful and convinced that Kenya is to remain an *African* country.

Karanja, my family, and all my friends who had given me encouragement or money were now aware of my plight. They were very sorry and hurt, but sympathetic. They agreed that I could use the money they had collected to go to India to attend a school where some of my friends had already entered. So on March 22nd 1949, I left Nairobi for Mombasa by train, bound for India.

When I arrived in Mombasa I felt that it was very different from Nairobi—not so clean, more Asians and Arabs and far fewer Europeans. People from up-country were referred to as 'bara' people, that is they were thought of as 'unsophisticated'. Just two years before I arrived, there had been a big dock strike in Mombasa led by a Kikuyu named Chege Kibachia. A *bara* man had come to the coast and organized the workers, thus demonstrating that tribalism could be overcome. When I arrived Chege was not there, however. He had been rusticated to the Northern Frontier District in detention, but people were still talking about him. Mombasa was a kind of meeting point and melting pot of Arabia, India, and Africa, and this was reflected in the way the people looked and dressed. For many centuries there had been trade with Asia across the Indian Ocean. The tarbush, Arabic gowns and mosques were everywhere. I stayed with a Kikuyu family who had been in

Mombasa for a long time. Having no money, I could not buy anything, but simply walked around and looked at the city. Life, except for the business world, was generally slower than in Nairobi. I prepared myself for the plunge into the Brown Man's World.

The S.S. *Kampala* left Mombasa for India on March 25th, and I was on it. I waved goodbye to a girl friend who had come to see me off and, when she began to cry, I did too. I was leaving Africa for the first time. I did not know where this journey would end. The boat pitched like a rock-and-roll dancer and it was very cold at night. I did not have enough blankets or sheets, and the facilities offered to the tourist class were not too good. However, I managed to get along. Most of the passengers were Indians and Pakistanis. They were very friendly. One was a school teacher in Nairobi returning to India to see his parents. He kindly offered me some blankets and sheets.

On April 1st we reached Karachi. Eventually, I arrived via Bombay and the Great Indian Peninsula Railway, at Allahabad on April 6th.

I went right away to St Joseph's where the school principal was waiting for me. On April 7th I began my schooling. A friend from Kenya was very happy to see me and we remained at school until May 14th, when the school was closed for the summer vacation.

Fortunately for us, the Indian High Commissioner in Nairobi, the son of Raja Saheb of Audh in Satara District of Bombay Presidency, had made arrangements for four Kenya students to stay with his family for the summer holiday. My friend and I were included in this invitation. The other two Kenya students were from Allahabad University and from Benares Hindu University.

On May 15th we left Allahabad for Poona via Kalyan by train. The train was so overcrowded that by the time we got to Kalyan, a long distance indeed from Allahabad, we were feeling dizzy and sick. We changed trains at Kalyan, from Bombay to Poona. There were thousands of people on that station, and our changing from one train to the other was like playing American football. It was rough, and in the process I lost my passport. Another member of the group lost one of his suitcases. (I wrote to the British High Commissioner in Bombay immediately

about my passport. He issued another one to me at once.)
The Poona train stopped at Rahimatpur where we were met by
two sons of the Raja Saheb with their new car. On our arrival at
the Raja's home we were kindly received and made comfortable. Everybody was curious about our looks, but in a very
friendly manner. In fact, some people were observing us so
closely and with such utter amazement as if we were grotesque!

We enjoyed our stay in Audh state greatly, for the Commissioner's family treated us very well. It was a very wealthy
family, and we also had an opportunity of learning something
about Indian rural life and customs, and of their attitudes
towards Africans.

The Raja had a large library, a museum, and also a temple
for the entire community in the surrounding area. The people
in this community were very much devoted to their religion,
so much so that one could see a large procession of people going
to the temple every evening. We were also invited to go to the
temple. We did not understand what was going on, hence we
did not attend it more than once. We spent most of our time in
the library and also in roaming about in the fields and on the
farms.

I had seen Indians in Nairobi, of course, and most of them
there were in business and professions, or worked as clerks and
artisans. Few were farming. Now I had a chance to see the land
from which our brown neighbours in Kenya came and the
types of farms their ancestors had. There was a sharp contrast
between traditional agriculture in Kenya and in India. My
people mainly used the hoe, but the Indians used a small
plough pulled by bullocks. We were very much interested
in the kinds of houses they lived in. Most of them were mud,
stone, and brick houses, roofed with corrugated iron sheets.
There was a great contrast between their poverty and the
wealth of our hosts. We were not able to converse with them
freely, but they were curious about us and tried to attract our
attention by shouting at us and they often stared at us.

During the meal times there were a series of customs to be
observed. We were to take our shoes off before we entered the
dining place. We were then to sit down, crossing our legs.
Facing us on the opposite side were our hosts who were also
sitting with their legs crossed. Our hosts were served first, and

ourselves immediately afterwards. We were served bountifully with an abundance of fruit (mainly mangoes and oranges), rice, raw sliced onions, ghee, and butter milk. The food was highly spiced and very hot. It was sometimes very difficult to stop the servants from heaping our plates with extra food. We drank a lot of water at meal times because the food left our throats astringent and dry. Our hosts laughed at us when we cried for more water. It was a lot of fun!

Coming from a 'meat-eating world' to one of vegetarians, our appetites soon began yearning for meat. Religious beliefs prevented our hosts from extending their hospitality to the point of cooking us some meat. What could we do? One of the four boys and I decided to trap wild pheasants in the bush. The village was isolated and there was no town where we could buy meat. At the same time, we did not want to embarrass our hosts. Indirectly, my daring friend and I discovered a near-by Moslem who was raising some chickens. We debated whether to tell the others so that we could all go and try to buy a chicken from him. The problem was to find a place to cook it even if we were able to buy it. We both decided against telling our other two friends. They were nice fellows but they were very conservative, and they used to frown on our ideas as fantastic and sometimes irritating. They wanted us to conform to the pattern.

We Chewed a Fowl in the Bush

Finally, with some difficulty, we persuaded the Moslem farmer to let us buy a chicken, but we couldn't persuade him to cook it for us, since we were staying with a Brahman family. He did agree, however, to slaughter the chicken and to pluck the feathers. We took the fowl with us, wrapped in newspapers, into the bush and built a fire on which we roasted it.

We ate the whole chicken and then buried the bones! We walked into the village observing farms and flowers and pretending that we had done nothing at all. Our colleagues never did find out. We did not eat much food that evening during dinner time, and everybody kept on asking:

'What's wrong with Mugo and his friend?'

'Are they sick? They are very quiet today.'

'Oh no! No! We are all right,' we protested.

'We have been fascinated by the farms and beautiful flowers,' we added, and then started changing the talk immediately.

On July 10th, after a most enjoyable holiday, we left for Allahabad, to resume our schooling on July 14th.

St Joseph's was a Catholic school for boys run by Irish Jesuits. There were only six Africans, most of the students being Anglo-Indians. The students came from many different social levels and the school had a high reputation for preparing students for college. We lived in the same dormitory with the students but we did not, however, make close friends with them, although in general the students were friendly.

Like schoolboys everywhere they were not particularly interested in the customs and politics of other countries. We talked about our school subjects and sports. Of course, we occasionally discussed girls. There was a girls' school near by and inevitably we imagined occasionally what went on over there. We all took part in sports. Perhaps it was our vanity misleading us but we felt that the Anglo-Indian girls gave us an extra loud cheer when we played well. The teachers were very kind and took an interest in seeing that we did good work. The humid climate was hard on us, however, and we often had stomach upsets. Besides, my mind was not really on India. India was a means to an end. My sights were set upon America.

Despite the fact that we were very well treated by the Indians, there were several things which we encountered in the course of our social intercourse which were a bit puzzling to us. Whenever we were taken to be shown how the Indians had progressed in education, agriculture, and other technical developments, our special guide would then turn around after he had shown us everything and ask proudly: 'Do you have the same thing in your country?' We found this and other questions very embarrassing. I observed, too, that the Indians were not easily receptive to criticisms. They were very sensitive and always wanted to dominate whenever we had a discussion. Their conversation with us seemed to centre around politics and praise of their leaders. Not that there was anything really wrong with these discussions, but they were sometimes boring. Perhaps we Africans are much the same. Like other emerging nations, Africa tends to be dominated by politics.

Our physical characteristics, too, caused tremendous curiosity among the Indians, so much that we almost suspected them of being a pathologically colour-conscious people. Frequently, they shouted 'Madras! Madras!' or 'Afriga! Afriga!' whenever they saw us passing by or shopping. They were sometimes so very excited that one evening we decided to discuss the matter with an editor of a local newspaper in Allahabad called *Amristar Bazaar Patrikar*, to see whether or not he could register our protest. The editor suggested that we submit our complaint in the form of an article. However, after much thinking, we decided to drop it.

On the other hand, on the rare occasions when we did meet groups of ordinary Indians and could sit down in a friendly atmosphere with them, there was no real unpleasantness. For example, upon one occasion, some villagers near Allahabad who had heard that there were Africans at St Joseph's, came to the school to see us, and they immediately invited us to the village as their guests. We accepted and when we arrived we were taken into a stone house with a corrugated iron roof. We had to leave our shoes at the door and went in and sat on mats. The food, plenty of it, was in bowls—mangoes, curried rice, and chappaties. The women were in their best saris and some of them were very pretty. The Indians sat on one side of the room and we on the other. The women were very shy but were curious about us. They made their menfolk ask us questions—'How do you like Indian food?' 'Do you have children?' They wanted to know how we kept our teeth so white, and one of them actually wanted to give one of us some rupees to be allowed to feel African hair. We took it as a joke and let them come and feel it as much as they wanted to—without charging. Most of the women were very light brown and both our skin and hair seemed new and strange to them.

The men were interested in how Africans and Indians get along in Kenya, what Africans think about Gandhi, and whether we were free from the British rule. When we said that the British were still there they wanted to know did we have people like Gandhi to lead us? They were also very curious about our religion and seemed surprised when some of us said we were Christians. They felt that this was very strange. Did we not have our own religion? They wondered why we were Christians. I felt that we were not only a little bit weak in our defence as to why we were Christians, but also confused. When we had finished our meal they brought out some bicycles built for three and rode us home in tandem. They asked us to return some day—next time in our national costume. We enjoyed this evening with an Indian family very much.

A few months after our return to Allahabad, many Kenya students started coming to India. Most of them were sent by their parents. Others had grants-in-aid offered to them by various interested Indian business men in Kenya. The influx had begun as early as 1947, when the Indian Interim Government, under the leadership of Nehru, had offered five annual scholarships to the East African territories. This offer, a gesture of friendship towards the East Africans by the Indian Government, was gladly accepted.

There were, however, some people in East Africa and Kenya in particular who had complained, before the announcement of these scholarships, that the Indians had also participated in the commercial exploitation of the Africans in Kenya, and that they had contributed nothing to African progress.

To understand the African misgivings about the Indians in Kenya, we should not forget that the Indians' presence there goes back to the time of the Kenya-Uganda Railway. Over 20,000 Indian 'coolies', as they were called, were brought in to build it. On its completion, most of them decided to stay in Kenya permanently. They have been generally disliked by the Kenya settlers, mainly because their frugal manner of living and characteristic shrewdness make them keen competitors.

Africans have accused the Indians of concentrating on commerce, and thereby impeding African commercial progress. The Africans, however, couldn't have competed with the Indians because they did not have enough capital.

The Indians have argued that they did not have any political control in Kenya, and that they themselves, like the Africans, were also victims of colonial administration in Kenya and in India.

When the Indian Government offered scholarships to the East African territories, most Africans assumed India realized that it was a good diplomatic move. Undoubtedly, the attainment of Indian independence opened another channel for the Kenya Africans to further their higher studies, at least to those very few who could afford to pay for themselves and could not easily get into a college since there was only one college, Makerere, in East Africa for about 10,000,000 Africans.

Coming from a country like Kenya, in which colonialism was very 'raw', to a newly independent country like India was, to say the least, a tremendous experience to me emotionally and psychologically. There, for the first time in my life, I felt a free man—free from passes or being pushed here and there as if I was an undesirable animal. Yet, I found that many Indians were not really free. While I continually appreciated the Indians' hospitality and good will towards the Africans, and was conscious of the fact that the Indians are classified as among the coloured peoples, I could not help being worried and disturbed by the way in which many Indians were, and still are, treating the 52,000,000 so-called 'Untouchables', despite the policy and legislation of the Government. This struck me as a horrible national stigma despite its religious justification.

In Allahabad I met one Untouchable who specialized in reading peoples' hands, palmistry, and in telling them their fortunes. I wondered how he did this since he was not supposed to touch other people except Untouchables. However, I took his word. He approached me in a very courteous manner and started speaking to me as if he had kissed the Blarney Stone. He said:

'Sahib, good morning.'

'Good morning,' I replied.

His English was halting. 'Where have you come from?' he asked.

'Kenya, East Africa,' I replied.

'Ah, ha! I thought so,' he said. 'Now, Sahib, show me your hand, if you please, and I shall tell you some good news,' he went on.

'Good news?' I asked.

'Yes, very good news,' he answered.

'All right.' I stretched my right hand towards him as I was holding a history text-book in my left. He held my hand on his left hand and started observing lines in my palm as if he was reading a contoured map.

'Ha! Sahib, you are lucky!' he exclaimed.

'Lucky?'

'Yes, Sahib, you'll have a long life.'

'What else?'

'You are a very intelligent man, and you are also interested in political things,' he said. I felt flattered even though I did not trust the 'science' of palmistry.

'What else?' I asked him.

'Sahib, there is a nice beautiful girl waiting for you some-where,' he said.

Afterwards, he asked me for money. I gave him a rupee. He was very, very happy. He tried to persuade me to offer him some more money. I was dead broke myself! He started holding his stomach with his right hand and kneeling down as if he had stomach-ache, saying: 'Sahiiiib, Poverty! Poverty!' His gestures became more and more persuasive. I started walking away from him, but he wouldn't let me, saying sadly:

'I wish that the British did not have to leave India. There were many jobs for us.'

'No, you are absolutely wrong!' I said.

'No! No! No!' he protested. He was under the impression that if he said this, I would perhaps give him some more money. I made him reverse that statement. When he did, I offered him another rupee! He went away thanking me and as happy as the cat that swallowed the canary.

It was only too painful to see such people roaming in public places begging and hungry while great sums of the money were in the hands of the wealthy rajas and banias and while Ortho-dox Hinduism was hampering the Government in its efforts to institute social and economic reconstruction of the Untouchables.

My conscience bothered me a lot after this experience. For example, I did not understand why in the world I had to accept the honour of his calling me 'Sahib'. This 'Sahib' reminded me of a Swahili word 'Bwana'. The Europeans in Kenya had attached tremendous social and psychological connotation to the word 'Bwana', and they used to feel great self-gratification whenever they were referred to as 'Bwanas' by the Africans. In fact, a European would have found it very, very difficult, and perhaps lowering of his dignity, to refer to an African as 'Bwana'. We were 'natives' without even a capital 'N'. We were not even *Africans*. We were 'natives'. It took an African member of the

Kenya Legislative Council to have the Africans referred to as the 'Africans'! And here was Mugo accepting this title—'Sahib'. It was a very disturbing feeling.

The atmosphere of an independent India created a tremendous impression on me. Its effects were also evident everywhere. Roads which were known before independence as 'Clive Road' and 'Viceroy Road' were now known as 'Gandhi Road' and 'Patel Road'. Streets known as 'Cunningham Road' and 'Minto Street' were now known as 'Mukherjee Road' and 'Naidu Street'. Naturally, all this reminded me of our road and street names back in Kenya.

As regards social, economic, educational, and political reforms, I should say that the Government was pre-occupied with political reconstruction much more than anything else. It was a remarkable thing that the Indians were seriously determined to maintain a parliamentary democracy on Westminster lines at all costs. But, the problems of internal reorganization, languages, population, Kashmir, Untouchables, were very acute indeed. The Central Government with the aid of its capable and well-trained civil service seemed to be in firm control.

While in Kenya I had heard it said by the settlers, in their attempt to discourage the Africans, that 'the Indian politicians with their demagogic cry of Jai Hind, should be made to understand that they cannot hold an independent India for a month'. How wrong and irresponsible was this assertion! If anything, the Government was trying to be only too democratic in its parliamentary approach. Independent India inspired me greatly.

Little Dirty Bed in the City

During the Christmas holiday in 1949, four of us decided to remain in Allahabad. An Anglo-Indian family accommodated us at a reasonable fee.

Our hosts were very kind. A retired school teacher and his Irish wife, their son was attending Ewing's Christian College in Allahabad. They were widely read people.

Like other young men anywhere else in the world, we

were constantly curious about the social side of life. In India, there seemed to be a barrier between the young men and the young women. It was even worse for us, since we were foreigners.

One day, on a very humid evening, a close friend of mine, whom I shall refer to as 'K', decided that we should try to break some of these rigid customs, in an attempt to find out about Indian social life. But how? It was very difficult but we decided that we had not come all the way to India for an education only to return to Kenya without understanding the social side of it.

After various laborious attempts, we failed. Finally, an idea hit us:

'Supposing we try to understand life in the city down town?' we asked ourselves.

'Who can we ask for directions? If this is known around here, where we are so conspicuous, we shall be laughed at.'

A few miles away there was a restaurant. We used to go there sometimes for tea or coffee. There was a friendly young man on the counter who asked many questions about our country. Gradually, we started joking with him.

One morning as we were having some coffee, he came to our table and asked:

'How is the world treating you?'

'Fine,' we replied.

'How do you like the Indian women over here?'

'Women?' we asked, apparently without interest.

'Yes, women,' he repeated. 'I hope I don't hurt you by my questions,' he added apologetically.

'Well, we don't get hurt so easily. The women look all right to us. Some of them look very pretty and well dressed,' we answered.

He laughed. 'They are very difficult over here,' he added.

'What do you do?' we asked slyly.

'Anything,' he answered.

'Such as?'

'Anybody can go to the city. The rickshaw men know all about this city.'

'What about dancing places over here?' we asked.

'There are very few dance places in Allahabad. It's not like

133

Calcutta or Bombay,' he said. 'There's only one social hall for the Eurasians and the Indian Christians in the city.'

'Where is it?' we asked.

'Along the western side of the Mukherjee Road,' he replied.

Some customers came in and the young man returned to his work. We gained three things from him: social hall for dances, the rickshaw men, and—the 'city'.

On Christmas Eve, as our hosts also mentioned, there was a big dance in the social hall, to which we went. It was free. There were many Eurasians, of all ages. Everyone started looking at us curiously. We sat down by one of the tables and asked for some soda.

We decided to join the dancing crowd. The music was very good. I think they were playing 'Tales from the Vienna Woods'. It was lovely. There were unattached girls sitting near our table and we asked them for a dance. We had only danced a few steps when other men came and took our girls away and started dancing with them. There was nothing that we could do, but go back to our table and wait for the next dance.

At the next dance the same thing happened. We felt badly about it. We noticed that the Eurasian men were very jealous of us and we decided to leave for home not wishing to return to a place like that.

On Christmas Day K and I decided to visit this enigmatic place called 'city'. We felt that we should not tell the rest of our plans. My friend K was a very daring man indeed.

In a situation such as this, we thought that we should dress ourselves up to our necks and even wear hats so that no one would recognize us. It was getting towards a quarter to eight in the evening. When we finished dressing (the rest had gone to a movie), we were walking towards the road which led to the city centre when we saw a rickshaw man coming. We asked him to take us down town. He did not understand English, but he had terrific insight! None of us could understand Hindi. However, we happened to know one name in Hindi which helped the rickshaw man (we referred to him as our man) to guess what we were after. That name belonged to the members of the fair sex in general.

Both K and I had long coats. I carried a small flash light in my pocket. Our man drove us off, and as we approached the centre of the city he turned left into a very narrow street. In a few moments we were passing large buildings with long windows. Lights were dim. We heard some music coming through the windows. We also heard people playing some instruments which we thought were guitars.

As we moved along, we saw girls with long hair and fantastic dresses looking through the windows on both sides of the street. Some were leaning against the windows. There was occasional laughter. We became a little bit scared.

Our man moved us along slowly, waving his right hand repeatedly to both sides of the street and saying something in Hindi. He was laughing and we thought that he was probably telling us 'look at all these'. The long blocks of buildings appeared endless. We went across another wider street than the one we were in before. We heard some whistling coming through the windows. There were many people, mainly men, walking to and fro. They seemed to be walking aimlessly. Most of them were Indians.

Momentarily, the crowd of people started lining up in the street watching us very curiously as if we were being driven in a carriage during a coronation day. That was not what we wanted. Nevertheless, we cast away our fear. We moved on. Music was still in the air. We also started smelling something burning like scented powder. We were now restless since we didn't know the direction or the destination of our adventure. But, our man seemed to know what he was doing.

Suddenly he stopped the rickshaw in front of a building. Immediately a lot of people gathered around us. They started yelling: 'Afriga! Afriga! Afriga!' My friend K whispered to me:

'The whole town will now know that we came here.'

'Should we ask our man to take us home?' I asked K.

'No, let's see what's going on over here first. After all, this is also a part of our education,' K replied.

'O.K.' I said.

At the entrance of the building, which had four storeys, there was an old woman squatting with a small stove burning what looked like charcoal. Actually, it was dried cow's dung.

To our astonishment, our man directed us to this old woman. As we approached her, he talked to her in Hindi. She couldn't understand English, but we presumed that she understood the real purpose of our presence there.

As it turned out, she was the one who could let us in the building, and her permission was absolutely necessary. She told our man to tell us that it was all right, but she needed some tips from us at once. Otherwise she couldn't let us in. We asked our man to ask the amount needed. She said one rupee each and that was only for her alone. Other bargainings were to take place upstairs with the individuals concerned. We gave two rupees.

All right. We had now secured permission to go to the *mysterious* upstairs. As we were climbing the stairs led by our man, we heard great laughter downstairs. We became fright-fully scared and silent.

On the fourth floor there were a lot of rooms and all the doors were closed. Our man knocked at one of the doors. In a few seconds, the door was opened s-l-o-w-l-y by a young woman whose face was aggressively radiant. When she focused her eyes on us we felt like falling down on our faces! She let us in. Our man led us inside. It appeared now as if we were going to receive our 'bachelor of social experience' degrees!

The room itself was beautifully decorated. It was very large, and had another door which led to other large rooms. Its four walls were decorated with reddish wallpapers on which were pictures or drawings of Indian models. There wasn't a single chair or table. In one corner four girls were sitting down and smiling at each other. They stood up and came to the centre of the room where we were standing with the one who had opened the door. Our man started talking to them in Hindi. They laughed heartily.

They were attractive, with long hair, highly decorated saris, and countless jewels. In a few more seconds, three other girls came in through the inside door. They were also well dressed with heavy make-up. Some could understand a little English. They all formed a circle at the centre of the room. Our man negotiated the fee for us. The bargain was reached at six rupees. We were asked to go to the centre inside the circle and make our choice. There were now eight women in all. I was leading my friend K and it was suggested that I should be the first to make a choice from the eight. We didn't know why this was so, but we didn't question.

K followed me and we felt as if we owned a harem. Strangely enough, my friend K could make his choice only after I had done so. I was unable to make a choice for the first and second round. They looked all the same to me. In the third round, I made my choice. My friend did not like it.

'Don't you see that she has a lot of pimples on her face?' he shouted to me.

'All right, all right. I shall make another choice,' I said.

'That shortish one is much better,' he advised.

'No. I don't like the way she looks,' I said.

'O.K. How about the one in the blue?' he suggested.

'Right,' I said.

My choice was made. It was my friend's turn now. He picked a girl with a transparent sari and the rest of the girls disappeared through the inside door. Our man went to wait for us downstairs. The two girls led us to the inside door through which the others had disappeared. Within, we found two other doors leading to different rooms. K was led to one and I was led to the other. We didn't know how we should meet again and how long it would take us. Anyway, we said good luck to each other.

The room to which I was taken was small, nicely decorated, but dirty. As I looked around, I noticed that there was a small bed which was also very dirty indeed. It looked as if some children had been playing on it. I couldn't understand why that room and its bed were so dirty.

A few moments later the girl touched my hair. She seemed to be fascinated by it. I touched hers too. At that moment she started unfolding her sari and other items. Immediately, my mind flashed back to Nairobi, and reminded me of my work at the Medical Research Laboratory in pathology and biology. I remembered quickly that I had dealt with specimens for Wasserman tests on people suspected of syphilis. I also remembered how we used to do tests for gonorrhoea, etc. As I glanced at the girl my mind flashed to what I saw under the microscope in the laboratory. The little dirty bed made me almost sick. I therefore lost interest in the entire adventure. By this time, the girl of my choice had undone her clothes and was waiting for me. I hadn't made any efforts to unloose my clothes.

I went towards her. She was on the little dirty bed. I took out my small flash-light which I had in my pocket. I asked her whether I could examine her. I did not know how much diagnoses I could have obtained by means of a flash-light, but I was afraid of 'picking up something'!

The girl allowed me to examine her and, evidently, she noticed that I was scared of disease. She howled at me:

'Mister, mister, me no disease, me no disease!' At that time she was holding her legs high up. I was confused and, after weighing the matter carefully, I decided against prosecuting the action. I told her that I couldn't do a thing and that I was having some stomach trouble. She didn't seem to mind about it, clothed herself and led me out through the large room to the staircase. She didn't refund my six rupees. She went back. A moment later I heard my friend K coming down saying:

'Hey you! Why didn't you wait for me?'

I was on the first floor waiting.

'Come on,' I called to him.

He came down hurriedly, and when we looked at each other we almost burst out in loud laughter! We opened the entrance door and went out. Our man was waiting for us outside. We stepped down to the rickshaw. There were a lot of people around. They laughed loudly as we were leaving. We were shy and looked ashamed, but we outwardly manifested an attitude of carefree fellows.

We asked our man to drive us back fast. On the way back we started relating our experiences to each other. When I told K how I used a flash-light he laughed, laughed, and laughed, so that he could speak no more until we arrived home, where we paid our man and went to bed.

In the course of my stay in India I maintained correspondence with my American contacts, Messrs George F. McCray and Julius C. Graham, and Professor St Clair Drake. I was restless because I was constantly anxious to go to the United States for my higher education, and I had been definitely informed by Mr McCray that my scholarship at Roosevelt University could not be transferred to India. I kept on praying to Ngai. I had one thing and one thing only in my mind—that come what may, I would obtain a university degree. I did not think that any power on earth could ever stop me from pursuing this objective.

My friend, Mr Graham of Ohio, reassured me that if I could get enough money for my fare from India to England, he and the members of some Negro churches at Hubbard and Youngstown, Ohio, could raise the fare to the United States. This reassurance gave me more courage. I wrote immediately, telling Karanja and The Beautiful One. They told me that they were certain about raising the fare to England and they eventually sent me £50.

On February 11th 1950, I left India for England on the S.S. *Chitral*. Before my departure I had written to Mr Charles Njonjo, son of Chief Josiah Njonjo of Kikuyu, who was then studying law at Gray's Inn in London, asking him whether he could make some arrangements for me to stay until my fare was sent from the United States.

It was a long voyage from Bombay to Tilbury. There were many Australians, Indian students who were going to England for technical education, and Jews who were emigrating from Burma to Israel. I made several friends among these Jewish emigrants. They were hopeful and confident about their future in Israel. I enjoyed talking international relations with them. One of them who had a very pretty daughter, said to me:

'Mr Gatheru, I think it's a good idea for young people like you to go abroad for higher education, and then return to serve your country.'

'Yes, it's a wonderful thing,' I said.

'How many college graduates are there in Kenya—I mean the Africans?' he asked.

'Six only among more than five million Africans,' I replied.

'Six!' He stared at me in amazement.

'Yes, six only,' I replied.

'I should think that you will be a very important man when you return to your country.'

'Not necessarily so important, but I shall do my best in my small way,' I said.

'I have very high regard for people like you with that sort of spirit,' he said.

I thanked him.

'There could have been no Israel if there were no men and women with a strong determination, conviction, and spirit,' he went on.

'I agree with you entirely,' I said.

'I wish you well in your endeavours,' he concluded.

'Thank you very much, I shall remember your words,' I said.

This reminded me of what an old Kikuyu wise man had told me in Nairobi just before I left for India:

'Mugo, now that you are going to foreign countries, don't you ever forget our troubles over here.'

'I shall not,' I replied.

'All right, find an envelope and put some Kenya soil in it. Save it very carefully in your suitcase as a token of remembrance of your beautiful country, which must be self-governing like India and America, where you are going to further your education.'

'I shall very definitely do that,' I confirmed.

Some time around March 3rd 1950, after a rough Mediterranean voyage, we passed through the Straits of Gibraltar, which the ancients called the Pillars of Hercules, the little bottle-neck between the Mediterranean and the great ocean. It was the gateway to the White Man's World. Behind me was the great melting-pot of the Mediterranean and the great sub-continent of India—Brown Man's World. Now I was heading for White Man's World.

XI

White Man's World

ON March 5th, we arrived at the port of Tilbury, near London. Now, for the first time I was in the White Man's World—the United Kingdom. After customs clearance, we travelled by train from Tilbury to London.

I was so excited at being near the end of my journey and so worried about my future fate that I fear the scenery along the way made no impression on me.

In London I had hoped that Mr Njonjo would be waiting for me, but since he was not at the station I decided to take a taxi to his address. Njonjo was in Scotland but I found a friend of his who was living in the same building. He was an Indian student studying for the LL.M. degree at the University of London. Since he did not have the keys to Njonjo's room, and was not sure when Njonjo would return, he decided to get me a room in one of the students' hostels. He took me to Kensington Square Gardens where I remained until Njonjo's arrival two days later.

Njonjo moved me to Hallam Street, where he got me a better room at one of the hostels provided by the Welfare Section of the Colonial Office to accommodate overseas students. There were many students from the West Indies, Nigeria, the Gold Coast (now Ghana), Uganda, Zanzibar, but none from Kenya or Tanganyika. I made friends among these students. It was largely due to them that my stay in London was so enjoyable. This was the first time I met fellow students from other parts of Africa. I had to come to Britain to make my first Pan-African contacts.

In general, the African and the West Indian students were very angry with the Labour Government, which was in power at that time, because of the Seretse Khama affair, the Central African Federation, and political crisis in the Gold Coast, and they urged that the British people vote the Labour Government from office over these issues.

In England I found myself in a culture which was very different from the Indian culture. The Indian culture appeared to be less dynamic, but sympathetic—while the English was very dynamic and aggressive. It was much more aggressive and demanding than I had experienced in Nairobi when I first encountered urban life.

As regards the British people, I must say that they impressed me very highly, in particular by their courtesy. I found it very difficult to understand them, however. I was amazed at the difference between the British people in Great Britain and in Kenya. In Kenya they were very arrogant, if not snobbish and shortsighted. Their general outlook appeared as if it were circumscribed by their selfishness, which in turn made them appear illiterate, though there were, of course, exceptions here and there. As for the freedom of speech, press and assembly, I thought that Great Britain was the classic example, even though I had not travelled all over the world in order to make a comparison.

I visited Hyde Park where different groups of people gathered to expound their varied political and religious philosophies. I was surprised to see African speakers up on their stands side by side with white men, speaking their minds vigorously and without fear. Speakers there were saying just what they wanted to say and drawing crowds to listen to them.

My six weeks in England were wonderful! I visited the BBC, St James's Park, the British Museum, the Haymarket, and Madame Tussaud's. I asked someone to take me to No. 10 Downing Street to see where the authority comes from. Most of the students were very busy, and had it not been for the kind attention of a blonde Scottish secretary at the hostel I would never have seen London. I was very grateful to her, and even now look back on her friendliness to me as the high point of the trip. She did much to open my eyes to the fair-mindedness and friendliness of liberal British people. I think what impressed me most in my rambling around was that Nehru and Gandhi were among the famous ones at Madame Tussaud's. I spent most of my time reading and walking by myself.

In my history classes over in Kenya I had learnt how Great Britain was able to dominate the world, particularly by her navy, from the time of the Spanish Armada up to 1945. It was really incredible to me that such a tiny country could have done all this. Now that I was there, I started observing for myself the underlying causes that generated the British people's success. I attributed this success, perhaps too hastily, to their stable government, unity of purpose, scientific achievement, diplomacy, and a grim, supreme tenacity.

On March 13th, I obtained a United States visitor's visa, No. 0900/55939/257 or 1-94 No. V-104333 from the American Consul in London. I also received $40 from Mr Graham for pocket money while in London. On April 17th, I received a letter from the Cunard White Star Company Ltd, of London, telling me that my fare from England to the United States had already been paid by Mr Graham, and that I should go to their office to collect the ticket. I was very happy.

On April 22nd, I left London by train for Liverpool to embark for the United States. That evening the M.V. *Britannic* left for Cobh in Ireland where Irish passengers were to embark. I wanted to see Ireland very much. I had heard of 'Erin go Bragh' many times in the past and it made me feel that some day the Kenya Africans, too, may like to say 'Kenya go Bragh'!

Our voyage from Cobh to New York was also very pleasant. There were a lot of beautiful American girls from Boston and California. Some of them were curious about why I was going to America and they asked me many questions about my country. I was a bit ill at ease when talking to them. Partly because I wasn't too sure about the correctness of my English. But I gradually gained self-confidence.

I recalled what I had learnt over in Kenya in my geography and history classes about people like Christopher Columbus who had sailed the Atlantic Ocean to the New World. Now that I was doing the same I felt like a human document. I was being a part of history myself, not just reading about it. I was extremely happy about it.

On April 30th, I arrived at New York. I did not know anybody there. However, Njonjo had given me an address of an American girl whom he met in London, a lady belonging to a well-to-do white family who had become interested in the welfare of Africans when she was visiting London. At the port I found that Mr Graham had sent me $20 through the American Express Company Inc. and Professor Drake had sent me $35 through the Western Union.

So after our passports were examined and we had gone through the customs I decided to take a taxi to the address which Njonjo had given to me. Unfortunately, the girl was not in. I asked the superintendent of the building, a white man, whether he knew when she would come back. He said that he did not have any idea. I insisted that he open her apartment for me so that I could leave my suitcase inside it. He said that he could not do that but if I wanted, I could stay in the lounge until she came. I remained there from 7.47 p.m. to 11 p.m. that night. The girl did not come! The superintendent tried to call various hotels and the Y.M.C.A. for me without success. Finally, he suggested that he take me to the police station and said that the police authorities could get me a place to sleep for the night. We set off for the police station. I did not feel frightened at mention of the police. I just assumed that this was a New York custom. I also trusted the superintendent. On our arrival we were informed that there was no place for me to stay that night. The police suggested two other places and we went to both of them, unsuccessfully.

By this time the superintendent was getting tired. But he was very friendly to me. He paid the taxi driver who was driving us to all these places and bought me two packets of Chesterfield cigarettes. He was a German immigrant who had been there twenty-five years. By this time, having met friendly white people in London and on the boat, I was not surprised at receiving kindness from him.

Since I did not know anybody in New York, I had already decided to leave immediately for Chicago. My chief reason in trying to contact the girl was that she might advance me enough money for my fare to Chicago, since the money Professor Drake had sent to me could not be obtained from the Western Union office until the next day. I had less than $20 and it was running out, pretty fast!

144

Finally, the superintendent and I returned to the building. We found that she had come back. The superintendent introduced me to her. She remembered Njonjo immediately. She and I thanked the superintendent for the trouble which he had taken.

After the girl had asked me about Njonjo, London, and my voyage from Liverpool to New York, and where I was going to attend college, she made some coffee for me. She also got in touch with her boy friend and asked him to come to her place in his car so that they could make arrangements for my accommodation until the following day when I would leave New York for Chicago.

In a few minutes, he arrived and she introduced me to him. He was a very pleasant psychology student at New York University. All of us drove to his apartment where I was accommodated nicely until the following morning.

On Monday, both of them drove me around New York City. I saw many Negroes on the road. When we drove through Harlem I was surprised to see so many. I wanted to stop and go over to one of them and say: 'I am your brother.' I was naive. I felt I'd like to start telling them about their brothers in Kenya. But I did not want to bother my friends to stop. Having seen them, I felt that I was not alone now, that if I got lost I could go to them and could get what I wanted. But it was not till I got to Chicago that I had my first chance to talk to an American Negro. I enjoyed seeing New York City very much.

In the evening, my friends took me to the station and offered to pay my fare to Chicago with a hope that Professor Drake would refund it. I accepted happily and thanked them very much for their kind generosity.

On the following day, I arrived at Chicago, where Professor Drake was waiting. Immediately I said to myself: 'He looks like a Kikuyu from the Fort Hall District in Kenya or like a Chagga from Moshi near Kilimanjaro in Tanganyika.' Both of us were very happy to see each other. I thought that if we were in Black Man's World over in Kenya, perhaps we could have strangled a spotless fat ram to celebrate the occasion! I thanked Ngai.

From the station, Professor Drake took me to a cafeteria for late lunch. He asked about my experiences in Kenya, India, England, and New York. He was very kind to me.

145

After lunch, he took me to a near-by Y.M.C.A. where I was to remain until the following morning when he would get me proper accommodation.

At six o'clock, both Professor St Clair Drake and Mr McCray came to see me. This was my first meeting with Mr McCray, a man who had been corresponding with me for a long time. I had seen his picture, so I knew how he looked. It was like meeting an old friend. He was typically African in colour and features. I found him very interesting and widely read—especially on African and West Indian affairs. After two hours of tremendous discussion, both gentlemen left me.

On the following morning, Professor Drake came to the Y.M.C.A. and I checked out for a small, nice apartment in Maryland Avenue. He helped me to put things in order, after which he took me down town to Roosevelt University. There he introduced me to various professors and students. About forty per cent of the students were Jewish, one-fifth Negro, and many other races were also represented. Everyone was very friendly to me. Some students kept on telling me: 'Mugo, now that you are here, you should study economics and political science.' But, one student from Kansas said: 'No, he should think of studying geology or engineering, they need this kind of training over in Africa at the present time, don't they?' I told them: 'We will see.'

Professor Drake took me around to various departments and finally to his own Sociology Department where he gave me a small section of his office as my study room. He also brought me various books on politics, economics, philosophy, history, English, anthropology, and sociology. To me, everything was strange, exciting, and confusing. Professor Drake helped me to get along very well. He also taught me how to enunciate various words and names in the American way so that I could be understood. He really paid as much attention to my welfare as my aunt, The Beautiful One, and Karanja did in Fort Hall. In a few days I was calling him 'Drake' just as he called me 'Mugo'. Difference in age was no barrier to our friendship.

Unfortunately for me, my scholarship at Roosevelt had been cancelled after the authorities had learnt that I could not avail myself of it due to various difficulties in Kenya. Nevertheless, Drake kept on negotiating with the university officials with the result that I was offered a scholarship for the summer of 1950, only. He also tried to raise enough money from various people in Chicago both for my school tuition and for my maintenance. A noted American educator raised almost $400 for me through Drake. Drake made special efforts to write to various people, churches, and organizations. The Afro-World Fellowship members were very generous, but the organization was broke! There were important people among its membership, however, and later they did raise some money to assist. At the time, the president was a Negro woman lawyer who was the first Negro to represent the United States in the General Assembly of the United Nations.

In the summer of 1950, I took three courses. They were not aimed at a degree but merely to acquaint me with the American system of education. I did not do too well, except in Anthropology. I was very worried about money and whether I would be able to get a scholarship for the rest of my education in the United States. At the same time the American idiom was very strange to me. It was as hard to understand as Cockney.

A student would make a remark like this: 'That "cat" may wash everybody away', meaning that student will beat everybody in the test. To me 'cat' meant an animal that people keep in their houses. I did manage to cope with it eventually. I made several good friends among the professors and students.

In the evening after the classes were over, Drake and I would go to a cafeteria or an hotel to eat. We would start discussing my lessons and, of course, sociology, anthropology, and politics. He 'opened up my mind' about innumerable things that were unknown to me. In particular, he warned me that as a scholar I should refrain from using value judgments carelessly without a critical examination. During that summer, we discussed Nietzsche, Toynbee, Freud, Hegel, Marx, Jesus Christ, Martin Luther, William James, Abraham Lincoln, Nehru, and scores of other people whose names I was finding in my reading.

Instinctively, perhaps, I thought, wrongly, I would feel more at home if I made more friends among the American Negroes than the other Americans. They all behaved alike. I had then to start approaching all of them on the basis of human beings, white and black, and not on the basis of race. In other words, the very fact that the American Negroes looked like my tribesmen did not imply that I could understand them automatically.

As I look back, one of the most difficult things to adjust to and learn was the way of Americans with their women. Socially, I didn't act so naively in Chicago. I made a friend, a Negro student named Browne, who fixed up some dates for me. I learned about a lot of new things in Chicago ranging from the use of deodorants to how Americans kiss. But I learned! I was now initiated into the ways of white men in their own homelands—Great Britain and America.

Social Life in Chicago

Drake was always worried about whether I was really happy in Chicago and not constantly thinking about my educational problems. He urged Browne to keep me busy socially after our studies and he was also keen to teach me some American social conventions which he thought were important so that I could deal with my 'dates' intelligently.

One evening I had a very important date with a pretty American girl. I told Drake about it. He was very happy. I said I might take her to a film and later on to a coffee bar or to my place for a glass of beer. He advised:

'Mugo, take it easy with the American girls if you date them for the first time.'

'What do you mean?' I asked.

'You don't invite them to your room for a drink unless you really know them very well,' he said.

'That does not mean that you cannot take a chance if you so wish,' he added.

'I shall use typology,' I said.

'What?' Drake exclaimed.

'Typology'.

'You mean you will try to size her up first before you make any such suggestion?'

'Exactly,' I replied.

'Fine,' Drake said. 'Incidentally I would also advise very strongly against using these long words until you are very familiar with them—especially the word "typology" which you have just used. Remember also that your breath must smell sweet, and that your armpits are well taken care of.'

148

'I shall use Listerine to wash my mouth beforehand,' I said.

'All right. Here is the money,' he said.

'Twenty dollars!' I exclaimed.

'Yes; why the surprise?' he asked.

'It's too much,' I said.

'Better to have too much than too little,' he said.

'Thank you.'

'How well up are you in your kissing methods, just in case?' Drake asked.

'I think I can manage,' I said.

'Are you sure?'

'Yes, I am.'

'I do not want you to make a mistake because I know that the Kikuyu are not used to kissing, since it is not one of their customs,' Drake said.

'I shall try to do what I used to see Europeans do in Nairobi,' I said.

'When you hug a girl, and you must be sure that it is the proper moment and at the right time, you can then kiss her gently. There are different ways of kissing. For example, what is called the "French way" is different from a friendly kiss,' Drake said.

'What's the difference?' I asked.

'The difference is the way you play with your tongue.'

'Tongue?' I asked.

'Yes. Sometimes you can put your tongue in a girl's mouth or you can let her take yours into her mouth.'

'How do you do that?' I asked.

'Like this.' Drake put a red marking pencil in his mouth by way of demonstration.

'Do you get the idea?' he asked.

'I do.'

'Good luck. Make no mistake,' Drake said.

I went to the girl's home and found her waiting for me. I took her to a film. It was my first date in the United States. When the film was over we went to a coffee bar. The girl asked me many questions about Africa, India, and Great Britain. Finally I suggested to her to go with me to my place so that I could show her some photographs on Kenya and India.

When we arrived home, I showed her my picture book,

which she enjoyed. I offered her some beer. She said that she did not like beer too much, but that I could go ahead and have some. However, she agreed to have two glasses only later on. She looked friendly and I felt at ease talking to her.

I started teasing her and she also teased me back. I felt I wanted to kiss her and then I withdrew lest she thought I was 'fresh'. But, temptations were overpowering me. Finally, I hugged and kissed her, following Drake's demonstration.

During the 'session' I realized that the girl had a removable artificial plate of front teeth. I put her tongue in my mouth and in turn she put mine into hers. As her gums did not have sensation, her teeth fell on my tongue. She kept on pressing me. I felt pain since she was actually biting me without realizing it. She continued, and it was exceedingly painful. I did not want to tell her to stop or that she was biting me, but outwardly made it appear as if I was really enjoying it!

In the end, the kissing was over! I excused myself to go to the lavatory to spit some blood from my tongue. I was uncomfortable throughout the evening, but I did not create any impression that could make her know of my painful tongue. Everything was all right. From that time on, I was always leery about kissing, whether a girl had false teeth or not.

The Americans like kissing very much, and in many cases their way of kissing looks like birds trying to pull each other's beaks!

XII

Becoming an American 'Collegian'

WHILE my friend Browne was giving me my social education, Drake was writing to several colleges about me. He wrote to Tuskegee Institute, Hampton Institute, and the predominantly Negro Bethune-Cookman College in Daytona Beach, Florida. The first two did not promise us anything, but the last one offered me a partial scholarship with the understanding that Drake and the rest of my friends in Chicago would raise enough money to cover other expenses. Drake felt confident that he could do so and we accepted.

Drake and Browne bought me several things I would need and early in September 1950 I left Chicago for Daytona Beach. We didn't have enough money to buy a train ticket so a Negro preacher lent me his 'clergy'—that is his permit to ride on the train at a reduced fare. He said, laughing: 'Just don't talk much but if the conductor calls you "Reverend" act like a preacher.' Drake saw me off. I felt very sad. I didn't want to leave Chicago, but what else could I do? I needed a small school where I could get special attention. The cost of living was too high in Chicago.

It was a long way. I enjoyed seeing the beautiful scenery and the wonders of Yankee technology but I was lonesome on that train. That loneliness made me feel homesick for the first time in my life.

The following morning the train arrived at Daytona Beach. I took a taxi immediately to the college, which was not very far from the station and went to the president's office. He was very happy to see me and said: 'Welcome to Bethune-Cookman.'

He was a forceful man, a Negro about six feet tall, with a dynamic personality. He took me around the campus area, and finally to the office of the registrar. I was assigned to a dormitory called Cookman Hall. The following morning I was enrolled as a full-time student.

Student Life in Bethune-Cookman

I was interested in the social sciences so I associated myself with the Social Sciences Department. I took sociology, political science, biology, English language, and literature and history, under Mr Hacker, otherwise known as Major Hacker. He had been in the American Army in Europe during the Second World War, and was now giving a course in comparative political institutions.

The classes were large, with sometimes almost forty students, but I was able to follow lectures without any language trouble. A Nigerian student and I gained a high reputation among the young ladies because of our hard work; but we were always penniless and could not take any of them out. It was a very embarrassing situation.

I described my plight to Major Hacker casually as I felt free to talk to him on any subject. I said we were like a nation which can conquer another nation but at the same time doesn't have enough troops to hold its conquest. 'Enough troops' in this case meant enough money. Bethune-Cookman did not have as extensive facilities as Roosevelt College, but the location of the college and Daytona Beach were very beautiful. And the education was a sound one.

The professors and students were very co-operative and friendly, in particular a teacher in the History Department, Miss Erma L. Rodriguez. Her brother was also associated with the college and he operated a small department store with a soda fountain near the college. After classes Miss Rodriguez helped him. When she discovered that I was a poverty-stricken student from Kenya, she asked her brother if I could help them to wash dishes part-time. He agreed, and paid me $1.50 (about ten shillings) per hour for two hours a week. I was very impressed by their kind and sympathetic attitude. Sometimes Miss Rodriguez gave me soap, toothpaste, cigarettes, milk, and bread free of charge. I was embarrassed to receive all these gifts, for her generosity was overwhelming!

But, in some ways life at Bethune-Cookman was not too good. I made good marks and good friends, but I was always penniless. There were more women students than men but I was afraid to have a girl friend. In order to be on the safe side, I decided to always go to the library or to my dormitory immediately after dinner. The girls were amazed at my behaviour as they did not understand my motive. Some felt that I was perhaps shy or anti-social.

There were two things that I enjoyed most while at Bethune-Cookman. First, there were frequent trips by car around the town of Daytona with Major Hacker, and from Daytona to Orlando and Tampa. I think that Major Hacker planned these trips in order to help me get rid of my financial worries. From these trips I concluded that Florida was one of the most beautiful states in the United States, though I feel that my country, Kenya, could compete with her. I saw many beautiful lakes like those that one would see in the Southern Kinangop, in the lower part of the Aberdare Range in the Rift Valley Province.

While driving, Major Hacker would tell me about Freudian psychology and its contribution to the field of social science. He would also tell me of his war experiences in the Second World War. I liked to listen. These were very interesting talks, but they reminded me of the horrors of war—more and more.

The second thing I enjoyed was the splendid college choir, under the direction of Mrs Hacker. The choir and the whole student body had to meet in the chapel once a week and also on Sundays. In the chapel, on the side where the choir sat, was an inscription inspiring me each time I read it: 'Enter to learn, depart to serve.' Each time I saw it, I said to myself: 'Surely this inscription must apply to me, too.'

The songs the college choir sang were also inspiring. I particularly liked to listen to the Negro Spirituals. For example, the one that went like this: 'I have shoes, you have shoes, all God's children have shoes; When we get to Heaven, gonna put on our shoes, and walk all over God's Heaven.' I said: 'Gonna walk all over God's Kenya!'

There were two other songs that inspired me greatly: 'Old Man River', and 'I will never, I will never, I will never turn back no more ... ' These particular songs kept on reminding me of my past experiences with certain officials back in Kenya. I said to myself that even though Canutists were fighting my great efforts to obtain an American education, I should not look back any more. I should not burn with hatred against Canutism, which had been perpetuating ignorance, frustration, and hatred. Spinoza said:

> Love tends to beget love...
> to hate is to acknowledge our
> inferiority and fear; we do not hate
> a foe whom we are confident we can
> overcome ...
>
> He who wishes to revenge injuries by
> reciprocal hatred will live in misery;
> but he who endeavours to drive away
> hatred by means of love, fights with
> pleasure and confidence; he resists
> equally one or many men, and scarcely
> needs at all the help of fortune.
> Those whom he conquers yield joyfully.

As my poverty and loneliness overpowered me, I wrote several letters to Drake telling him that I wanted to come back to the north badly. He insisted very strongly that I should spend another year at Bethune-Cookman—after which he would try and see if I could get a scholarship in one of the northern colleges. I refused to agree with him on this point, because I felt that the pressure was too great. For instance, bills for board and lodging were very high and the college authorities kept pushing me harder and harder for payment. They argued that their previous experiences with the foreign students were such that they could no longer be sympathetic. In fact, eight Nigerian students had accumulated bills of more than $17,000 in four years! This was paid later on by the Nigerian Government through the good office of the adviser to Nigerian students in Washington, D.C. There was no such Kenya adviser!

Drake got annoyed about my insistence on leaving Bethune-Cookman. But I quoted the Kikuyu proverb—'Mutiga Njeru akoraga njeru', which means: 'There are as good fish in the sea as ever were caught', but here is my great friend who is trying to remind me of another proverb which says: 'Muhoi ndaga thimaga'—'Don't look a gift horse in the mouth.' I retorted: 'Muikari muti gitina niwe uui kiria thambo iriaga', which literally means: 'He who stays at the foot of a tree knows what ants eat'.

While Drake and I were exchanging correspondence, I wrote to the registrar of Manchester College in Indiana about admission and scholarship. This college had been mentioned to me by a white friend. He had also told me that the registrar was his friend and if I needed to go to Manchester I could use his name for any references.

After formal application, I eventually received a letter of admission from the registrar of Manchester. He indicated, however, that the school could not guarantee a full scholarship, but that there were many job opportunities on the campus and he felt that I could fight my way through. This sounded pretty good to me but Drake continued to be adamant. His idea was that I should work in Chicago for the summer so that I could have enough pocket money to keep me going at Bethune-Cookman and, on his part, he would raise enough money for board and lodging, since the president of Bethune-Cookman had indicated in writing that my tuition scholarship could be extended indefinitely.

After I had weighed the matter carefully, I felt that Manchester College was offering me much more than Bethune-Cookman. Hence I made up my mind to go there at the end of the school year.

To go to Manchester by bus from Daytona Beach I needed $36. I did not have the money, but in my suitcase I had a good, new, blue suit, which a lady well-wisher had bought for me in Chicago for $48. I borrowed $36 from a Sierra Leone student, leaving the suit as security. I thought after I had arrived in Manchester, I could then persuade Drake to raise the money to pay this debt.

I bought my bus ticket to Manchester but did not mention this to anyone at Bethune-Cookman. Miss Rodriguez had gone to Atlanta to attend a teachers' conference. I wished to say goodbye to her, but this was impossible.

On June 3rd 1951, at about midnight, I left Daytona Beach by bus for Indiana. I had only fifty cents in my pocket! But I did not feel worried. I remembered the words of the Apostle Paul: 'The race is neither to the swift nor to the strong, but to him that endureth unto the end.'

In the bus, I was sitting in the very back seat all the time, and it was a long, boring trip. I knew there was segregation and discrimination against Negroes in the South. In many of the towns where the bus stopped, I remained in the bus when other people got out for coffee or ice-cream. I only went out of the bus when I was going to the men's room. I did not even feel hungry. However, I bought a bottle of Coca Cola at Macon, Georgia, another one at Nashville, Tennessee, another one at Louisville, Kentucky, and a cup of coffee at Columbus, Ohio. It took us about two and half days to go from Daytona Beach to Manchester. When I arrived on the campus I was taken directly to the registrar's home by one of the students, and we were gladly received. The registrar introduced me to his wife and three children. He was a very intelligent and nice man. His wife gave me some food and made coffee for us all. We talked at length, and at about 10.30 p.m. I was taken to one of the dormitories. It had been newly built and was very clean. The college itself was an all-white institution, and everyone was very, very kind to me. I was the first African student to have ever entered there.

The following morning, after we had eaten, I was taken to the registrar's office. It was suggested that I register for two summer courses and a part-time job. They asked me how much money I had, and I said ten cents but that I hoped I would get some money before long.

The dean said that the college would give me a loan of $25 for personal expenses until the money came. I registered for two courses, one in the History Department and the other in the English. The dean was a very practical man, suave, witty, sympathetic, with a Ph.D. from Harvard University.

After two days, I wrote a letter to Chicago telling my friends there that I was in Manchester and that I had registered for two courses. Professor Drake sent me money for my fare from Manchester to Chicago so that we could evaluate the whole situation carefully. I told the college authorities of this fact. They were not too happy about it. They said that summer courses required a lot of reading and that I might lag behind if I went to Chicago. They added that I could go if it was absolutely necessary, but that I should return very soon.

Two students gave me a lift to Fort Wayne to catch the bus.

I bought my ticket, but as it turned out, the bus for Chicago was to leave the following morning at 4.30! I bought some papers and settled down to read them at the bus station. In the evening I decided to go to a movie, and afterwards I had some coffee. As I was coming out of the restaurant about 10.45 p.m. and walking back to the bus station, two Negro soldiers approached me and asked if I knew a bar near by where they could buy some beer. I could detect their Southern accents, even though I had not been in the United States a very long time. I directed them to one bar which I had seen near the movie house, but they did not seem to understand me, so I took them personally. As we entered, the barman came directly to us. They asked him if they could have some beer. He said: 'Yes, I can serve you two because you're in uniform, but I can't serve him,' referring to me. This was in the North, in Fort Wayne, Indiana, in June 1951. I did not worry about this; I hadn't even wanted any beer to begin with, my main idea was to show the two gentlemen where the bar was. I left the two G.I.s drinking beer. They did not protest against this incident or say anything about it.

I returned to the bus station, where I stayed until the bus left for Chicago where Drake met me about 11 a.m. We were very happy to see each other. We went immediately to Browne's apartment, and he fixed a delicious dinner for all of us.

When we had finished Browne opened three cans of beer, and we started a discussion on my going back to Manchester. They both seemed to feel that the best thing for me to do was to take a full-time summer job in Chicago and then to see whether it was a good idea to return to Bethune-Cookman. There was also another alternative open to me. Lincoln University in Oxford, Pennsylvania, was thinking of offering me a full scholarship for the fall of 1951, for which I was to teach Swahili in their African studies programme. Professor Drake had started these negotiations that spring when he went to Lincoln to see Ghana's Kwame Nkrumah get his honorary doctorate. After we had weighed all the pros and cons, we decided that I should not return to Manchester College. But my desire to go back to Manchester lingered in my mind for a long time. I am sure that my benefactors there, the registrar and the dean were very hurt and I must here place on record the distress and inconvenience that my youthful confusion must have caused them.

Browne suggested that I could stay with him in his apartment throughout the summer. I was grateful for his offer. The following morning, we went to the Federated Waiters' Union office. The union officer asked me to pay $13 as my union dues. I borrowed this money and refunded it later.

Adventures with Food for the Mind and Stomach

The union got me a job at the Hotel Sherry, near Lake Michigan. I went for an interview and the white head waiter told me to report to him on the following day at 11 a.m. He sounded encouraging. I had to wear a black pair of trousers, white shirt, and bow tie. A red coat would be provided by the hotel.

I returned to Browne's apartment. He was still at work, so I called Drake and informed him of the good news. He told me to come to his home. I went over right away and he lent me the bow tie and the black trousers.

When I returned to Browne's apartment he too was jubilant at my news.

The following day I went to Hotel Sherry and the head waiter gave me the red coat. He then took me to the dining-room and showed me all the things a bus-boy should be familiar with. There was only one other bus-boy besides myself. The head waiter asked me if I had any experience and I said, 'No', but that if I were given a chance I would do my best. He told me not to worry.

When lunch-time came I was assigned to my section. I was not sure that I would be able to remember all the things I had been told, but I kept my morale up. The dining-room started getting busier and busier. The manageress of the hotel came along with her husband. The head waiter pointed her out to me and said: 'Be careful of her, she is the boss of this place.'

I began to be afraid of her. She kept on moving from table to table, and I think she was trying to find out whether every customer was satisfied with the service. The bus-boys took the trays of used dishes. We had a very tiring time, and there was much tension. I made many mistakes, but the head waiter was satisfied with my efforts.

Dinner-time on this first day was worse. Many people were expected and a buffet was being prepared. The manageress asked me to go to the kitchen and bring her a 'Jello'. I did not know what a 'Jello' was, so I asked her. She gave me an infuriated look. Very confused, I hurried to the head waiter and asked him to help me. He took me to the kitchen and told me what it was and where it was kept. I then took it to the manageress at once. The head waiter probably saved my job.

I had the same section as before and there were four waiters working with me. They were supposed to give me an equal share of their tips but somehow this did not seem to work out. Besides taking dirty dishes to the dish-washers in the kitchen, I gave ice water and butter to the diners. Some customers liked to use many ice cubes, and two of them on one occasion asked for more. I put some in the lady's glass first. But when I moved to put them into her husband's glass, two ice cubes fell on his fine grey trousers. I said that I was sorry so excitedly that the customers sympathized with me instead of getting angry. But instantly, the manageress came up wanting to know what the trouble was. She was furious. The head waiter was scared, and so was I. She went over to the head waiter and asked him how much experience I had had as a bus-boy. He replied that I didn't have any, but it was his feeling I could do the job if I were given a chance. She told the head waiter that she could not stand me. The head waiter pleaded on my behalf and she finally agreed that I could stay. He went to the man on whose suit I had dropped the cubes and also apologized. After that I handled ice and butter so carefully that I reminded myself of a surgeon performing a delicate operation on the table!

In two weeks I was almost a first-rate professional bus-boy. For instance, the other bus-boy did not show up one day. We had to call the union office for a replacement. A Sunday wedding reception was on the programme, and I assumed most of the responsibilities. Even the manageress was very pleased and said she hoped I'd stay.

About the middle of August, Drake received a letter from Dr Horace Mann Bond, President of Lincoln University, telling him that the university was offering me a full scholarship for the fall of 1951–52, and for the complete degree course.

'A full scholarship for Mugo?' I asked. Drake once again said: 'Yes.' The whole thing sounded unbelievable to me after I had struggled so much! We celebrated with a party on the 21st, my birthday.

I left Hotel Sherry with friendly congratulations and good wishes from the manageress and head waiter. I now had enough money to buy some clothes, shoes, and a big trunk. I also sent $36 to repay the loan for which I had pledged my suit. My Sierra Leone friend never gave me my suit back. But I didn't really care.

XIII

Becoming a 'Lincoln Man'

WHEN I entered Lincoln University in the fall of 1951, I was happy. I also felt that things were going along fairly well back in Kenya. I received occasional letters from home which indicated that the Kenya African Union was growing in members and in power. As I read copies of *Baraza* and *Sauti Ya Mwafrika* which friends sent to me, I was able to follow the situation. Little did I realize that before another year and a half had passed, Kenya would be in the midst of a bloody civil war, that some of my friends would be in concentration camps, and that I, myself, would be on the verge of being deported back to Kenya. Yet, a year after I entered Lincoln, the American headlines began to flash out the words Mau Mau, and the Kikuyu became the most talked about people in Africa. I found my personal fate bound up with the fate of my country. But before telling the story of my bad luck—of how the shadow of Mau Mau fell on me, I should speak of my good fortune in being a student at Lincoln University.

Lincoln is a small school out in the country about forty miles south-west of Philadelphia, Pennsylvania. It has a very beautiful campus, and a long and distinguished history. In fact, its intellectual genealogy is exceptionally impressive. It was founded in 1854 by Presbyterians who wanted to see some of the Negroes who had run away from slavery given the opportunity to have a college training. It trained people for leadership in the new nation of Liberia which had been started by ex-slaves in Africa. The officials of Lincoln have always had an interest in Africa and many West African leaders have studied there, the most famous of these being Dr Nnamdi Azikiwe of Nigeria and Dr Kwame Nkrumah of Ghana. The Minister of External Affairs in Ghana also studied there, as did a number of members of the Legislature in Nigeria. Lincoln had just started an African studies programme and wanted to attract African students who could assist in teaching if needed. I was to help out with Swahili classes if any.

At the time I went to Lincoln it had a Negro president who was passionately interested in Africa—Dr Horace Mann Bond. He had the reputation of never turning a qualified African student away. He'd find scholarship money somewhere. I should add that Lincoln also had the reputation of being a first-class liberal arts college, with high standards. Many conservative Europeans in Kenya who disliked Lincoln University because it has turned out a number of nationalists, sometimes sneer at Lincoln and call it an 'inferior' institution. They are misinformed. Lincoln is fully accredited and famous for the high proportion of its graduates who have become successful lawyers, doctors, lecturers, and ministers. At the time I went there it was all male, and this, plus isolation from big city life, meant that students studied hard without distractions. I was very happy to know that I was going to be a 'Lincoln man'.

When I left Chicago in September 1951, several of my friends took me to the train. We were all in a jolly mood and promised to write to each other. I had saved some money from my summer's work, and for the first time since I'd been in America I felt some security. But I was so anxious not to waste any money that I ate very little on my long trip. I got a glass of orange juice, however, when we passed through Pittsburgh. When we rolled through the big tobacco farms between Pittsburgh and Philadelphia, around Lancaster, I became homesick for Kenya for the second time because the land reminded me so much of home. I was also extremely fascinated and impressed by the American methods of farming.

The train reached Philadelphia in the afternoon. I had a three-hour stop in Philadelphia before taking the bus for Lincoln, but I did not wander far from the station. Since I was now close to my destination, I decided to spend a little money, so I bought a hamburger, a cup of coffee, magazines and newspapers. But my mind was really on other things. I was thinking of how I was sitting in the city of the Liberty Bell, the city where the Declaration of Independence had been signed that freed America from imperialism. I knew, too, that this town was called 'The City of Brotherly Love'. Had it been daytime, I would have gone out to see this historic city. But it was dark and I was waiting for a bus. So I just tried to imagine what it must have been like on that first Independence Day when people were celebrating with fireworks and picnics and prayers as I had read.

Finally, my bus came. We arrived at the gates of Lincoln at midnight. I dragged my suitcase along and found two students who were still awake. They took me off to the proctor of Lincoln Hall who remembered my name right away since a notice was already posted on a bulletin board announcing that I was available for Swahili classes. He took me to a room which accommodated two students and handed me a copy of the rules and regulations. I selected one of the beds and went to sleep. This was my new home. I was glad to be there.

On my first morning at Lincoln I rushed over, immediately after breakfast, to Dr Bond's office. As I went in, Dr Bond arose and shook my hand with enthusiasm. I knew that I had found another real friend in him. He said that he was glad I had come to Lincoln and he hoped I could now settle down to study without having to spend so much time during the school term in working for a living. Neither of us knew, on that morning, what life really had in store for us, that we should soon be engaged in a heavy battle to keep me there. I thanked him for having granted me the scholarship of $895 a year.

My most vivid memory about this meeting with Dr Bond is that his office was very clean with four large shelves of books, and there was a large portrait of Abraham Lincoln behind his chair inscribed: 'With malice toward none; with charity to all.' I have never forgotten this scene or the inscription.

The registrar, too, received me kindly. He was a white man but by now I had realized that in America, as in Britain and elsewhere, one could expect some white people to have forgotten the colour-bar completely, while others were intensely prejudiced. He sent me on to the man who was to be my academic adviser, and who later became one of my closest friends, Professor Thomas Jones of the History Department. Professor Jones was a devout Quaker, a long-distance runner of Olympic calibre, a Ph.D. from the University of Pennsylvania, and an excellent teacher. He and his wife told me to make their home my home. I did. The fact that they were white and I was black never was of any importance to them or to me. I might add that Lincoln, unlike Bethune-Cookman, had both white and coloured teachers and one or two white students. I was now to have the new experience of attending a school in the American North.

Professor Jones told me that he was glad to see a student from Kenya at Lincoln. They had never had one before. There were students present from Nigeria, the Gold Coast, Sierra Leone, and Liberia. (I very soon wrote back to Kenya and encouraged a close friend of mine to apply.) I selected History and Political Science as my major field and my studies included lectures and classes on modern European history, English literature, introductory sociology, and French. All students had to take Biblical literature, too. I was also placed in a Philosophy class, and enjoyed this very much. I began to get familiar with the ideas of Kant, Spengler, Nietzsche, Hegel, and Spinoza, great men of the past, and those of present-day thinkers like Toynbee, Northrop, Whitehead, Sorokin, Bertrand Russell, Kroeber, Collingwood, and Crane-Brinton. I sometimes reflected on what a different world this was from the world of my childhood as a goatherd in Kenya, or of my youth when the knife bit me during my circumcision. The reading forced me to think about the destiny of myself and my country and mankind. During the second term of the first year my reading became very heavy but I did not mind it. I had a compelling lust for a higher education. This was my chance and I would not miss it. I finished the year with quite good grades in everything except French.

Lincoln closes its dining hall for two weeks during the Christmas vacation, and very few students remain in residence. I had written Drake about what to do during Christmas. He arranged hospitality for me at a Quaker graduate school, Pendle Hill, near Philadelphia, and I made a brief stop there. I then decided to go on to New York to visit an anthropologist friend of his who was teaching at Columbia, so I went to Philadelphia to get a bus. The weather was bitterly cold. The streets were very slippery. It was snowing. I kept falling to my knees in the slippery snow. I was miserable. So I retreated back to Lincoln to wait until the weather was better.

Drake had told me that his mother in Staunton, Virginia, wanted me to go to her home for a few days, so I decided to go there instead of New York. When I telegraphed Drake that I was in Virginia, he wrote as follows:

> ... I've asked my mother to introduce you to the young people thereabouts. I don't know that there are many home from college, but there may be ... You will see from looking at our house that not all Americans have central heating and inside baths and toilets. I hope you don't suffer too much.

He didn't need to write to me in that apologetic fashion. This turned out to be one of the happiest Christmas seasons I've ever had. Mrs Drake treated me like a son and stuffed me with chicken, cake, pie, and all the other nice things that Virginians eat for Christmas, and I was kept well supplied with Christmas spirits. A number of kind people invited me to their homes. I went back to Lincoln well fed and well rested. On this trip I had made many new friends among the American Negroes. This was something I was beginning to like most about America—my new friends, both white and coloured. I could study better in the knowledge that although far from home I had friends—in Florida, in Chicago, at Lincoln, and in Virginia.

As the summer of 1952 approached, I had to make up my mind whether or not to work again at Hotel Sherry in Chicago. I decided to stay on at Lincoln and to work at the Post House near by as a kitchen helper. Lincoln was planning a summer conference on African affairs, and Drake was among the scholars —European, African, and American—who had been invited to lecture. This was a chance to attend some of the sessions and to see Drake and his family again. The head of the Department of Social Welfare and Community Development in Ghana was present, as well as Dr George Edmund Haynes, the American Negro connected with the International Y.M.C.A. who had written a book called *Africa Continent of the Future*.

Drake and I presented one lecture together on Kenya. In preparing for the session, I translated a number of important items from *Baraza* and *Sauti ya Mwafrika* which brought us up to date on what was going on in Kenya. The Kenya European papers were referring to what they felt was a too aggressive attitude on the part of the Kenya African Union, and *Baraza* was warning Kenyatta in its editorials to try to curb the activities of local units of the organization. There were also the usual letters to the editors from Africans complaining about the injustices of too few schools, lack of opportunity for Africans to advance, and of the need for equal pay for equal work. There was much interest in our discussion because some of the American papers and magazines, too, were beginning to report that the Kenya Government was getting disturbed over the activities of young Kenya Africans who were being accused of organizing 'subversive associations'. They were being accused of taking 'oaths' not to inform against a fellow member; neither to assist nor to sell land to any European; and to fight to expel the Europeans from Kenya. On June 12th 1952, Sir Philip Mitchell, who was retiring as Governor, made a speech in which he said:

The Government views with concern the recent threat to law and order occasioned by the activities of proscribed societies. Urgent and continuous attention will be given to the task of maintaining the fullest confidence in the peaceful administration of the colony. Measures to this end must include more extensive policing of the African Land Units (i.e. the Reserves) ...

Just about the time the Lincoln conference began, Michael Blundell, one of the leaders of the settlers had said in the Legislature:

There is among us today a subversive organization which is like a disease spreading through this colony; the leaders of that movement have a target, and that target is the overturning of the Government ... within nine months ...

All that we knew about any of this was what we read in the newspapers, but what we tried to do was to give the conference as much background information on Kenya affairs as we could.

In the evenings Drake and I had many long discussions about sociology, anthropology, and politics. I also took the opportunity to extract from him a detailed explanation of the rules of American football so I could enjoy the game better when the next term began. Lincoln had always been proud of her football teams, and as a Lincoln man I felt I should be intelligent about such matters.

Like Major Hacker, Drake kept telling me that I should not get so intoxicated with study and politics that I never would get any fun out of life. So we used to end up our discussions listening to records—Pat Page, Bing Crosby, Doris Day, Lena Horne, Nat King Cole, Marian Anderson, and Josef and Miranda. I am a record fan to this day.

Before the 1952 autumn term began, I had a chance to see New England and New York. An Economics professor at Iowa State College named Dr Elizabeth Hoyt had visited East Africa on a Fulbright grant. She worked with the Institute for Economic and Social Research at Makerere College in Uganda and visited Kenya. She had been particularly impressed with the energy of the Kikuyu people when she went to Kenya Teachers' College. When she got back to America she tried to get to know some Kenya students studying in America. So I received an invitation to visit her summer home at Round Pond in Maine for a week before school began in 1952.

I went to Maine by bus and found Dr Hoyt waiting for me at her gate. She was a motherly person, her hair almost white. Her home, which had belonged to her father, was built in the old New England style and was surrounded by woods. She took me into supper and after we had finished she began to tell me about her many trips to South America, Europe, Australia, New Zealand, and Africa. When I went up to crawl into bed the blanket looked familiar. It was from Kenya, made in a town called Nakuru. Dr Hoyt had bought it when she was in East Africa. This blanket made me feel very much at home during my stay.

Dr Hoyt and I talked for three days. She told me about her work and writings on economics and anthropology. I began to admire her as an alert and energetic scholar. She asked me to tell her about conditions in Kenya, and about my own aims and aspirations.

On the fourth day at Round Pond, another lady from Iowa came to visit Dr Hoyt—she was an agriculturalist and displayed as great an interest in Kenya as I did in agriculture. We explored Round Pond thoroughly while Dr Hoyt was completing the typing of a manuscript. Then we all drove to Portland Maine where I caught a bus for New York, while the ladies went on to Canada. I rode down to Boston where I had a few hours and here, as in Philadelphia, my mind went back to the days of the American struggle for independence. The Boston Tea Party was uppermost in my mind.

When I arrived in New York, I decided to walk around to see Times Square, New York University, Columbia University, the Empire State Building, and the Museum of Natural History, and later to take a bus to Lincoln University.

The Empire State Building reminded me of the name of an American magazine I had read when I was in Nairobi, in 1946. It was a copy of *Scientific American*. I thought very deeply of the amount of engineering ingenuity that the Americans had put into that building and New York City in general, and arrived at the conclusion that they really were 'scientific Americans', as the title of the magazine had implied. As I expressed my utter amazement at this fantastically spectacular building, somebody near by said: 'You should see the George Washington Bridge and the Brooklyn Bridge too,' which I did. All this persuaded me that the Americans, if they were interested, could 'technologize' Kenya entirely in fifteen years!

XIV

Under the Shadow of Mau Mau

ON my arrival at Lincoln I had a pleasant surprise. George Mbugua Kimani, the friend whom I had left in Nairobi, had already arrived from Kenya on the full scholarship Lincoln University had awarded him. I had assisted in the negotiations for the scholarship with the president. Kimani is one of the most brilliant students I have ever met. He is a born mathematician, self-educated until he came to Lincoln. He passed with distinction the tough London University Matriculation Examination by correspondence, and yet he had never had a formal high school education before. To me, Kimani is one of the classic examples of what supreme determination and ambition can do.

With Kimani was another friend of mine, Njiiri, son of Senior Chief Njiiri of Fort Hall District in the Central Province, Kenya. Njiiri and I had been together in India and had attended St Joseph's in Allahabad.

I was very happy to see them both. We held endless discussions. Njiiri registered in the Department of Sociology and Kimani in the Department of Mathematics. We were Kenya's 'Lincoln contingent'; on the surface we seemed very happy.

I say we were happy on the surface because, in private, we were very disturbed and worried. From August through November of 1952 political events were moving very fast in Kenya. We could only try to piece the truth together from sensational newspaper accounts, the weekly news magazine summaries, and an occasional letter from home. What was very clear was that on October 20th 1952, the Governor of Kenya declared a state of emergency in the country and rounded up all the leaders of the Kenya Africa Union on the charge of helping organize a secret society dedicated to the slaughter of Europeans and the overthrow of the Kenya Government. On October 22nd, Kenyatta was arrested. There had been a few accounts of attacks by Africans on Europeans or other Africans. Now there were accounts of the massive use of troops to round up Africans and to intern them. In the absence of reliable information we were naturally disturbed and confused. We rushed for the paper every day.

On September 5th, the Member for Law and Order of the Kenya Legislature had made a speech in which he said:

> Within recent weeks charges against over a hundred persons for administering or participating in the administration of Mau Mau oaths have had to be withdrawn because witnesses have disappeared or have been intimidated into changing their story.

Rumours were beginning to circulate that the Kikuyu were planning an uprising. By the end of September, thirty-seven Africans were alleged to have been killed by Mau Mau terrorists for refusing to co-operate. We three students at Lincoln read the news greedily. We were wondering just what was happening back home.

Mau Mau: The Nature of the Kikuyu Oath

Much has been written about the Mau Mau oath, so much that to many the oath itself is more important than the rebellion against British colonial rule and the problems and pressures which caused its violent explosion. Few who condemn the oath with assurance could explain one good reason for the rebellion or why the oath had such a strong psychological effect on the people. Judgment may be necessary but must we have such judges? It is not appropriate for me in this book to analyse the origins of the Mau Mau rebellion but I can at least explain the genesis of the oath.

First of all, the taking of oaths was not new to the Kikuyu. It was an integral and powerful part of our society, as in most societies at one time or another in their development. The variety of oaths was large to suit the many serious occasions of life, a binding force providing an important moral sanction of society. They were an essential part of tribal law, like the ordeals of fire and water of early English society. Basically, the oaths fell into two categories, major and minor.

If a man denied responsibility for the pregnancy of a girl, the Council of Elders would administer a minor oath to test his innocence. If the man lied, the punishment which he himself had invoked would fall on him between seven days and seven months from the oath. His body might erupt with boils, his animals (his wealth) or even he himself might die; whatever its form, the punishment was inevitable.

The major oath was used to settle land disputes, allegations of larceny and other criminal offences and to test witch doctors suspected of using black magic to poison others, on their own account or hired to do so. Again, the Council of Elders, having failed to solve the problem by arbitration, would administer the oath. However, the major oath had such terrible consequences, involving the man's family and even his entire clan, that he had to obtain their permission before submitting to it. The punishment to follow a major oath dishonestly sworn would fall three and a half years after the oath, 'imera mogwanja', and would be incalculable in its effects.

The psychological effect of the oath was literally terrifying to the Kikuyu. If a man lied, he lied not only to society but also to the ancestors' spirits, whom we have seen could cause great suffering if displeased, and still more he lied to the Creator, Ngai himself. Once taken, it followed that an oath was irrevocable. There was no possibility of mental reservation or de-oathing; during the Emergency, the colonial administration held 'de-oathing' ceremonies, the only effect of which was to confuse the people with one further variety of fear. Certainly, few felt that the ceremonies absolved them and their families from the evils to follow the renunciation of their original oath.

The origin of the rebellion lay in the arrogation of African land by the White Settlers. Later, further grievances were added because of political, economic, educational and social repressions. For thirty years, the struggle was peaceful but barren and therefore largely unnoticed in England, discounted even by the Government who encouraged still more settlers to emigrate to Kenya after the Second World War. Curiously, therefore, the outbreak of violence came as a surprise to the British public and their rulers who were outraged by the 'wholesale return of the Kikuyu to savagery' and their desire to 'slaughter all the white people in Kenya'. None of this was true for the general people who wanted only their basic human dignity, and who were tired of waiting. If an impartial view is needed, consider Professor Margery Perham who delivered the Reith Lectures in 1961 (now published as *The Colonial Reckoning*) in which she said: 'How deep must have been the frustrations of the Kikuyu to drive them to practices which quite deliberately violated the sanctities of their own sexual and tribal life.'

Professor Perham is primarily referring to the excesses of the later and more extreme forms of the Mau Mau oath which were administered rarely and only to ensure the continued support of doubtful followers, but she is correct about the deep frustrations. It was logical that at such a serious time in the history of the tribe that the Kikuyu should seek to bind themselves to the success of the rebellion by the traditional, most solemn method of the Kikuyu oath—for that is all the Mau Mau oath was essentially, the Kikuyu oath adapted for war, a religious expression or moral intent. It is so long since the English themselves had need for rebellion that each time it occurs they fail to recognize its legitimacy and urgency: America, Ireland, Palestine, India, Cyprus, Kenya. However, once the initial shock has worn off, and the case is proved finally, we may give thanks for the pragmatism of the English and their real and fundamental belief in democracy. The English have inevitably come under attack most often because of all the Great Powers they have had the largest empire to dismember. The lesson is for all to learn: all peoples have their dignity for which they will eventually resort to violence. It has happened too often for this world. Let there now be an end to violence and let every man eat today.

Then, on September 23rd 1952, at about 11 a.m. the shadow of Mau Mau fell upon me. I had just finished my English class and was on my way to another class when a white man walked over to my professor and said: 'Where is Mr Gatheru?' The professor pointed me out to him. He walked over to me and showed me a card. It identified him as an agent of the United States Immigration Service. My heart sank. What did this agent want with me? He told me that he had been sent by the Immigration Service from Philadelphia to check on certain facts about my visa. He advised me to go and have my lunch first and to get excused from the rest of my classes for the day because the checking on these facts was going to take a long time. I didn't want any lunch. I said: 'Let's start it right now.'

I invited him to come to my room in one of the dormitories and I offered him a seat. He offered me a cigarette. Then he pulled some papers out of his bulky brief case. I could not help noticing that he had a long list of questions in his hand. I started getting really frightened. I sensed immediately that the same Canutism that had hounded me in Kenya was after me again. Here I was, happily established in Lincoln and now the long arms of Canutists seemed to have reached across the sea, grabbing for my throat, trying to drag me back to that office in Nairobi where I had fought the battle to come to America years before. My heart was beating furiously. I felt in the pit of my stomach as if I had eaten a big meal that was weighing like a rock inside me. Did all of this mean that now, perhaps, I should never be able to get the higher education for which I had struggled so much?

The agent began to question me as though I were before a grand jury:

'What's your full name?'

'Reuel John Mugo Gatheru,' I replied.

'How did you come to the United States?'

'I came to the United States by way of India and England,' I answered.

'Why didn't you come to the United States directly from Kenya instead of going to India?' he asked.

'After I was offered a scholarship at Roosevelt College, I went to the American Consul in Nairobi to seek for information about the U.S. student visa. The American Consul advised me that in order to obtain a student visa, I had to get a certificate of good conduct or political clearance from the Kenya Government. I tried to obtain the necessary clearance, but all in vain. Hence I went to India with a hope that if I did not obtain a U.S. visa, I could further my higher education in India.'

'Who financed your trip to India?' he asked.

'My friends and relatives,' I replied.

'You seem to have been very active in politics in Kenya, can you tell me something about your activities in Nairobi?' he asked again.

'Well, first of all I went to Nairobi in 1945. I joined the Medical Research Laboratory as a learner laboratory technician. After some two years I left the Medical Department and joined the Kenya African Union as an assistant editor,' I replied.

'What sort of literature were you editing?' he asked.

'A weekly newspaper published by the Kenya African Union,' I replied.

'Any other literature?' he asked.

'Not to my knowledge,' I replied.

'Are you familiar with a magazine called the *African*?' he asked.

I now realized that this inquiry was inspired from Kenya and not the United States.

'Yes, I am. Some time ago I wrote to the American Consul in Nairobi asking for some addresses of the leading Negro newspapers and magazines. I then wrote to some of the papers and magazines, asking for pen-friends who were interested in discussing politics or current affairs in general. One of these papers was the *African Magazine* published by some American Negroes in New York. I took a particular interest in it and asked the editor whether he could send me some twenty-five copies to try and see whether the Kenya people would be interested in subscribing,' I replied.

'Did many people in Kenya try to buy copies of the *African Magazine*?' he asked.

'Yes, even the Kenya Intelligence Department,' I replied.

'What happened then?' he asked.

'I learned later on that the magazine was banned in Kenya and in the Belgian Congo.'

'What was the Kenya African Union?' he asked.

'A country-wide political organization headed by Jomo Kenyatta whose main purposes were to secure the African rights and self-government through constitutional means,' I replied.

'Were you a member?' he asked.

'No, I was not a member officially, but there was nothing to prevent me becoming one.'

'How could you be an assistant editor without being a member?' he asked.

'I was not compelled to join as membership was quite voluntary. But do not think that because of this I did not fully support the union's policy.'

'Was the Kenya African Union a Communist body?' he asked.

'No, it was not,' I replied.

'Do you know of Communists in Kenya?' he asked.

'No, I don't,' I replied.

'Is there a Communist Party in Kenya?' he went on.

'No, there is not,' I replied.

'What's the population of Kenya?' he demanded.

'About 5,000,000 Africans, 100,000 Asians, and about 33,000 Europeans,' I replied.

'Were you then an agitator for the Kenya African Union?' he insinuated.

'I was not an agitator from the point of view of the Kenya Africans, but the Kenya settlers may have thought me one. After all, even George Washington was an agitator here in your country,' I replied.

He laughed appreciatively but said nothing.

'Have you ever carried on any political agitation in the United States, in India, in England?' he asked.

It was now clear to me that he thought that I had some kind of revolutionary aims.

'No,' I answered.

I thought that even though my answers were genuine and clear, this man had a preconceived idea that I was a Communist.

'Don't you think you lied to the American Consul in London in not revealing you had been refused a U.S. visa in Nairobi?' he asked.

'No, I did not lie to him. The truth is that I was never refused a U.S. visa. The American Consul merely told me the requirements for a U.S. student visa. Specifically, he asked me to get a certificate of good conduct from the Kenya Government to the effect that there was nothing against me in Kenya politically. I was not able to obtain this document and so never made a formal application for a U.S. visa,' I said.

'What form of government would you like to see in Kenya?' he asked.

'A republican type of government,' I replied.

'Who are your friends in the United States?' he asked.

'They are both white and black,' I answered.

'Have you ever addressed or attended a meeting in the United States?' he asked.

'No,' I answered.

'Who is Professor St Clair Drake?' he demanded.

'He is an American teaching Sociology at Roosevelt College in Chicago, Illinois.'

'How did you happen to know him?' he asked.

'Through correspondence,' I replied.

'Is he white or Negro?' he wanted to know.

'His father came from Barbados and was related to Sir Francis Drake, and his mother is half Red Indian and half Negro,' I replied.

'How do you support yourself financially?' he asked.

'I have a college scholarship,' I answered.

'Are you supposed to perform some duties on completion of your college career, that is, after you have gone back to Kenya?' he asked.

At this I became angry. What kind of 'duties' could he mean? Why was he asking what I'd do when I went back home? Did all of this have something to do with the fact that there were disturbances in Kenya and, if so, what could he want from *me*?

'What newspapers do you read?' he continued.

'*The Chicago Defender*, the *New York Times*, the *Christian Science Monitor*, the *Washington Times-Herald*, the *Nation*, the *Afro-American*, the *Philadelphia Inquiry*, the *Evening Bulletin*, *Ebony*, the *Time-Life Magazines* and the air edition of the *Manchester Guardian*,' I replied.

'What are the politics of the *Chicago Defender*?'

I was rather surprised that he picked this particular paper out of such a long list.

'Off hand, that is a difficult question, but I would say that it expresses the current political views of American Negroes, and it also appears to be sympathetic towards Africans,' I replied.

'How many countries have you visited besides the United States, Britain, and India?' he went on.

'None,' I replied.

'What are your major subjects here at Lincoln University?' he asked.

'History and Political Science,' I replied.

'For what degree?' he questioned.

'The B.A. degree,' I replied.

Why this, I wondered? I still don't know, but it seemed obvious that the investigation had been initiated from overseas, that some kind of information must have been given to the immigration authorities by someone who knew me back in Nairobi.

The interrogation lasted from 11.15 a.m. until 2 p.m. The man was friendly in a detached, diplomatic way. I took his cigarettes and smoked them, but I was very angry at some of the questions. In fact, I was angry about the whole procedure. I asked him what was behind all this and he said it was just a routine matter and that I should not worry. This was hardly the truth as we shall see later.

I reported the matter to Dr Bond. He was disturbed and worried, but he said: 'Just sit tight and wait.' He became very busy. He put everything else aside, including correspondence, and made several long calls to Philadelphia, New York, and Washington. He was thoroughly angry, particularly at those questions with which the immigration agent tried to implicate me with Communism. At that time, American public opinion was very afraid of Communism, so no one mentioned Communism without checking who was around. It was like an un-circumcised boy mentioning sex relations to circumcised young men in the old Kikuyu society—if such a thing could ever have happened!

On October 20th 1952, only four weeks after my interrogation, the Kenya Government declared a state of emergency; two days later over a hundred leaders and officers of the Kenya African Union were imprisoned, including Jomo Kenyatta. I felt in my inner soul that these events must be connected with my interrogation although the immigration agent had said it only concerned my visa. Why were they concerned about my visa anyhow?

I had entered the United States in 1950 on a visitor's visa. I asked for this kind of visa in London in order to come to America to discuss schools and finances with my friend, Professor Drake. Hundreds of people came into America every year on visitors' visas. The Consular official had asked me if I had ever been refused a visa by the United States. I said 'No'. This was the truth. Since I could never get a 'good conduct certificate' from the Kenya Government, the United States had never had a chance to refuse me. I just dropped the matter and went to India. But that little word 'No' was to rise up to plague me years later, as we shall see.

After I entered Bethune-Cookman College I went to the local immigration authorities and asked for a student visa. They changed my visitors' visa to a student visa courteously and gladly. I never broke any immigration regulations and each time I went to get my visa renewed I had no trouble at all. I never tried to hide anything from anybody. Once, I lost my passport and applied to Kenya for another one which they sent through the British Consulate General in Philadelphia. They knew exactly where I was. Everything I did was open and above board. You can imagine my surprise when on November 5th 1952, six weeks after my interview with the immigration agent (and barely two weeks after the state of emergency had been declared in Kenya), I received a letter from the Immigration Office in Philadelphia which read as follows:

Dear Sir,
          Pursuant to instructions received from the office of the Commissioner of Immigration and Naturalization at Washington, I request that you depart from the United States as soon as possible.

    I am obliged to say that unless such departure is effected within thirty days, this office will be obliged to take the necessary steps to enforce your departure.

What did this mean? What had I done to warrant this expulsion? Was it connected with the things happening in Kenya? Did the United States Government think that I had something to do with Mau Mau?

So, amid all my worries about the fate of my people at home, I now had my personal worries. I could hardly believe my eyes when I read that letter. I had struggled along until I had reached my junior year at Lincoln University. The fall term had just begun and now the United States Immigration Office was telling me to get out. Where was I to go? To Kenya? I would certainly be thrown into a concentration camp immediately as a former assistant editor of the Kenya African Union newspaper. To Britain? What could I do there? I had no scholarship or means of support.

I wanted to stay in America to prepare myself to serve Kenya after the Mau Mau crisis was over. Now, I faced deportation. I had come to love Lincoln University and I wanted to get my B.A. degree from there.

I went in haste to Dr Bond. He read the letter carefully and I could see that he was getting more annoyed. He took the phone and made a call to Philadelphia. The immigration authorities refused to tell him why I was being ordered out of the country. He said he'd never take this lying down. He started to work immediately to set up a committee to defend me. He told me once again not to worry and not to lose my nerve. He said to go on with my classes and to study hard and that the history professor—Tom Jones—and some of the other professors would take care of my case. I understand that he got into touch with Professor Drake and Dr Elizabeth E. Hoyt right away, and that Dr Hoyt sent on some money immediately to hire a lawyer.

Although Dr Bond told me not to worry and to study, I was very worried and could not keep my mind on my books. I recall my professor in economics class telling me: 'Mugo, please do not worry so much. They can't just come here and grab you by your neck like a cat. They will give enough notice when they decide to come for you.' Then, too, my picture began to appear in the newspapers and reporters began to call on me for interviews and sometimes I had meetings with my 'Defence Committee'. It was rough. At night I could not sleep. I thought of numerous things as I was tossing around. Why am I suffering this much, I would ask myself? This was the price of my past activities in Kenya. I was paying the hard way because, while in Kenya, I had learnt of the burning injustices of colonial rule and the disparity of white settler supremacy in a country where the population is almost totally African. A great desire came upon me to talk about these injustices that my people had

179

suffered for so long. Without access to the radio, the movies, to television, the only way to speak to many people was to write and have my writings published, and that is exactly what I did. I wrote mainly 'Letters to the Editor'. These were duly published by solid, conservative, pro-settler papers as amusing examples of a typical African 'agitator's' tactics. But some people were not amused. Still others became highly interested. I was not trying to subvert democracy. However, I did want to break the Kenya settlers' economic and political domination of my people. I had never injured the United States, but the political persecution I had known in Kenya followed me and in America I suffered still.

The students at Lincoln University were my real salvation. I was now a sort of hero, and they all came round and said: 'Give them hell, Mugo. We are with you.' This gave me real strength, and I even began to enjoy the struggle.

People all over the United States rallied to my cause, and I fear that sometimes I really felt too important. Even the *New York Times* carried stories on me and I began to hear that the Kenya papers were writing about the case too. The attempt by the immigration authorities to smear me with Communism did not stop people from supporting me. The American people were intelligent enough to understand that one did not have to be a Communist to appreciate the fact that the Kenya settlers had more arable land than the Africans or that the living conditions in the Nairobi African locations were appalling! This was just everyday common sense.

As the crisis intensified in Kenya, I read every scrap of news every day on what was going on, and sometimes the news about myself was mixed with the news from home.

During my ordeal the people at the British Embassy were always kind and courteous. They claimed they had nothing to do with the threat to deport me and even offered to find me a place at the University of Manitoba in Canada if I had to leave America. I never found out how much they knew but suspected that the trouble was instigated by officials of the Kenya Government.

My American friends fought so hard to save me from deportation that on February 4th 1953, I received a letter from the immigration authorities to say that:

as a result of further consideration given to your status under immigration laws, you may ignore letter of this office dated November 5th 1952, requesting you to depart from the United States as soon as possible. In this connection, however, your attention is directed to the fact that your authorized stay in this country will expire on April 30th 1953, and you will be expected to depart by that date.

We had won a partial victory. I had been saved from deportation; I was glad, but I was lonesome too. I had heard a Negro spiritual sung at Bethune-Cookman College: 'Sometimes I feel like a motherless child, a long way from home.' Now, I felt that way.

There was one fly in the ointment. My visa was to run out two months before school closed. What was I to do? I had one of the best immigration lawyers in the United States—Jack Wasserman. The immigration order said to leave as soon as the present visa expired. My lawyer said he wasn't going to risk my being refused another student visa. He wanted me to finish Lincoln and get to my master's degree before going home. He decided that the thing to do was to ask for a permanent visa—not because I wanted to immigrate to the United States, but to give me time to finish my school work and to give me the right to work as much as I needed to earn money. There was nothing illegal in this request for a change of status.

When Jack Wasserman applied for a permanent visa two things happened: firstly, the immigration authorities decided to fight against it tooth and nail and secondly, some of my friends who didn't understand why I was asking for a permanent visa decided that they could no longer support me in my fight. I also lost some of my supporters because by now I was interested in the American girl whom I wanted to marry. This was unexpected but many people resented the idea of my marrying a girl they did not approve of, and from certain quarters support, both moral and financial, began to fall off steeply. As so often happens in such cases, enthusiastic interest on the part of many disturbed citizens deteriorated into indifference. People, too, feel that if the victim of injustice shows the slightest deviation from their own standards, this releases them from a moral obligation to support the victim. I did, however, stick to my guns.

However, my real friends never faltered: Professor Jones and Professor Drake took over responsibility for raising funds and Jack Wasserman decided to carry on even though we had no money just then to pay his fees. He filed a declaratory injunction and thus what became the suit of Reuel Mugo Gatheru v. Herbert Brownell, Jr. Attorney General of the United States, began.

I was furious over the implication that I might have been a 'subversive alien'. Perhaps someone from Kenya had told the American immigration authorities that I was a 'subversive', and perhaps the Americans didn't know that the term meant something different in Kenya and South Africa. In America it meant to be a part of the world-wide Communist conspiracy. In Kenya and South Africa, a man was 'subversive' if he asked for the right of Africans to vote, or pressed for more schools or equal pay for equal work; in other words, those rights enshrined in the American Constitution which one day will be put into practice in the Southern states of America with the support of the Federal Government!

Judge John W. Holland heard my application for a declaratory injunction and his vigorous, clear judgment dealt firmly with the allegation of subversion. A direct accusation of Communism had never been made against me as it could hardly have been substantiated and the judge found only one important issue: 'Had I secured a visa fraudulently in London by not telling the American Consul I'd been denied a political clearance document in Kenya?' He said:

If the plaintiff is committed to the philosophy of Communism it would have to be inferred. The ways and means of communistic organizations are various. I am not making any findings as to that issue if it was in the case, which it is not directly. But from the evidence it is my opinion that he was not a follower of communistic thought, but as a student he was actively interested in the philosophy of government and antagonistic to colonization, and was active in his native land in securing reforms of government, not by the overthrow of the government by force and violence. This I say in his favour as my opinion. But that is not the issue in the case.

The plaintiff is an intelligent person as shown by the record. He was a student in his native land. It is true that he didn't go through more than high school, as I recall, in his native land, then got out in certain activities. I believe that those activities contemplated or incorporated some activity connected with the acquiring of knowledge, but that I think is more or less immaterial here. But he was a student. He was not only a boy who had gone through high school, but he was one who desired to gain knowledge. He wanted to improve himself. He took an interest in public affairs, and particularly was he desirous of aiding and securing reforms in his local government, not by force and violence but reformations favourable to his people in his native land where British Colonial rule obtained. He was particularly desirous of extending his educational facilities by becoming a student in the United States. He sought to extend his acquaintance by developing friends through correspondence. However, his over-zealousness in this regard proved his downfall so far as the issues in this case are concerned. His failure to acquaint the authorities in London who were responsible for his visa being granted with the facts about his efforts in his native land to secure a visa was a decided mistake on his part. He was duty-bound in answering the questions propounded to him in London to relate the facts about his previous efforts, especially the fact that he had not been able to secure a political clearance document.

This was an opinion in the highest tradition of the liberal American judiciary, although Judge Holland still felt that I should have told the American Consul in London that Kenya wouldn't give me a 'political clearance'.

In the summer of 1957, my lawyer received a letter from the Attorney General's office stating that the Government did not care to argue the case and that, if we'd drop the suit, they'd drop all their attempts to keep me from retaining my visa. They would no longer try to prove that I was an undesirable alien illegally in the United States. *I had won my case* but the victory belonged to Jack Wasserman to whom I shall never cease to be grateful. For five years I had had the feeling that I was living with a big hammer hanging over my head and that it could fall and crush me at any time. I never knew when something might happen that would mean the end of my college career.

I am grateful to all my friends who made it possible for me to stay in America and to complete my studies there. I can't forget how scared I sometimes was and how sometimes I felt so much all alone. But I had faith in my lawyer and in my many friends. I knew that if we lost it would not be because they hadn't tried as hard as they could to save me. This whole experience 'made a man out of me'. I do not regret it.

People sometimes say to me, 'Mugo, how did you ever manage to get your first degree and then another with all that pressure on you?' Sometimes I wonder myself. In the summer before my last year at Lincoln University, I decided to look for work. Since my immigration status was not clear, I was permitted to work the whole year round if I wished to do so. I secured a job in the Bronx working for the American Wool Corporation. The work was hard but it was made pleasant by my foreman, a hard-working and kind West Indian from Jamaica.

When I returned to Lincoln for the autumn term of 1953, I was a bit nervous. This was a very important year for me, my final year, in which I was to receive the B.A. degree for which I had struggled so very much. I studied constantly, despite the news from Kenya where the state of emergency had now lasted a full year, and even took two extra courses which required much outside reading.

My great day, equal to that on which I was initiated and circumcised, came on June 8th 1954. On this day the B.A. degree in History and Political Science was conferred on me. I shall never forget that day in my life. I was happy, yet I felt a little sad that neither Drake nor Browne came to my graduation. I did not have any family in the United States, even though my people in Kenya had sent me letters and cards of congratulations. I actually felt lonely, especially when I saw that all members of my graduating class (there were fifty-four in all) had their relatives present. I was grateful, however, that Kimani and Njiiri were with me. I needed their presence very badly. I was happy and sad by turns and Kimani and Njiiri also did not pretend to hide their feelings. My uncontrolled joy and sadness mingled with hearty laughter, forced my eye-lashes to glisten from dampness. It was fantastic.

XV

Mugo as a Kikuyu 'Psychoanalyst'

I WAS now ready for my post-graduate studies for which I chose New York, mainly for its fine university but also for the city itself with its magnificent Museums of Art and Natural History and, above all, for me, the United Nations, the only state among the states with no allegiance to the union.

But before I started attending the university, in the summer of 1954 I worked for the New York Standard Manufacturing Company in Brooklyn as a general factory hand, making hampers, baskets, and stools. I kept on this job even when the summer months were over and in the fall I registered at the university, in the Political Science Department under Professor Thomas R. Adam. Besides my main post-graduate subjects in political science, I took three others in analytical psychology which I enjoyed very much, particularly when I discovered an interesting similarity between the practices of the Kikuyu medicineman or *Mugo* and those of American psychoanalysts.

A Kikuyu medicine-man insists on knowing the entire background of his client, his clan, totems, parents, grand-parents, brothers, sisters, dreams and so on. Only with this knowledge does a *Mugo* consider himself ready to advise.

I remember two cases which illustrate this similarity, one of which took place at Stoton where our village was and the other in Fort Hall, in the Kikuyu Country in 1936.

At Stoton, my father had a friend who was said to be the ugliest man in the entire village. He had also a reputation for eating like a horse. He was tall, physically strong, with a lot of hair, a head oval like an egg, and very heavy jaws like *Proconsul Africanus*. Forty years old, he was hard-working and as a

185

result had a lot of goats and sheep. In fact, he was a very wealthy man but unfortunately unusually ugly and quite unable to find a girl to marry even though there was a surplus of women in the village. To add to his troubles, Kikuyu girls do not like a man with an insatiable appetite for they fear that one of them marrying such a man will spend her entire day cooking for him. Naturally, all this depressed him very much.

In the village everybody called this ugly man 'Nuthi', 'The Shapeless One'. He was quite happy with this nickname as his real name was even worse.

In Kikuyu society a family never gives the name of a child who has died to one born later. They fear that the evil spirits, or *ngoma*, who took the first child might be tempted on hearing his name again to take the second. For this reason, the second child is called Kariuki if a boy, or Njoki if a girl, both names meaning one who has been reborn. If by mischance the second child should also die, the family will not risk calling a third child by one of the usual family names but will protect him by giving him the name of a tree, a river, or even an animal. In this way they hope to deceive the *ngoma* into thinking that the unfortunate child does not belong to the family against which they have a grievance.

Nuthi was the third of three sons, the first two of whom died at birth. His parents decided to take no chances and called him 'Hiti' or 'Hyena'. When he was still only a little boy, Nuthi's parents died leaving him in the care of his long-widowed grandmother. He grew up in a Kikuyu village among other boys and girls who naturally made fun of his name. His grandma did not like him either. She used to shout at him:

'Get away from me, ugly Hiti,' or 'Come here, ugly one,' or 'Don't walk in front of me, you dirty creature, you are not like my child.'

Unfortunately, although his grandma was tyrannical, young Nuthi had no one else to turn to. He had no brothers or sisters. He was lonely and dejected.

When Nuthi was fifteen years of age his grandma became less offensive, perhaps because of her own increasing years, and at the age of seventeen Nuthi decided to go through the *irua* or circumcision ceremony. That year my father also was a candidate and their age-group was called 'Kihiu mwiri' or 'Knife on

the body' because during the ceremony the circumciser's knife
slipped and cut one of the other boys deeply in his thigh. The boy
shouted loudly: 'Knife! Knife! On my body!' This was contrary
to the Kikuyu tradition that no candidate should speak or show
any sign of fear while being circumcised and so the entire age-
group was named after the incident. It is said that the relatives
of the injured boy were so upset that a riot broke out in which
the circumciser was badly beaten and was saved from worse
only because the old men advised against shedding blood during
such an important and serious ceremony.

Although she detested him, Nuthi's grandma was pleasant
during the *irua* ceremony, partly because of public opinion and
partly because of the solemnity of the occasion. However, later
she reverted to her old ways and not even Nuthi's new status as
a 'Mwanake' could alter her dislike of him. Six months after
the ceremony she died. Unfortunately, Nuthi was away from
home at the time and was unable to hear her last words and
ask her blessing. As a Kikuyu, this was a serious matter for
Nuthi, particularly as there had been bad feeling between
them.

Nuthi was now left alone with only a few friends who cared
for him, mostly members of his age-group. He was a kind and
intelligent man but, although all the others of his age-group in
the village got married, young Nuthi could never find a girl to
whom he could propose. He was ugly. He kept looking for a
girl, but all in vain. He was very ugly.

When Nuthi was forty-five years old, my father was confirmed
as *Mugo* and received a visit at Stoton from a famous medicine-
man called Kirungu. Encouraged by my father, Nuthi decided
to ask Kirungu to help him find a wife. Kirungu was quite
willing to help as by chance he too was of my father's age-
group and therefore interested in Nuthi's welfare. The consultation took place in our yard.

In appearance and dress Kirungu reminded me of nothing
so much as a Welsh miner. He had a round head and a small
beard which made him look like a hornless billy goat. Two of
his upper teeth were chipped and people used to tease him as
'King'ethu', 'One whose front teeth were missing'. He had
travelled all the way from Kiambu District to the Rift Valley
and on to Stoton, giving advice to the Kikuyu Squatters

working on the European farms, carrying his *mwano* or the medicine basket with him. Usually, medicine-men employed aides to help them carry their medicine baskets wherever they went, but Kirungu travelled alone.

When he stayed with us, Kirungu's *mwano* was kept separately from my father's. Neither he nor my father was supposed to go around the other: in fact it was considered dangerous for anyone to go around a medicine-man in case he should be contaminated by the powerful magic radiating from the medicine-man's body. One could, however, shake hands with a *Mugo*, and a *Mugo* was, of course, allowed to embrace his wife without any danger. But otherwise, no one was supposed to go around him. (I doubt whether medicine-men would dance, say, a waltz as inevitably they would go round and round each other!)

As I look back now, I think it was about eleven o'clock in the morning when Nuthi came to our house for consultation. My father, Nuthi, and Kirungu sat down in our yard near the men's house, *thingira*. Kirungu asked my father to go to a small 'ikumbi'—store—to bring out his *mwano* for him, which my father did.

Kirungu pulled out a piece of soft sheepskin from his *mwano* and spread it flat upon the ground, then a gourd full of *mbugu* and finally a small bundle containing a white powder called 'Iraa' with which he rubbed his palms. Nuthi then told his life story: that his parents and near relations were dead, though he had some distant relatives living in a town called Naivasha in the Rift Valley Province; how he had been brought up by his grandma who had treated him harshly, cursing him often and living only long enough to see his circumcision. He told how his absence at his grandma's death had made him doubly depressed because he did not know what she had said, or would have said as she lay dying. After his grandma's death Nuthi had become a Squatter and was then working as a forester with other Kikuyu in Stoton. He had a number of goats and sheep and was therefore quite wealthy but he had never been able to impress any girl whom he had thought of marrying.

'How do other people treat you now?' asked Kirungu.

'Some are nice to me, but most do not care one way or the other,' Nuthi replied. 'They tell me that I'm ugly and laugh at me for not finding a girl to marry like the rest of my age-group.'

'Do you think any of these people sincerely respect you?' asked Kirungu.

'I should think so,' Nuthi replied.

'Why do you think so?'

'I do not know. Perhaps because I do not bother anybody, and I always ask them to drink with me when I have some,' replied Nuthi.

Kirungu then took up his big gourd full of *mbugu* and removed the fly-whisk which had covered it. Muttering all the while, he pointed the gourd towards the sky and to the four corners of the earth as if he was shooting a flying bird. Finally, he poured some *mbugu* on the sheepskin and asked Nuthi and my father to watch their direction as they scattered, and to count them.

'How many are there?' he asked.

'There are nine,' my father and Nuthi replied together as if they were schoolboys reciting to their teacher.

'What do you think your grandmother would have said to you if you had been at her death bed?' asked Kirungu.

'I don't know. Perhaps she might have cursed me since she didn't like me.'

Kirungu shook up his gourd repeatedly like a chemist with a bottle of medicine. Again he poured out *mbugu* and this time five came out. He did not ask for them to be counted. He only watched them as they spread. There was a tense silence and then he called solemnly:

'Nuthi! You have plenty of goats and sheep. You also look strong enough to be a fine warrior. Why then should you worry so much? There are many men with two or three wives who are not as well off as you. Go and brew some drink. Then find a spotless ram. Invite your closest friends and ask a *Mugo* to perform a ceremony to appease the spirit of your grandmother for it is she who is responsible for all your misfortune.'

'I'll do so,' replied Nuthi eagerly.

'The ram must be strangled by a Shaman and pieces of its roasted meat must be thrown down in the kitchen, near the front door, in the yard, and near the gate. A medicine-man must help you and, before any of you eat or drink, some drink must be poured on each spot where you have thrown the pieces of meat,' Kirungu advised. 'The ceremony will purge your bad luck and before this harvest is over you will have a wife.'

Nuthi was overjoyed to hear this and asked:

'Shall I find a wife in Stoton?'

'No,' answered Kirungu. 'Soon after the ceremony you must make a trip to Kikuyuland where you will find her.'

Nuthi promised to follow Kirungu's advice exactly and Kirungu's fee was agreed at five lambs and one castrated he-goat.

A *Mugo's* fee could be agreed before he gave his advice but either way no one ever dared refuse payment. In most cases fees were very moderate.

As advised, Nuthi made a trip to Kikuyuland after the ceremony and there he made friends with a number of girls, which was quite a new experience for him. He now became confident where in the past he had been very shy and reserved. He proposed to the girl whom he liked the best and she agreed to marry him. Nuthi was very, very happy. Unfortunately, Nuthi's reason for being in Kikuyuland became known in the girl's location where the young men were jealous of Nuthi's success with such a pretty girl and tried his new-found happiness. They would say:

'Why do you want to marry such a man? He's ugly and old and they say he eats like a horse. You'll be cooking the rest of your life.'

'I don't mind,' the girl would reply. 'I love him very much. If he eats a lot, that's all right with me—a man with a big appetite will work for his food and it is this kind of man I want to marry. If he works hard for himself, there will always be enough food left for me, too. A man who eats little might produce little—in which case he would not be a hard-working man.'

The young men of the village were defeated and Nuthi and his sweetheart were married. When the news reached Stoton that Nuthi was married, people talked about it very much. Some were pleased whilst others were sceptical. Everyone wanted to know whether the girl was pretty, or whether Nuthi had taken the first girl to accept him because of his bad luck in the past.

I remember very well when Nuthi and his wife arrived at Stoton. It was in the evening when the sun was setting. He was leading and she followed him. She was very pretty. Then everyone liked them, even those who had ignored Nuthi before. Clearly, Kirungu's influence had helped Nuthi if only by building up his confidence.

Most of the Kikuyu ceremonies and purifications involve the strangling of spotless animals, principally fat rams or lambs. For instance, before one was initiated into manhood or womanhood by circumcision a ram had to be strangled, partly as a matter of custom and partly to propitiate the spirits of the dead to ensure the prosperity of the candidate. Some of the meat was roasted by men of the household and the rest by a specially chosen woman from the village who was related to the candidate either by family ties or by clan. The woman's part in the ceremony was very important: she was not supposed to be angry about anything at the time of cooking the meat lest she should attract the wrath of the dead spirits by her anger. These matters were part of a living belief and not mere formalities.

It will be recalled that my aunt, The Beautiful One, had been barren for a long time until she met Karanja. Her first husband had consulted many Kikuyu medicine-men in an attempt to find out why she did not have children, but had found no remedy. In all this time my aunt was very unhappy indeed. Her husband became ashamed and began to ill-treat her. He would shout angrily:

'What's wrong with you, you skinny barren woman? I wasted the dowry which I paid to your parents.'

Later, my aunt married Karanja and explained her difficulties to him. Karanja was sympathetic, loving, and would have done anything to help her. He was certain that the famous medicine-men of Fort Hall could find a cure.

In a village opposite Karanja's home and across the River Kayahwe there was a famous and powerful medicine-man called Kimani. His fees were higher than those of other medicine-men, but Karanja decided to consult him. His elder brother was a friend of Kimani and so they went together.

On their arrival they found Kimani very busy advising other clients and waited their turn patiently. After some hours Kimani was free and Karanja and his brother explained the situation to him. Kimani's *mwano* was ready. He produced a long gourd full of *mbugu* and held it in his arms. He asked

Karanja about himself and my aunt. Karanja related his own story but he did not know enough about my aunt's background. Kimani told Karanja that her story was vitally important and that they could not continue without it.

Fortunately, my father's eldest brother had gone to Fort Hall to visit Karanja and my aunt and, being the eldest son of my grandfather, he knew our family history well. His name was Nyutu and Karanja sent for him immediately.

When he came, Nyutu told my aunt's story, even mentioning the woman who had cooked the ram at my aunt's circumcision ceremony. Kimani stopped him at that point and pointed his long gourd towards Mt Kenya to the north, Mt Nyandarwa to the west, Kilima-Mbogo to the south-east, and then poured down some *mbugu*. He asked Karanja, his brother, and Nyutu to count them. There were four.

'The woman was related to your wife's family but she was angry while she was cooking the meat.'

'What did she do?' asked Karanja.

'While she was cooking the meat she took a small piece of meat and tied it secretly in her leather skirt. Later, she buried the meat at the foot of a tree near the village, pretending that she was burying your wife's future children and this is why your wife is barren.'

'What can be done?' asked Karanja eagerly.

'We must re-enact your wife's circumcision ceremony. First, you must get a spotless fat ram which my helpers and I will strangle in your yard. We shall then roast some of the meat. The rest will be cooked by a woman of your wife's clan who will bury a piece under a fig tree. She will do this alone, secretly, but we shall later ask her to take us where the meat is hidden. The woman will dig up the meat which represents your wife's children and give it to us. We shall then return to your home where I shall bless the meat and throw it under your wife's bed. This ceremony is very important and it should be done after your wife's menstruation is over,' Kimani explained.

A day was fixed for the ceremony and Karaja, his brother, and Nyutu returned home, satisfied by Kimani's interpretation. On the way, Nyutu told Karanja that the woman responsible for my aunt's misfortune had always been ill-treated by her husband and had eventually committed suicide.

Now the whole story was clear and Karanja and my aunt were ready for the 'purification' which is called 'Kuhakwo ng'ondu'. Kimani and his two aides arrived and performed the ceremony as planned, smearing oil from the fat tail of the strangled ram on the legs, hips, hands, face, and neck of my aunt. After only a few weeks my aunt conceived! It was exciting, incredible, and thrilling. I did not myself attend the ceremony but I know they believed completely in Kimani's diagnosis and that he was responsible for the cure.

I think it must be clear why I felt at home when I began my post-graduate studies in psychology. The similarity between the methods of our Kikuyu medicine-men and those of the American 'witch-doctors' is strong and perhaps one day someone will publish a comparison of their respective successes.

At the university I was also interested to find the extent of the problem of maladjustment in the industrial society of the white man. Before I was able to study this problem for myself, I knew that some leading anthropologists thought it unwise to attempt rapid industrialization of African societies lest their well-integrated pattern of life should be disturbed; they considered that Africans had a greater need of a proper knowledge of land use, simple methods of keeping accounts, and better methods of hygiene. Apparently, they had no need of electricity in their houses or of running water so long as they could draw it from wells. I think that the limited value of this view is today more widely recognized and therefore I would mention only that in my experience, problems of maladjustment occur almost as frequently in a so-called simple, agricultural community like Kikuyuland as they do in the sophisticated, industrial societies of Europe and North America. I can only assume that this has not been apparent to the experts because they have not known what to look for, unused as they are to the kind of community in which I was raised. These problems of maladjustment occur in both kinds of community but in each case take different forms. For example, in the earlier chapters of my story I explained that my father was a polygamist, and that the institution of polygamy was, and still is to a lesser extent, accepted in the Kikuyu society. It was one of the sources of a man's social pride, prestige, and self-gratification, as well as having economic advantages.

However, it is unlikely that any man has the capacity to share his sincere and genuine love among several wives equally. My own grandfather had nine wives of whom two were his favourites and of these two he preferred one to the other. This in itself created complications but further difficulty arose because the discrimination by grandfather showed between his wives extended also to their children.

Among my uncles, sons of my grandfather, there was ill-will and personal rivalry. The whole problem centred around inheritance. First sons inherited first shares and often these shares were bigger than the rest. The shares were of land, goats, sheep, cows, and any other property.

When a goat, cow, or sheep was strangled for eating, the sons of favourite wives would receive bigger pieces of meat than the rest; and they would also be the first called upon on an occasion. My grandma was the most favoured. I used to enjoy seeing my uncles getting bigger shares than the rest, especially of meat. At that time I too had a special position whenever I visited my grandfather. He would send one of his sons to call me when he had strangled a goat or a sheep so that I could eat with his children. In fact, I used to taste the meat immediately after him because I was the first son of the favourite daughter of his favourite wife. He used also to give me special food of a kind eaten only by rich Kikuyu of his generation called 'Rukuri' which was a mixture of liquid honey and fat slices of meat cut from the tail of a fattened ram, or nicely roasted fat ribs of a castrated he-goat. He could not give this food to an ordinary man however hungry that man might be. It was stored in a 'Kihembe', a round wooden drum covered with stretched leather on one side.

Three of my grandfather's wives he liked noticeably less than the rest and treated them accordingly. Their children also suffered the same fate. One of these three wives had a son who was her only child and the others had two sons each. The one with only one son was treated worst of all and eventually she ran away from my grandfather and went to Nairobi where she became a prostitute. Her son, back at home, was ill-treated and picked upon for every trivial mistake. He suffered a lot and was lonely. So eventually he, too, ran away from home. He went to a mission school of the Church of Scotland in the

Kikuyu district of Kiambu. There, he became a Christian and was educated. His mother planned all these things for him from Nairobi and paid for his school fees and maintenance. He was then quite happy.

When the sons of one of the other unfavoured wives heard of their half-brother's adventures, they too ran away and joined him at his mission school, leaving their mother behind. Their mother stayed with my grandfather, but he argued with her constantly and complained of her two irresponsible sons, saying she should be ashamed of them. Still she stayed but life was extremely hard for her. I don't know how she tolerated it. One day I saw her gums bleeding after she had been beaten across the mouth. I was very sorry, but my grandmother told me to go into the house and stop watching.

The two sons of the third unfavoured wife did not go away. Instead, they built their mother a hut about two miles away from my grandfather's home. They were tough, strong young men and I could never understand why they were so disliked. They worked hard and became wealthy by the Kikuyu standard of that time. Other people in the neighbourhood liked and respected them which embarrassed Grandfather considerably as his disfavour was known. He would therefore invite them on important occasions, but they would never go to him. They were happy and satisfied with their own independent way.

The sons who were favoured at home were given every opportunity and assistance to marry as many wives as they wished. They were in the prime of life and despised their three half-brothers who had gone to a mission school. They were, however, less scornful when they spoke of the two half-brothers who were successful and were living separately with their mother.

Across the small stream from my grandfather's home there lived a contemporary of his, another rich man with a lot of wives and children. Each man hated and was greatly jealous of the other. They often tried to hurt each other indirectly and, whenever they met in a part of the village where drinking was taking place, they would eventually quarrel and fight. Both also were medicine-men of high calibre but my grandfather was able to humiliate the other more often.

One night it was raining incessantly and the thunder and

lightning was terrifying. My grandfather heard footsteps in his big yard which was surrounded by living-huts and granaries, the whole fenced round with thorn trees called 'Matura' which I have not yet seen outside Kenya.

The footsteps which my grandfather heard were of more than two people and so he took his spear and a long sharp knife called *Ruhiu rwa njora* and woke two of his younger sons who had been sleeping in his *thingira*. He woke them quietly and told them in a whisper what was going on outside and to collect their weapons. The rest of the sons were sleeping separately in their own *thingiras* and could not be reached. It was still raining and the wind was blowing hard, whistling through the trees.

My grandfather and his two sons looked out through slits in the *riigi* which was woven from small thin sticks, rather like a basket, and which served as a door. They saw five men standing in front of their *thingira* and one man in front of each *thingira* where one of the other sons was sleeping. All the men were armed and looked as though they were standing guard for thieves working inside. To his horror, my grandfather saw that there were also men near a small store in which his *mwano* was kept. The store had already been opened. This was very serious. Neither my grandfather nor his two sons could recognize the culprits outside.

'How can we get out?' my grandfather whispered to his son.

'We should use arrows,' one suggested. His brother agreed.

'No,' my grandfather said. 'We must not shed blood now because they have already opened the store of my *mwano* and we don't want to pollute *mwano* with their blood.'

They waited, confused and tense. In the same *thingira* there was a fattened castrated he-goat called 'Kinyaga'. His name was descriptive because he was striped in black and white, rather more broadly than a zebra.

Kinyaga wore a bell tied to his neck. When he heard my grandfather and his two sons whispering he thought that they were going to feed him. He ran towards them and, of course, his bell rang. The men outside were sure they had been heard and started to run away. My grandfather and his two sons came out quickly and made a tremendous noise waking the entire family. It was still raining. All the men came out with knives, spears,

bows and arrows. They needed lamps and so the women made
'Iciinga', or bundles of firewood with the fire flaming to one
side, as torches for the men to use in the dark. However, by then
the culprits had disappeared into the bush. The huts and stores
were inspected to find out what had been stolen but everything
seemed in order. No goats or sheep were missing, the women
and children were all right but, to everybody's horror and
desolation, *the important* mwano *had gone*!

The whole family was frightened and unsure. Nobody knew
what to do.

'It must have been one of my rivals,' said my grandfather
sadly, 'but I have no evidence and shall never know.'

'I wish they had stolen some of our goats and sheep instead,'
said his eldest son.

'I wish we could have got them,' another son said striking
and waving his long sword as if ready to cut somebody into
pieces.

My grandfather ordered everyone into the huts in case the
culprits had spread some poison in the yard for the family to
step on. In the morning he called all his sons and their mothers
into the *thingira*. He even sent for the two who were living
separately with their mother, and when they all surrounded
him he said:

'My dear sons and wives, we are in grave trouble and the
entire family is in danger. My *mwano* has been stolen, I feel as if
I have no family or property any more. I shall consult a *Mugo*,
not so much to help me recover my *mwano* for it can never be the
same again after being stolen, but to tell me what I must do to
save us all from the evil that has come upon us.'

All of them listened grimly. They looked as if they had been
paralysed. My grandfather got ready to see Kanyita, the
famous *Mugo* and the others dispersed in confusion and
despair.

When Kanyita heard the story, he laid a leather goat-skin
at one corner of his yard near the *thingira*. My grandfather sat
on a stool in front of him. Kanyita pointed his gourd towards
Mt Kenya and then to the four corners of the earth and,
shaking the gourd slowly, poured some *mbugu* on the skin. They
spread. Kanyita told my grandfather to hand one of the *mbugu*
to him and examined it carefully as if it were a test tube in a

laboratory. My grandfather watched Kanyita quietly as he examined the *mbugu*, murmuring to himself.

At last Kanyita spoke:

'Son of Nguuri,' he called my grandfather respectfully and seriously. 'Your tragedy is great. Your *mwano* has been stolen not by an ordinary thief but by one who knows you well, your rival and a dangerous enemy.'

'What must I do now?' asked my grandfather.

'I was just going to tell you,' replied Kanyita. 'A spotless ram must be sacrificed to purify your family from the bad medicine and cleanse the footprints left in your yard by the culprits. You must then have another *mwano* conferred on you by two or more medicine-men, after which your entire family must go to another part of the country. You see, when your enemies got hold of your *mwano* they walked around your entire household with it—to poison you with your own magic so that all of you would die.'

My grandfather was panic stricken, particularly when he heard the second part of Kanyita's decree. All the family were upset by Kanyita's words and also when they saw how far my grandfather's health had been affected. He looked like a man who had been sick for months.

Grandfather now prepared a spotless black ram and on the appointed day Kanyita and two others performed a long and complicated ritual reinstating my grandfather and making another *mwano* for him.

By coincidence, it was at this time that the Kikuyu Squatters decided to leave 'Kwa Maitho'—'The Place of Him Who Wears Glasses' and my grandfather also left in the middle of the night for a township called Londiani. Some of his sons refused to follow him and went to European farms in other parts of the Rift Valley Province. This produced a great schism in his family which he no doubt attributed to the stolen *mwano*. Only two of his most favoured wives went with my grandfather.

At Londiani his health deteriorated. He was a broken man and eventually died in misery. All of his grandsons, except those who were at the mission school, came to honour him at his funeral but they still disliked each other.

When the news reached the three who were studying at the Church of Scotland mission, they also were sad although they had bitterly resented my grandfather's treatment of them. They completed their studies and returned to the Rift Valley Province. The two who were brothers became clerks on a European farm, and the other was so liked and trusted by his employer that he was made overseer of the large farm, perhaps the first African to be so, in charge of several hundred labourers and Squatters.

Eventually, some of his half-brothers came to work on the overseer's farm. He did not turn them away but he used to make fun of them, telling them they could not keep their wives in the bank like money and that they should know that money had replaced the economy of polygamy. Nevertheless, although he was strict with them because of their past ill-treatment of him, he was a just man and helped them whenever he could do so.

Clearly, many polygamous marriages were successful but, as in the case of my grandfather's home, many others brought unhappiness and even disaster. If the family quarrelled, inevitably the children suffered, particularly those of different mothers. These internal dissensions are rarely apparent to a stranger.

XVI

My 'Star' Started Shining

THE Committee on Friendly Relations Among Foreign Students in the city of New York got me a job as a bus-boy in the cafeteria of the United Nations in June 1955. It was a very hard job, especially for a student doing post-graduate study at evening classes after work. However, it was better than I had had before, because I could at least get free meals in the cafeteria.

Despite my job I maintained a very good academic record at New York University, and I was also very happy to be a part of the United Nations. I met many people from most parts of the world and made several friends. Some wondered why I could not get a better clerical or professional job in the United Nations Secretariat or in the Division of Non-self-governing Territories. I applied to both these divisions, but was told that no positions were available.

In June 1956 I left the United Nations cafeteria and joined Dun & Bradstreet, Inc., a credit rating agency in the heart of Wall Street. A white American lady named Mrs George D. Henderson arranged this job for me through her husband who was one of the corporation's executives. This was really a very important event because it was the first time in the course of my stay in the United States that I had had an easy and fairly well paid job. I worked as a clerk in the mornings and attended my classes in the evenings. Mrs Henderson had heard of me through the Committee on Friendly Relations Among Foreign Students. She had read about these 'enigmatic Mau Mau people', the Kikuyu of Kenya, in *Something of Value* by

Robert Ruark, and when she heard that there was a member of this fantastic tribe in New York City she decided to meet him. I shall not fail to remember Mr and Mrs George D. Henderson.

In actual fact, my 'star' was shining brilliantly in 1956! I received a grant-in-aid of $1000 from the African-American Institute, Inc., of Washington, D.C., to enable me to do my research work at New York University. The Institute is a private, non-profit-making organization which gives grants-in-aid to the African students on a competitive basis.

At the end of 1957 I met an American girl from Philadelphia at a small party in New York City. I did not pay too much attention to her at the time, but she created so strong an impression on my mind that I continued to think of her often. She was fair, well built, beautiful, with hazel eyes, and had a B.Sc. degree in Pharmacy. Her name was Dolores and she was working as a pharmacist in New York City.

I took her out several times; we went around Manhattan on one of the Circle Line boats and eventually I asked her to marry me. We talked earnestly about such a serious step. I told her in detail about myself, my people in Kenya and that I was resolutely interested in helping them solve their various problems in any way possible. She was very interested in all this and in turn told me about herself. At last we decided that we should get married right away.

I told my relatives in Kenya about our engagement and they sent us their blessing, expressing their eagerness to receive us affectionately when we went to Kenya.

We agreed that our marriage should take place in October 1958, that is, before I left the United States for the United Kingdom to study law. We also decided that, since there was not enough money for both of us, I should go to Britain first and prepare the ground for Dolores who was to follow later.

We decided also on a church wedding and approached several church ministers in New York City to find out whether they would solemnize our marriage.

The first minister we telephoned told us that he could marry us but that he wanted to talk to us first before he made up his mind. We made an appointment to see him and called at his office which was also a part of the church, on the second floor. The office was a small clean room with a telephone, type-writer, many books neatly stacked on the shelves, a shining table, and four comfortable chairs. The minister himself was a tall, slim man with glasses, brown greying hair, clean shaven, and about fifty-five years of age. He wore a brown suit, white shirt and red tie striped in white and greeted us warmly on arrival.

We told him of our determination to marry. He listened politely and then asked to talk to us separately. I left the office leaving Dolores behind and went down to the first floor to wait my turn.

The minister then questioned Dolores closely. He asked, for example, how long we had known each other, about her home, parents, relatives, her neighbourhood, educational background, and whether she had ever been outside the United States. The interrogation lasted for nearly thirty minutes. Finally, Dolores came down to the first floor. I went up again, climbing the steps quickly.

As I sat down I saw the minister writing something in his note-book and, holding his pen, he said:

'Sit down, Mr Gatheru, and tell me about yourself.'

'Thank you. Where shall I start?' I asked.

'How long have you been in the United States?'

'I have been here since April 30th 1950,' I said.

'What have you been studying?'

'History, political science, sociology, and psychology.'

'I see, you sound like a real scholar. What are your future plans?'

'I'm now planning to go to Britain to study law, after which I shall return to Kenya,' I said.

'What will be your specialty in law?'

'Criminal law.'

'Criminal law!' he exclaimed. 'Are there a lot of criminals in Kenya?'

'No more than there are in New York City, but I happen to take a special interest in criminal law as a subject.'

'I see. Are you sure you're ready for a marriage with all the responsibilities it entails?' he asked.

'I'm absolutely certain about that,' I said.

'Will your relatives approve of this sort of marriage?'

'They have already done so,' I answered.

'When do you intend to get married?'

'On October 19th 1958.'

'O.K. Mr Gatheru, I shall be free on that day at about 2 p.m. Is that all right with you?'

'Yes. It is all right with both of us.'

'All right, see you then.'

'Thank you very much,' I said.

'You're welcome.'

He opened the door for me and I walked out and down the stairs to where Dolores was waiting for me. We left looking forward happily to our wedding on October 19th.

On the following day the minister telephoned Dolores and said that he wanted to see her alone immediately. She got in touch with me at once and I agreed she should go. At the minister's office he started asking her further questions.

'By the way, I'm a little bit concerned about you. Why should you want to marry this man particularly?' he asked.

'Because I love him and he loves me,' she said.

'Don't you think it may be difficult for you to adjust yourself to a man from a different country, culture, and race from so far away?' he asked.

'Not at all. I have thought about all this carefully, and I know that everything will be all right.'

'What will your relatives think about all this?'

'I don't know. What I do know is that I am in love with Mugo now, and that's all that matters.'

'I see. Does your sister have a boy friend?' he asked.

'Yes, she has.'

'Who is he?'

'He's an American boy.'

'Of what kind?' he asked.

'What do you mean by "of what kind"?' she asked in her turn.

'We have all kinds of Americans; for instance, the Puerto Ricans, white Americans, the Indians, and the Negroes, you know.'

'He's a white American boy,' Dolores answered.

'Do you think he will continue his friendship with your sister if you marry this African?' he asked.

203

'That's their own business. I have my life and they have theirs. I love all of my relatives dearly, regardless of what they may think of my marriage to Mugo,' she said.

'I would suggest that you think twice about these matters,' he replied.

'I have nothing to think about again. The decision is made.'

'Don't you think that perhaps you are marrying this man because Negroes are generally said to be more sexually active than whites?' he asked, adding: 'You could very easily get a boy of your own race.'

'I'm sick and tired of these references to race. Don't you think that people of whatever race can genuinely love each other for whatever they are?' Dolores asked angrily.

'All right. I did not mean to interfere, but I wanted to clarify certain points which concerned me on your behalf,' he said. 'See you on October 19th 1958.'

'Thank you,' my fiancée replied and went to her apartment much disturbed.

When I telephoned her in the evening to find out the situation she was very angry and even wanted us to go to a minister or priest in another church. I went to see her at once. We talked the matter over, and I finally persuaded her to keep calm and forget about everything she did not like in her talk with the minister.

We started shopping and inviting our friends to the wedding which we wanted to be small, quiet, and simple. We were excited and happy. On October 19th, at about twenty to two in the afternoon, we went to church by taxi. On the way I noticed that the driver was watching us curiously in the mirror. No one said anything. On our arrival at the church we found our friends waiting for us, and in a few moments our marriage was solemnized. We were declared man and wife. Another new chapter was now open for Mugo-son-of-Gatheru.

An African student who was studying political science in the New School for Social Research and was also married to a well-educated American girl had offered us their large apartment for our wedding reception. Several other friends who had been unable to join us at the church arrived later in the evening at the apartment. We all enjoyed music, dancing, beer and wine, and some food. At about eleven o'clock my wife and I took a taxi to our own apartment which was between Third and Second Avenues on the second floor of a large block of flats along Third Street, near the important Fine Arts School called Cooper Union in Cooper Square. The section was occupied by a variety of European immigrants to the United States, among others, Poles, Italians, Greeks and Irish. Its streets were surrounded by numerous delicatessens, music, butcher, jewellery, and drug stores; and in between these there were a lot of small coffee bars, ice cream fountains, and beer and liquor stores.

Our apartment had two rooms, a kitchen, bathroom, and lavatory. There were a telephone, radio, refrigerator, one dining table, a bookshelf full of books, a cupboard, a wardrobe, and a bed.

Opposite the four windows on the western side was a graveyard which was separated from the building by a big stone wall. From our apartment one could see the memorial stones shining in an expanse of grass and green trees and we could hear birds singing in the trees.

That graveyard was the second oldest in Manhattan. At night it scared me, especially when Dolores visited her relatives in Philadelphia and left me alone in New York City. Even today, I hate passing through or being anywhere near a graveyard if I am alone at night. I always fear that some *ngoma* may try to talk to me! Dolores used to laugh when, looking at that graveyard in the evenings, I asked her to make sure that when I died a long panga (knife) was placed by my right hand so that when I got to '*ngomo*-land' I should be able to fight with them and perhaps try to incite some sort of revolution there!

There were a lot of other tenants in the building. Some of them looked like serious artists. Others merely played their radios and gramophones very loudly. Living opposite to us was a very pretty girl who was working as a model for a New York firm. The peculiar thing about her was that she bought most of her personal effects such as dresses on a hire-purchase plan so eventually her bills accumulated astronomically. In fact, it was said that she owed over $1000 to various stores in the city. She had a regular mail of threatening letters from her creditors. One day we saw her packing her belongings as if she were going away for a vacation. We said nothing of course as it was none of our business to interfere with other people's affairs. However, the packing went on and one Friday night she disappeared. She forgot to leave a note about her rent for the landlord who was astonished to find her apartment quite bare save for the keys and a lot of small things lying on the floor. He contacted the police, but the girl could not be traced.

XVII

My Brothers of the New World

ONE finds black men living throughout the White Man's World. I am one of these but I am a temporary resident completing my education, and I shall soon return to my own country in Africa. There are, however, millions of people of African descent with permanent homes in the United States, Great Britain and elsewhere, and I am of course greatly interested in them and in their fate. In America alone, where Africans first came in 1619, there are at least 18,000,000 Negroes, or one-tenth of the population, and these I call 'my brothers of the New World'. America's power and prosperity owe much to their skill and labour.

For reasons which must be obvious, all people of African descent are united by a bond of mutual sympathy which is today, with the practical example of the United Nations, assuming a positive force and influence quite unexpected at its birth in humiliation and subjection. I was therefore well-disposed towards 'my brothers' but it was not until I went to America that I realized that sympathy and good will alone do not necessarily make for true understanding. We had some curious ideas about each other.

Until recently, the knowledge that my people had of American Negroes was scanty, derived largely from out-of-date books of the late nineteenth and early twentieth centuries. Educated Africans knew of individuals like Booker T. Washington, George Washington Carver, Paul Robeson, Joe Louis, Dr Ralph Bunche, Richard Wright, Langston Hughes and Marian Anderson. However, for Africans, such people were symbols only of the success which a black man might achieve when given a proper chance to develop his natural abilities.

I remember well a biology lecture at the Medical Research Laboratory in Nairobi when the European instructor stressed the difference between a European child of twelve and an African adult. If a European child was so greatly superior to the average African, how much more so must be a European adult? When I asked about Paul Robeson and Dr Bunche, I was told to remember that they were Negroes who had been brought up in a white man's culture and that I should recognize the difference between creating and copying.

When Dr Bunche came to Kenya in 1938 to do research work for his doctorate, he was given the Kikuyu name of 'Kariuki', one who has returned. People were happy to welcome him wherever he went and hoped that many more American Negroes would come, and stay, in Kenya. Dr Bunche too enjoyed his time with us and wrote a long account of it for *The Journal of Negro History*, published by Howard University, Washington, D.C.

However, Dr Bunche's visit, although exciting for us, was an isolated occasion and the man himself exceptional by any standards. It was not until the Second World War that we were able to meet American Negroes in any number. Then they came as soldiers to Kenya and we tried hard to meet and talk with them. Although military restrictions made this somewhat difficult, I remember one special occasion in 1944 when more than a hundred of them came to Gethunguri School at the invitation of Mr Peter Mbiyu Koinange. The villages through which they passed went wild with rejoicing to see them. The women and girls ululated as if a new Kikuyu baby had been born! This mass demonstration certainly represented our attitude towards the American Negroes, our symbols of success. We thought of them merely as more emancipated members of the same community as ourselves and in fact when I arrived in America I had a vague expectation that they would act much like my fellow tribesmen in Kenya. I was disappointed to find that they did not and that they were in my inexperienced eyes more like white men of a different colour.

But, however naive I may have been about them, I was still more surprised to find how little the Negroes knew about my people. Often enough, their knowledge of us was as primitive as the conditions in which they imagined the whole of Africa was still living and many indeed were ashamed of our common ancestry. At college, the Negro students were very keen to know about African customs which I would attempt to explain to their utter amazement and sometimes incredulous laughter. One particular student from Nigeria with particularly heavy tribal marks on his face was the centre of great curiosity in the dining hall and on the college campus. Many of the Negro students seemed incapable of understanding why intelligent people should wish to 'disfigure' themselves in this way: it was certainly not an 'American' thing to do! This ignorance of the life, and inability to understand the values, of other peoples is not of course limited to the Negroes in America. Personal contact is essential to understanding and this is made difficult by the geographical isolation of the country. Certainly there is more ready understanding of Africa in Europe, but this is again only a matter of degree.

Ignorance of Africa in America is unfortunate and, among the Negroes, even occasionally tragic. In my opinion, atavistic movements of the 'Back-to-Africa' variety, like the Garveyists, based as they are on frustration and pessimism, are grossly misconceived. Their followers have little idea of the serious problems of adjustment they would have to face in Africa and even less understanding of the people with whom they would like to live. (Nor, need I add, do I favour the black Moslems with their policy, curiously reminiscent of South Africa, of separate Negro states in the union!) The American Negro of today is undoubtedly a man of the West who stands as little chance of successful assimilation into African society as his white fellow countryman, a Chinaman or European so born. We shall always be most happy to welcome him in Africa, he is indeed our brother, but, as present Negro leaders realize, their true hope for equality must lie in the dynamic fight now being waged for complete integration in American society.

My own encounter with the alien society of America was difficult, the experience strange but exciting. I have already told of my upbringing in the rural community of a Kikuyu medicine-man's family and of my struggle to adjust to the urban life in Nairobi when I began my laboratory work in

1945. Despite this, and also the greater strangeness of my time in India and England, my stay in America was perhaps the most stimulating and trying of all. I worked hard to understand the Americans, their methods of education, their colourful and kaleidoscopic society. All this was necessary if I was to gain the knowledge vitally important to me and to my country. Perhaps this necessity supplied the impetus but I think I can say that, for a Kenya tribesman, I succeeded quite well in my purpose! Never at any time did I lose my identity as a Kenyan but, so conscientious was my effort to learn all I could of this great country, that after a while I even caught myself reacting like an American, at least in circumstances essentially American, and without any conscious desire to do so.

Everything I saw in America added to my knowledge, meeting people, going to the movies or shopping, travelling by bus or train, or listening to the radio. In all my endeavours, I have been guided by the aphorism of a Greek philosopher, once quoted to me by my primary schoolteacher at Kambui in the Kikuyu Country: 'Whatever a man has done, a man can do,' which means almost the same as the Kikuyu proverb: 'Kirema Arume Nikigariure.'

The wisdom of these two sayings made a lasting impression on me and I shall never forget them. They taught me to look beyond my own parochial horizon and stirred in me that burning need for fresh ideas, like medicine or wine, which led me to America. There I learnt a further lesson, namely, to understand others one must be tolerant of them and judge them only when one knows the needs that they need and can feel the way that they feel.

One thing in the White Man's World still remains a mystery to me. From the time I first heard of it at Stoton until now, I must confess I have been unable to accept the concept of Christianity. I am not an atheist or agnostic. I believe in One God, the Creator, just as my great-great-great-grandparents did, but I regard Christianity as I do history or law, as a source from which I may advance my knowledge and intellectual capacity. However, I was deeply impressed to find that Christianity has been a strong unifying force among American Negroes and that it actually serves to give them a 'tribal' cohesion. They truly understand the Bible and hymns to mean what Mwangi and

Mwando were telling my people they meant before I went with Karanja from Stoton to get educated in the Kikuyu Country.

On a more material plane, I could not help being impressed by the obvious American mastery in the fields of technology, education, business management and agriculture, let alone communications, transport and hygiene; in fact, I was like Alice in Wonderland. I wished I could see my country as highly industrialized as the United States. In this hope there was no question of slavish imitation of Anglo-American culture, merely a desire that Kenya should have the benefit of the better things produced by Western civilization, whilst at the same time maintaining the best of her own way of life. We too have our glories and our pride but, while tradition has its virtues, we must be prepared to abandon that which is barren and accept that of others which is good and conducive to my people's prosperity.

Having obtained an M.A. degree at New York University, I decided to study law in Great Britain instead of taking the further degree of Ph.D. A white American friend Mr. William X. Scheinman, who had a manufacturing business kindly offered sufficient help to make this possible. I was now getting ready to return to the Old World.

In November 1958 I departed for the United Kingdom by B.O.A.C., very sad at leaving behind my professors and so many sincere friends and, of course, my dear darling wife.

On my arrival in London, I took a furnished room in a West Hampstead house owned by a lady who had come to England several years before from Germany. She was an Austrian Jew by birth, now well-off, but she told me that she had had to flee by night from Berlin where she not only left behind her entire belongings, but also her small baby son and husband. Her husband was an 'Aryan' and, therefore, he and the baby were not in such great danger as she was. She finally came to Great Britain by way of Switzerland, practically penniless, and physically weak. I was very moved by the story of her sufferings.

After I had been in London for four months, my wife joined me. Immediately, she obtained a job in a London hospital as an assistant dispenser, and I enrolled at Gray's Inn to read law.

During my studies in Britain I have been able to make

friends among the British people whom I have found to be very kind, generous, and sympathetic. Some of these friends have taken us in their cars to see life in the countryside outside London. I was particularly impressed by the English villages which I once saw in Bedfordshire when one of our friends took us to see his father's farm. I wished our villages in Kenya were like those English villages.

For us, life has been very busy. At first, my wife worked eight hours a day, five days a week and half a day on every other Saturday, while I studied law. After one year in West Hampstead, Ngai gave us our first baby daughter whom we named Wambui Mumbi Gatheru—the mother of the Kikuyu people. She was born three weeks prematurely in a Hampstead hospital, a few miles from our home, on January 6th 1960. As soon as Dolores arrived home from the hospital she developed an infection in her left breast and went to see the doctor, who suggested that a district nurse should attend my wife at home.

After four days, the breast started swelling. It was very painful, my wife's head was spinning inside, and everything seemed to be going round as if she would faint at any moment. The visiting nurse came regularly to wash the breast in warm water and dress it, and she advised my wife not to breast-feed the baby any more. This did not help. The breast swelled bigger and bigger every day and became an angry red. We called the doctor again who, after an examination, said that is was too late to avoid an operation and that Dolores would have to go into hospital for an incision.

After the operation she returned home on the same day, but she continued going to hospital for daily examination and dressing. This went on for a week, but the breast continued painful and hard and soon there was danger that the other breast also would become infected.

Dolores was obviously getting weaker and weaker and her face began to show her pain. On the doctor's advice she was admitted to one of the Hampstead hospitals until she should become better.

I was now left at home with a three-week-old tiny baby to take care of, for I did not want her to go to hospital with my wife. I felt that I was qualified to do the job as well as any nurse, but I think I might have been extremely possessive too.

Apart from taking care of such a delicate baby, I had to prepare for my law examination which was coming in May. From Dolores's hospital I learned that she would not come home for perhaps another two weeks. I could not visit her as I did not have anyone with whom I could leave the baby. We were 'dead broke', my dining term had just begun at Gray's Inn—I was frustrated and dejected. My difficulties seemed overwhelming.

Our bed-sitting room was very large and it was cold and very difficult to heat, although there was an inadequate gas fire. I bought an oil heater, but it did not improve the situation. It was at that time that I wished so much—in fact, very, very much—that British houses were centrally heated as most of the houses are in the United States. I thought that if I were to run or to stand for a political office in Britain one of my slogans would be *Make Britain's Homes Centrally Heated*.

The baby was so small that she could not take a large amount of milk at once. I had to keep on feeding her practically every hour and a half. I made formulas many, many times, and I changed her nappies constantly. I gazed at her features always. She was very pretty and, as I looked at her, I thought she was my mother's image. This was a great consolation in all these difficulties.

The night was particularly trying. For example, the baby would cry, I would get up very quickly, try to light the gas fire, hold her, and then warm her milk. After feeding her I would change her, and put her to sleep. In a few moments she would cry again and then vomit and soil her pyjamas, sheets, and blankets. I would again change her quickly (but I had to relight the gas fire first!) and feed her all over again near the fire lest she catch cold. Sometimes this would happen several times between 1.30 and 3.0 in the morning. The room was still very cold. I therefore decided to keep the gas fire lit throughout the twenty-four hours. I also used to sleep throughout the night in my trousers or pants, a shirt with a tie and a sweater; sometimes I also wore my shoes so that whenever the baby cried I could get up quickly without feeling the cold too much.

Unfortunately for me, she caught a cold and her tiny nose was so completely blocked by mucus that she could not sneeze. I was frightened and called the doctor right away. He said that there was nothing serious so long as she was able to drink her milk, and that I should go on drying her little nostrils by means of cotton wool fixed on a tiny tooth pick. He also suggested some nose drops as a last resort. Only after a week and a half of hard work did the baby's cold disappear.

In two neighbouring rooms there lived two tenants who got up for work very early each morning, and I had to be extra careful not to let the baby cry lest they should be disturbed. In fact, the landlady had warned me about them before our baby had come and therefore, whenever the baby opened her mouth, I would jump up, quickly heat her bottle, and put it in her mouth to stop her crying!

In the hospital, my wife did not show any sign of early improvement. It seemed she would have to remain in hospital indefinitely and I was very worried. I continued nursing the baby. I was sleepless, tired, broke, and desperate. I meditated every night on the troubles I had had since I left Kenya on March 25th 1949. If my father had been living in London at that time, he would perhaps have suggested that I should strangle a spotless brown or black fat ram in our bed-sitting room in West Hampstead in order to appease some bad *ngoma*—spirits—which were causing all these troubles and which were also making my wife and the baby sick. The trouble would have been, though, that perhaps the Borough Council of Hampstead would have refused us permission! Furthermore, for geographical reasons, it would have been difficult to throw pieces of meat in the direction of Mt Kenya from West Hampstead, London.

Fortunately, a Canadian lady, Mrs Steves Peitchinis— whom my wife had met in London before the baby came, agreed to take care of the baby for at least three hours a day so that I could go to Gray's Inn to complete my dining term. The kind lady did this for a week. She also bought many things for the baby and put a large sum of her own shillings in the gas meter. She was a real life-saver.

Finally, after four weeks, Dolores started to improve, although the doctors still feared that the second breast might become infected. Indeed, after some improvement, the first breast showed signs of re-infection but at last she recovered. She came home, but had to go to hospital once a week for observation until she was completely cured.

The baby continued to grow strong, healthy, and sensitive. One of our neighbours had a dog which barked often, particularly at night. This always wakened the baby. The postman's morning ring on the bell had the same effect and I did not know what to do.

Fortunately, despite these tribulations, I was able to pass all my subjects in the Bar Examination Part One without much difficulty. I did my studies in the evenings almost unaided since I had to take care of the baby during the day, and could not attend classes. Political changes had been taking place in Kenya and the 'Canutists' side had been losing ground drastically. (It will be recalled how a certain 'Canute' gave me a hard time in Nairobi.) This meant that I received no help from the Kenya Government until, with the aid of the United Kingdom Kenya Students' Adviser, Mr T. C. Colchester, I was able to obtain a £500 loan from them so that I could continue my legal studies. This, however, was not enough to enable my wife to stop working and look after the baby while I studied and attended classes.

After two years in West Hampstead we moved to Hammersmith where we obtained a much bigger room. I felt sad to leave the birthplace of my daughter. In fact, I still feel sentimental about it because it was there that the placenta of my daughter was disposed of as soon as she was born; if she had been born in the Kikuyu Country, the placenta would have been buried near our gate by the old woman who had acted as a midwife. At the hospital I was told that it had been burned. I wished it had been buried instead of being burned.

The months have passed and we are still in Hammersmith, but not for much longer now. As I write today, the first day of June 1963, the end of my journeying is in sight after fourteen years away from my country, Kenya, and I can say that I am a happy man. On this day, I sit in London and thousands of miles away, in space if not in spirit, Jomo Kenyatta stands in Nairobi on a platform draped in scarlet and, as the very first Prime Minister of Kenya, swears 'true allegiance to Her Majesty, Queen Elizabeth the Second, her heirs and successors according to law. So help me God.' May God indeed help him and all my people to that peace, prosperity, and happiness which alone can make sense of my life and those of others who have laboured so hard for this day. I am happy also because my studies are now ending, I shall shortly take my final examinations and I shall be home to help in the building of a new Kenya nation. And I am happy. I am happy because I now look upon the face of my son. My first son, Gatheru, Gatheru-son-of-Mugo, for this is one tradition which I shall not be the first to change.